ALF & MABEL

TERRY LANDER

Published by Lyvit Publishing, Cornwall

www.lyvit.com

ISBN 978-0-9926029-5-6

None of the information included in this book is related to actual places, persons or events and any resemblance to anything or anyone, living or dead, is entirely coincidental.

No Part of this book may be reproduced in any way, including, but not limited to, electronic or mechanical copying, photocopying, recording or by any information storage or retrieval system now known or hereafter invented, without prior consent from the publisher.

This book is sold subject to the condition that it shall not, by way of trade or otherwise, be lent, re-sold, hired out or otherwise circulated without the publisher's prior consent in any form of binding or cover other than that in which it is published and without a similar condition including this condition being imposed on the subsequent purchaser.

All Material © Terry Lander 2015
Cover Design © Suky Goodfellow

"The present becomes the past instantaneously. Look back by all means but remember that you're moving forward."

For Mary

ALF & MABEL

ONE

He recognised the tone even if the voice was a little blurred, however he was sure that by turning round he would see that same figure, albeit a few years older, bearing down on his position. Mabel sighed next to him and clutched her drink tighter; sure the speaker would knock it out of her hands given his reputation for clumsiness that was legendary throughout the school the couple had attended with their idiot friend, Henry. As sure as ships that sail have to port, here he was at the reunion ready to throw his weight around and make everyone feel uncomfortable while he had the time of his life.

"Alf-wee!"

The nickname itself came from a very innocent incident during their second year of school. Alf's mother had saved for months to buy him a wax jacket to see him through the next two winters and had measured him when she started putting the money aside. Unfortunately, by the time the pot was full enough to buy the jacket, Alfie had grown a good three inches which meant the jacket only came down to his waist. As waterproof as wax jackets are they can only protect what they surround, meaning the water running off the jacket pooled on the front of his trousers and made it look like Alf had no intention of relieving himself properly when it was raining. Alf-wee was a ridiculous nickname, hence it stuck throughout school and into college until he finally left to pursue a career in telecommunications. Its re-emergence now was a sign of things to come whenever he met up with old friends and he pledged to grin and bear it for the evening, leaving Mabel to lecture him on the difference between remaining civil and soaking up bullying later that evening.

Henry had done next to nothing since he left school at sixteen, at first working for his father in the plumbing trade but leaving after he flooded his neighbour's bathroom to pursue a career in avoiding careers. Alf knew this but chose not to bring it up as fodder against the nickname for reasons that escaped him. Instead he smiled, turned and nodded politely, accepting Henry's hand and wondering if he'd had a bet with someone on how long he could shake it for.

Mabel was in the year below Alf and the two of them had only met properly during their college years. Both studied English and found themselves in the same class as the former had been selected for a progression class that saw her gain her qualification in just over a year. Their romance blossomed during the English Poetry part of the syllabus and continued well into their twenties before they married and started cohabiting. The two of them were clearly in love and both felt that even an idiot could have seen it. Meeting Henry disproved this theory tenfold.

"Alf-wee, how are you? Still single I see. No surprise really, you ugly old toad!"

Mabel cringed to think that Henry thought himself a better candidate than Alf. Time had not been kind to the former plumber who she still considered the weirdest looking individual she had ever met and it sent shivers up her spine when he suggested he was going to try and get a date at the event, pointing to Mabel when he said he would try her first but would probably fail. Alf took that as his cue to introduce his wife, Henry at first looking unconvinced and finally making some joke about love being blind. Mabel countered by suggesting it may have just been short sighted as she hadn't had the misfortune to end up with him; after which a little small talk was made and Henry retreated back to the bar to speak to Stink-bomb Sid and Dirty Gerty, both of whom had probably married each other quickly out of fear of loneliness.

The rest of the reunion was spent avoiding certain gazes and hoping against hope that some of their old acquaintances would be keen to catch up. Many of them had considered marriage to be an institution entered into after a career and therefore saw the couple's situation as incorrect with some even looking down on them both. This would change over time as they started to look for and, in most cases, find love yet their stance was solid at that point; all they considered was that they were living in a period when money had to be sought and partners were nothing more than an inconvenience. Alf and Mabel had seen past the apparent hassles of marriage and were happily settled; enjoying life and experiencing work they were extremely proud to talk about.

Seeing that their attendance was nothing more than an addition to the success of the evening in terms of numbers the two of them escaped through a side door and drove to a nearby café to make the most of their night out; turning it into an impromptu date, sipping coffee until the place closed and getting a bag of chips to share in the car before the short drive back to their hotel. They'd come a long way for the reunion and they were certain they'd get their money's worth and make the most of such an unusual jaunt. Once back at the hotel thoughts turned back to the people they'd been to school with and why they'd drifted so quickly when books and films often talked about friendships between school friends that couldn't be broken.

Henry wasn't much of a friend to Alf, that was for certain, but he was always around and was more of a reliable ally than a friend in the true sense of the word. There was safety in numbers and Henry never took any time off sick, choosing school over his father's overbearing nature and making his way to the woods to be alone after school just so that he didn't have to go straight back. It was a tough life for Alf's pal yet Mabel felt that didn't excuse him for being an arrogant fool as he grew up. She reserved the right not to use the word 'matured' in this discussion.

Mabel's own ally in school had indeed been her best friend, a slim and attractive girl named Betty who turned down offers from lads as often as she flicked her long, blonde hair. She often wore make-up, an unusual characteristic given the thrifty nature of the time, and Mabel often felt this was because she thrived on crushing the dreams of the males around her who fell for her immense good looks before falling victim to her crushing words. Their friendship had ended just before college as the two of them both knew they would be attending different establishments and Betty considered their friendship a waste once they were aware it couldn't continue past their final summer holiday. It was almost as if they were business partners headed in opposite directions, allowing each other the permission to take up new partners as they couldn't keep communications up after their departure.

It seemed Alf and Mabel's time in school was nothing more than a conduit for their meeting and the qualifications they gained were simply a by-product of having to attend for so many years, the most important reflection being that the two of them simply belonged together. Both had received offers of adultery and one night stands during their marriage but they had stayed strong, realising that they could not be dishonest with each other regardless of the situation. Alf had once caught sight of the local farmer's wife's undergarments while she'd been bending over to retrieve a letter in her garden and felt it necessary to inform his wife in case he was reported for being a pervert. Mabel had laughed, wishing to herself that she'd been there to see him blush as it gave her incredible satisfaction to point it out to him.

By the time the couple returned home after the weekend they realised fate had smiled down on them and vowed never to take each other for granted. Their marriage was still technically in its infancy, though they could have planned a fiftieth anniversary party if they'd felt the need as both were confident they would achieve the target. The next thing to discuss was children, which had been a consideration in earlier conversations and were surely on the horizon given Mabel's maternal nature. She was kind to everyone, giving homeless people the benefit of the doubt about their situation instead of assuming they'd given up on life as Alf did and she loved animals of all varieties. Sure enough, eleven months later, Mabel started to put on a little weight around her middle.

As she grew and struggled to perform her usual household tasks Alf took over and spent as much time at home as he could. Every lunchtime he was back from work to fuss over Mabel and make sure she had her feet up, a cup of tea in her hand and enough of a book left to keep her entertained. Once he disappeared back to work Mabel finished her tea and continued to struggle around the house to shoo the boredom and keep her sane. Her routine became so consistent that her feet would be back up by the time he returned from work, convincing him that she'd stuck to his rules and not overstretched herself. He failed to notice that it took her most of her nine months to read just one book, *Pride and Prejudice*.

TWO

Alf and Mabel weren't in their late twenties anymore. The reunion had been over forty five years previously and both had witnessed their hair colour slowly being replaced by a soft grey since. Alf's wiry frame had withered considerably and he now walked with a bit of a stoop, although his strength was still better than most his age. Mabel's slight frame was still evident yet she'd cursed the wrinkles that broke up her once perfect complexion on more than one occasion. Both had allayed the other's fears of their appearance yet they still found occasional opportunities to take a good look at themselves and attempt to wish the changes away.

Alf was now trying to find warmth after waking up in a bed he used to struggle to cool down in. He'd bought a giant fan from a local hardware store when he was younger and used it throughout every summer to keep his temperature regulated so he could get a normal night of sleep. As he got older he'd needed the fan less and less, eventually getting rid of it eight years before and thanking it subconsciously for the years of hard work it had put in. Now he was absolutely freezing in a month when he'd usually had the fan on its highest setting.

He pulled the duvet right up to his chin and shivered as he thought about getting a new duvet to cover the one he and his wife were currently struggling under. That is, he'd assumed Mabel was struggling with the cold. She hadn't complained and seemed to be unconscious still, surely to wake up in a cloud of mist and wondering why she could see her breath as Alf thought he'd done. He started to visualise warm places; Jamaica, Barbados, even Spain would have done at a push, yet nowhere seemed close enough in his mind to warm his suffering body. Ten minutes later he got out of bed, put on his dressing gown and slippers and went downstairs to check the messages on the computer Wayne had installed for him. Why the wretched thing had been enforced upon him he didn't know but he thought it best to use it as Wayne insisted on employing it as his chosen method of contact. If Alf didn't reply within a day Wayne would ring at some ridiculous time of night and wake the two of them up, disregarding all requests not to do so.

As predicted there was a message from Wayne requesting permission to bring over his new girlfriend for a family dinner. The thought made him shudder as he knew his son's taste in women and he was sure this new one wouldn't be any better. Wayne seemed attracted to lifeless, plain women who had no desire to do anything or go anywhere other than to the bank to draw money out for themselves. Where this selfish streak in people had come from eluded him and he was sure a forty year old computer nut like his son should have moved his attentions to more suitable candidates by now. He chose not to respond, leaving the tone and language to the expert as she would surely know how best to phrase such an answer. Seeing nothing else of importance, he turned the computer off and considered his other options.

When Alf was a boy he remembered having one TV in the house, in the corner of the living room, only showing whatever his father chose to put on. When Wayne was fifteen he'd wanted his own personal TV in his bedroom so the family promised to double whatever he could save and he finally reached his goal a year later. To Alf, TV was a privilege and he never took it for granted that he could watch whatever he wanted, whenever he liked. Suddenly, in the cold of the night, although admittedly it was much colder in bed, he had the box all to himself and there was nobody to compete with. Mabel was keen on watching documentaries and spent a lot of time flicking between animal channels and crime channels to get the full range of dog-eat-dog style programming in between their chats about the house and what their children might be getting up to. This left Alf pondering what type of program he might like to watch.

Being so late he knew there would be no programmes featuring clapping audiences or cookery shows which soothed him somewhat. He'd watched a war film when he was younger and seemed to remember a real sense of education while he was engrossed in the story, giving him a sense of satisfaction about the experience rather than that of a waste of time. His mother had used the phrase 'Idiot Box' more than once and this instilled a sense of guilt in him that he was unable to shift, although his mother wasn't there and he should technically have been asleep; his present situation was not caused by his own doing. An hour later and feeling somewhat rebellious, Alf retired back to bed having seen Hitler's men thwarted by the righteous and made a plea to his mind to base his dreams around being a pilot in World War 2 and blowing the insides out of Nazi occupied buildings.

On returning to his bedroom he decided to try and get back into bed in the dark, leaving Mabel resting to avoid a telling off for waking her. He'd spent many a night on the end of one of her annoyed speeches and didn't fancy it on a night when he couldn't get to sleep in the first place. He tried to remember *why* he couldn't sleep, damning his age for failing him so often before he finally recalled the chill in the bed. He hadn't felt cold getting out of bed and certainly didn't feel it now so wondered if it had been part of an elaborate dream where he was skiing or cooling off in a far away pool somewhere, both of which had occurred before. It did feel unbelievably real, however.

Alf went back to thinking about spraying bullets at enemy garrisons as he removed his dressing gown and slippers and almost slid back into bed, stalling at the squeaking sound emanating from beneath him. He froze on the spot as he hated the thought that something could bite him during the night yet he also felt that he should protect his dozing wife so as not to look stupid if she woke and had to deal with the problem herself. Recurring thoughts about the light situation struck him and he made his way tentatively on to the landing where he immediately flicked the switch and witnessed a small, white mouse barrelling across the floor. After darting into the spare room Alf plucked up the courage to follow it and grabbed a newspaper, hoping it would be a sufficient weapon against the beast.

The spare room was full of old bits and pieces Wayne had collected over the years and was planning to use in the future, giving the impertinent mouse ample hiding space and Alf a headache as to where it could be. It had moved with the pace of a cheetah and his own swaying, tired body had no real chance if he did get near it. The best he could hope to do was chase it downstairs and hope it found its way out, the hope fading with every second he spent searching beneath the boxes. Most of the components were completely lost on Alf as they all looked the same to him and he had less interest in the inside of the computers than he did the images they produced.

Resignation was the new word of the day and the mouse was clearly going to win this epic battle so Alf put his newspaper down and closed the door to act as a barrier despite it having been thwarted by the mouse once already. He cursed the thing for having been there in the first place and tried for a second time to get back into bed, removing his slippers and his dressing gown yet again but putting less energy into climbing in quietly.

He thought he'd heard Mabel speak as he went to lie back down but didn't catch exactly what she'd said so he recounted his tale of the mouse in hushed tones in case she was talking in her sleep. In his version of events the mouse had run in fear and he'd bravely chased it into the spare room, making it lose itself amongst the boxes and giving it the ultimate escape challenge. He even uttered the words, "We won't be seeing *him* again tonight, I can assure you of that", while still petrified that they might. Fortunately for him his prediction was right, not that he'd remembered much about it in the morning.

The chill was suddenly back upon him as he edged beneath the duvet and he frowned deeply, thinking back to the temperature as he'd removed it previously. He asked Mabel if she was cold as well but she'd clearly dropped back off as she was completely silent and still. Alf shivered for the last time before considering putting his socks on, wondering whether age had yet another inconvenience to throw at him. He'd already resorted to pyjamas after a happy lifetime of nude sleep and was starting to get concerned that he'd need a full suit and tails before he reached his final rest, putting the thought aside while he pulled on the socks he'd readied for the morning. He found that even that was to no avail, though.

Mabel and Alf had slept back to back since early in their courtship, mainly due to the problems they both had regulating their temperatures at night. Occasionally they'd fallen asleep in each other's arms after a tiring day or a few glasses of wine but it was particularly rare and therefore nothing they ever concerned themselves with. The problem was becoming so bad that he decided to cuddle up to Mabel until such time as she woke up, kicked him and told him that she was too hot. He didn't expect it to take long yet hoped he'd have enough time to at least warm up so he could get to sleep. With this he slid one arm beneath Mabel's neck and the other over her waist to rest on her stomach. That was when it hit him; Mabel wasn't under the duvet and her body felt very cold to the touch. *Very cold.*

THREE

Jill's birth was a particularly magical time for Alf. While Mabel was lying in hospital in agony, cursing him and the midwife who refused to make the pain stop instantly, he was drinking ale and playing darts with Gordon, the landlord of his local pub. He'd won three of the first four games and was set on finishing his opponent off when he realised the time and made his apologies having promised to be by his wife's side as soon after the birth as possible. Mabel had worn herself out swearing at the hospital staff and was catching up on her sleep when Alf finally made it to the hospital, swaying and smiling from ear to ear.

One of the nurses led Alf to the side room where his new family were resting and he thought to himself that, judging by the state of the sheets that had been collected beside her bed, he was glad he'd been assured that husbands weren't allowed at the births. He kept it to himself as he picked his young daughter up in his arms and grinned at her, taking in the scent and feel of her as well as the frown appearing on her face. He panicked slightly as she threw up down his favourite jumper, soon realising that it was perfectly normal and he should expect it more often as the weeks went by. Mabel stirred as he spoke to Jill and promised to take care of her, although she wasn't fully aware he was there until the morning arrived.

The doctor declared both Mabel and Jill well enough to go home after three nights in the hospital and Alf made sure the nursery was all set by the time they got back. He'd taken two full days to put the cot up, really struggling with the construction as it was designed by himself and seven of his friends during a heavy session one weekend and had to be perfected with a lot of sawing and planing. When it was finally complete he vowed never to touch woodwork projects again, forgetting his promise almost immediately when the wardrobe had to be altered to fit between the changing table and the cot to avoid blocking the window at the side of the room.

Baby-proofing the house had been a further nightmare as Alf went round on his hands and knees to find every sharp corner and hot surface he could get his hands on to ensure they were covered, modified or removed. He was paranoid about Jill's welfare and Mabel took great delight in exaggerating situations to panic him and cause extra work in order to get the whole house just right. Jill's arrival sparked a new bout of paranoia as the two of them watched their daughter, imagining how she would get around in just a few short months and relaying the possibilities to each other before action was taken, Mabel's information always being followed with a sly smile as she watched her husband hard at work.

Their arrival back home almost seemed as though it wasn't to be as they witnessed two accidents from the car, Alf having to take action to avoid both of them. The first wasn't altogether too bad as it was caused by a young driver who failed to stop in time and hit a waiting van from the rear, the impact being absorbed by the two vehicles and the occupants finding themselves with nothing more than heated tempers and bruised egos, particularly for the car driver. Alf was driving behind the two of them and predicted a collision although he failed to slow down more urgently. Fortunately his brakes were well maintained and he stopped in time, remaining inside the car while the other two sorted out their differences with their fists. The incident itself was nothing much to worry about and he soon got back on his way after the two of them sped off in bad spirits, however a more serious accident was waiting just up the road and it was something Alf couldn't help but get involved with despite his wife and daughter being in the car.

The cause of the accident was a middle aged woman singing along to David Bowie at the top of her voice, concentrating hard on hitting the right notes instead of the articulated lorry that was heading in the opposite direction. As she closed her eyes to briefly imagine being on stage she veered slightly to the right, catching the attention of the heavy goods driver and causing him to swerve to his left to avoid her. As he did so he caught a large rock at the side of the road that skipped him back over to the right and the two vehicles collided with an unforgiving force. Alf and Mabel were following the larger of the two vehicles and looked on in amazement as the right hand side of the car peeled back and trapped the woman between the seat and steering wheel to cause a considerable amount of discomfort before her body gave way. This time Alf didn't leave anything to chance, swerving off slightly to the right to avoid the back of the lorry in front of him.

As he stopped he told Mabel to wait in the car and checked around to ensure she was safe from other vehicles that may have driven near to where they were now parked. Knowing she was safe he ran immediately to where the car had split in two and confirmed that the woman was beyond saving before turning his attention to the driver of the lorry who was sobbing in the seat of his cab. As an onlooker he could safely confirm the fault of the woman but it was little consolation for the two of them as they imagined her family being told the bad news, the information of her poor driving being added later on to clear the name of the lorry driver. Before that could occur, the emergency services had to be called, an easy task using a nearby phonebox yet one that would lead to the road being closed for hours and the witnesses eventually having to find alternative routes home.

The whole scene was a complete mess with glass and discarded metal everywhere. The lorry driver was able to pull himself together before the authorities arrived to give his account but the clean up was long and arduous. The front of the lorry was crushed right back and the car looked like it had been split to get the contents out, the blood staining the upholstery, the bodywork and the floor. Other drivers were forced to abandon their cars in awkward positions much like Alf had, although most were happy to sit back and take no part in the events unfolding in front of them other than to give a statement when asked. Alf would have given more time to the clean up operation had he not been escorting his family home, an offer that was likely to have been limited given that it was the site of a fatal accident.

Getting back was a minor blessing in itself and the parents laid their newborn in her cot, fast asleep, as they prepared some hot drinks and a snack to help them sleep as well. They knew this would be great preparation for the sleepless nights they were about to encounter though they hoped for a good few hours at least to recover from the ordeal of the accident. Alf was fairing much worse than Mabel as he'd seen the woman and she was having quite an impact on him due to her injuries sustained during the collision. That night her face returned in his dreams as she goaded him about not helping sooner, a threat that was as illogical as it was empty but something that Alf genuinely considered a fault of his. The thought jolted him awake and he left the bed to explore the living room, hoping that a few pages of his book would take his mind off the events.

Eventually he started to relax and made his way back upstairs after reassuring himself that nothing could have been done and, in fact, his actions had probably helped the other driver a great deal. He couldn't help but take a sneaky look at his daughter as he passed her room and snuck up to her cot to check that she was alright. New parents were generally nervous, he knew that, though he didn't want to be one of the few that didn't take enough precautions and saw the worst happen. Sure enough, as he opened the door the hinge squeaked and Jill woke up. After a further half an hour consoling her and singing 'rock-a-bye baby' with as many lyrics as he knew she was back off to sleep, meaning he didn't have to wake Mabel to feed her.

As he climbed into bed beside her he was wary of pressing his cold body against hers and warmed himself up under the duvet before he sidled up behind her. As he did so he thought he heard her say, "Are you okay?", and replied, telling her all about how Jill had been woken and how he'd managed to get her back to sleep without having to wake Mabel. He then decided he'd done so well that she should know despite clearly having gone back to sleep so he started to shake her gently to wake her up while uttering her name.

"Mabel? Mabel? Ma…bel..?"

FOUR

"For Pete's sake, Mabel. Wake up!" he shouted, her body still cold and utterly immobile. When she slept she was dead to the world, however Alf couldn't feel her breath on the back of his hand and was certain he shouldn't try for a pulse as he was useless at finding it during his First Aid training and didn't want to worry himself unduly. He shook her a little more firmly before deciding an ambulance was in order as she was clearly unwell if nothing more. By the time he reached the phone at the bottom of the stairs his breathing had reached a record pace and his heart was beating twice as fast as when he'd seen the accident, making his palms sweaty and the receiver difficult to hold. After dropping it twice he decided to check for a pulse after all and made his way back up the stairs to the bedroom.

On the way up a number of thoughts struck Alf. What if they thought he'd killed her? Maybe these modern forensics would see something that wasn't there and they'd put him in jail for her murder. Worse than that, what if he'd accidentally killed her by dropping something in her juice without knowing and she'd ingested something deadly because of his stupidity? What if she wasn't dead and they paid to bury her, only for her to wake up after the soil had been shifted back on to the coffin lid. It was a real concern and one that wouldn't leave him from the moment it entered his head. He started to feel dizzy as he got to the top of the stairs and had to hold on to the banister to stop himself from falling, feeling sick along with it.

His fear of being buried alive came from his brothers when he was just seven years old. Whenever they were left in charge of him during their parent's absence he would be enticed into the shed at the bottom of the garden with his favourite toys and books and then locked in, only to be let out ten minutes before they were due to arrive back. Some days he would be left for hours as it meant his brothers could read in peace without having to entertain him, although he felt perfectly capable of entertaining himself and told them as often as he got the chance. During one of these lock-ins their father's compost heap, stacked high from a wet summer that had ruined most of his vegetables, toppled over and covered the window of the shed. Left in darkness for most of the day, Alf screamed to be let out and banged on the sides of the shed until he was finally heard and released, gasping for breath and fearing he'd eaten his last rhubarb and custard sweet. Since then he'd had panic attacks whenever the issue was raised in a book or even more violently when he saw people on TV being buried against their will. His transference of this fear was nothing more than a remarkable trait and it was this problem he was facing now which meant he had to find a pulse or face the issue once more in great, inescapable detail.

Mabel hadn't moved since his journey downstairs despite his hope that she would and so he ran to her side of the bed after collecting himself on the landing and felt hurriedly for a pulse. He checked her left wrist, then her neck, then her left wrist again before moving to the right wrist as a final check. While he was leaning over her chest Mabel let out a low moan very quickly that made him jump. Again he tried to rouse her, resulting in the same response he'd originally received. He refused to accept that his wife, who had remained loyal and taken him exactly as she'd found him, was lying there on their bed having exhaled her last breath.

Alf sat her up and rested her head against the headboard, inducing another slight expulsion of air that sounded like she was calling for him. Her eyes remained closed and her body was starting to stiffen, making her difficult to arrange as he'd intended. He thought about calling an ambulance once more until he looked closely at her face with its smile barely formed and fell forward towards her, embracing her and feeling her as he had just the night before. There was no heartbeat other than that which his memory sent from his mind, no temperature high enough to sustain a body's needs and no resistance from her muscles however he felt like she was right there with him, ready to wake up and ask him what he thought he was doing.

Alf started to worry unusually about arrangements. He concerned himself with the fact that nobody would be around at the funeral home to take his messages or to console him. He also considered that the ambulance employees (he wanted to call them 'paramedics', but wasn't sure if those were the people who threw themselves out of aeroplanes) wouldn't want to take a body that was definitely dead as they were there for emergencies given the amount of training they received. He confused himself with who he was meant to call at this time as it had never really occurred to him before; finally deciding that he didn't *have* to call anyone at all right now. Mabel had told him how much she loved him before turning off the light and they'd originally planned on spending the night together as they always did so he didn't see why that had to change right now. He was tired, still cold and wanted to get some rest so he could focus properly on the problem he was suddenly faced with. After all, it wasn't his fault he was in this position…unless he did poison her drink.

Alf took advantage of his newly established right and lay Mabel back down, asking if she was comfortable before remembering there was little chance of her giving an answer either way. He tucked her in and made his way back to his side of the bed, getting beneath the covers and moving the duvet between the two of them to stop him from getting cold again. He managed to cuddle behind his other half in this position without feeling any discomfort and closed his eyes in the hope he could find sleep again. He even considered that he may wake up to find this had been a terrible dream as he felt exactly as he'd felt every other night they'd been together. His mind drifting and hopeful, Alf fell back to sleep within the hour and his mind took him back to a time when they'd both been happier and healthier with the rest of their lives ahead of them.

After dawn broke Alf woke to find his wife in much the same state as he'd found her earlier that night, confirming it wasn't a dream or a reaction to the meal he'd eaten less than twelve hours earlier. He got himself dressed and considered dressing Mabel purely to keep her in her routine while she was still in the house. He managed to stop himself in time, realising that he'd have to move every inch of her body without thinking too much about whether the movements were natural or not as that would make the situation seem too real. He also knew that whatever outfit he picked out for her wouldn't have been right if she was alive, let alone as her final outfit. He knew that decisions on her clothing should be left to their daughter as she knew exactly what her mother would have put on rather than having a vague recollection of which items she generally wore together. This was too big a decision to be made on the off chance.

He tucked Mabel back into bed and decided to get himself some breakfast so he had some energy for the rest of the day. He was sure it would involve talking to a lot of people and perhaps convincing them that he had no part in her demise which he figured he would need a full stomach for. A week earlier Mabel had made them both a full English breakfast with sausages, bacon and three strawberry pencils (his own, unusual, addition) and he thought back to that, thankful that he didn't now have to make any attempt to cook as he would probably have burned the kitchen down given his condition. A bowl of cereal was simple to put together and even Alf was sure he could manage it alone despite shaking slightly from the trauma.

Returning to the bedroom after only spilling his cereal twice on the stairs he decided to watch the breakfast news in the company of his wife. There was a long story about a train accident and the tale of a nurse who was suspected of stealing hypodermic needles to assist her drug habit, both of which made him tut and sigh. He wondered what the world was coming to but remembered that he would evoke no response from his companion, choosing instead to concentrate harder on the images in front of him. The cereal was much as he'd expected and seemed to almost choke him by the time he neared the end, after which he wondered when he would ever get another cooked breakfast. He didn't consider it a selfish thought, more of an adaptation necessary for the coming months. He would have to ask Jill to cook one for him as she'd helped Mabel to take care of him when he'd had his fall. That's what he'd do.

FIVE

Alf was regularly asked to help his idiot neighbour, Ronan. The guy could barely string a coherent sentence together most of the time so, when he'd talked about clearing out his gutters, Alf knew he would have to offer a hand if only to stop Ronan from falling onto the roof of his car or into his beloved garden. The job was only meant to be a quick elevation on the ladder, scooping of the leaves and bird muck with a hand trowel and an easy descent. The problem was that Ronan saw no reason why he'd been asked to hold the ladder and had considered the ringing phone to be more important than the dreary task he'd been asked to perform.

Alf hadn't realised he'd let go of the ladder as he was swift and unusually careful, leaving the scene to talk to a woman he'd met three years previously. At the time he'd lied about his twenty years as an estate agent and had handed over a business card with the word 'plumber' scribbled out, maintaining that he'd ordered the wrong cards and was awaiting delivery of the new ones. His number hadn't changed and the woman was keen to employ him to sell her house as he'd seemed so knowledgeable about the business, although she could never have known how much he'd elaborated.

While he was telling her about interest rateable mortgages and domino effect insurance, two terms the woman would never hear again from genuine estate agents, Alf was vigorously digging several years' worth of muck from the gutters and wobbling every so often while assuming the neighbour he was working for was still present. Finally he came to a stubborn clump that required some extra attention and he called out to Ronan to steady the ladder. He was used to the man's ignorance and wrongly assumed he hadn't bothered to reply as he dug deep and dislodged the blockage more easily than he'd anticipated. He swung to the left and tried to catch his legs in the ladder for support before dropping further towards the ground. As he got halfway down he realised that he was alone and destined for a hard, flat surface so he braced himself and let go of the trowel before landing on his back with a thud. The noise escaping his mouth rang out through the houses and was heard by Mabel who ran outside to find him breathless beside the car. He quietly thanked his lucky stars that his treasured vehicle hadn't been harmed before he passed out having finally caught his breath.

He woke up a couple of hours later in the local hospital having suffered a fractured pelvis and a lot of bruising with his wife, three year old daughter and an annoyingly apologetic neighbour beside his bed. The pain covered his whole body and he noticed a nurse looking very sympathetically in his direction as she passed, suggesting this was not going to be a quick recovery. Mabel had taken a selection of books to keep him entertained during his stay and he found the hardest part of the whole incident to be the nights she couldn't stay with him, although she managed to hide herself away on two occasions to spend time in his company, sleeping uncomfortably on a chair once the nurses had left him alone while Ronan babysat Jill to make up for his part.

His return home was marked with a small party to which most of his friends and family were invited. On the whole he'd been away for almost six weeks and was so bored that he'd started drawing caricatures of the other hospital patrons who had all become jovially known as inmates due to their long stays. He'd never noticed a talent for cartooning during his life but had found it when the necessity of moving his hands took hold, the end results being kept by the subjects as reminders of his handiwork. Leaving them all brought a tear to his eye yet he knew there was a healthy amount of joy in his emotions as he was returning to the one woman who made him a decent meal.

The party was largely a group of people drinking his beer as they were sure the painkillers would mean he wouldn't get to it in time and other people joking about getting him a 'ladder safety' brochure, one of whom was Ronan. He'd have loved to name and shame his neighbour for leaving him like that, however he knew it wouldn't alter his circumstances and thought he could at least use it as an excuse never to help out again. If the people eating crisps without offering him a packet asked him to climb a ladder again he could always decline and claim off the insurance if they landed on his car as he would have done in this instance, although he quickly realised that he'd never have let go of the ladder if Ronan was on top of it.

Bitterness aside, Alf got on with the rest of the party and managed to speak to most of his guests. His Aunt Hettie could barely stop laughing to chat to him and it made for uncomfortable viewing, particularly for those who were trying to make him feel more at ease. He wanted to ask what had tickled her, feeling he wouldn't really want to know the answer and keeping quiet just in case. He'd always got on with his distant family yet this woman laughing in his face at such a colossal accident made him question her sanity in his head. He kept his answers to her short to make sure he didn't blurt out how crazy she looked as that would have killed the party when it was in full swing and he knew his wife had gone to a lot of trouble to put it on.

Not all of his guests were quite so vocal about their opinions of his situation and he found most of the conversations quite pleasant, dulling the memories of the hospital boredom and taking his mind off every now and then during the more general periods of chat. He forgot about the pain altogether when the young woman from across the road started singing as he found her voice to be very soothing, causing him to try and get a drink for himself and falling on to the floor in agony a split second after remembering why they were all there in the first place. His Aunt started laughing hysterically once more and the young woman did well to carry on singing throughout her horrendous racket as Mabel got him back on the sofa to lie back down once more, his pelvis singing out in sympathy.

Alf couldn't deny that he was pleased when his final guests left in a swarm to leave him with his pain, his wife and his daughter. Over the coming weeks he was tended to by both of them, the former cooking his meals and fetching glasses of water when they were required and the latter helping out by stirring the beans, whisking the eggs and taking big plates from the kitchen to the living room under the supervision of her mother. Alf almost wished he could remain in a cast forever, right up until he needed the toilet and had only ten minutes to get there before he could hold on no longer.

During this period Jill became fascinated with cooking and helped out whenever she could, spending occasions when she couldn't anxiously watching and taking mental notes. Being so young Mabel was careful not to give her tasks she couldn't perform yet she seemed amazed by the level of skill her young one was displaying. There was one small mishap where Jill spilt an entire plate of spaghetti bolognese over her father while he was lying in front of the football, though it wasn't too hot and the occurrence was laughed off as Mabel wiped the sauce from her still broken husband. Jill called herself 'Daddy's Little Helper' and tried to ensure he had everything he could have asked for.

Alf recovered almost completely from his injuries, aside from a small limp, and Jill was concerned that his good health would mean she couldn't help him out anymore. She kept offering him empty cups of tea as Mabel was too busy to make them, after which the two of them would go into the kitchen and Alf would help Jill to satisfy her unusual craving for support. Before too long Alf found himself helping them both with the meals and the three of them were sharing jobs and working like a real kitchen team. Just as Jill was really enjoying having her parents to herself a terrible sickness came over her mother, mostly in the morning but sometimes lasting well into the afternoon. Alf and Jill happily took care of her by making her makeshift meals, though the parents knew they would have to shatter their daughter's perfect world with the news of a sibling on the way.

They did so in the only way they knew, providing the world's biggest bowl full of ice cream and a milkshake that screamed out 'bad news'. To a three year old it was nothing more than a dream and, once she was loaded with dairy and sugar, the news of another life dependant on the trio was launched onto the unsuspecting target. It took a while for the young Jill to fully comprehend the enormity of the situation, though they were soon talking about how she could help to look after a new baby and how the two of them would grow to be best friends. One hour later and Jill finally realised that her parent's attention would also be divided into two, as would many other things like the big bowl of ice cream she'd not fully digested and the box of cereal she had all to herself. Suddenly the news became the bad news Alf and Mabel had expected and they had to deal with the biggest tantrum they'd ever faced.

SIX

"Do you remember that, Mabel?" Alf asked his wife before realising he wasn't going to get a response.

He was replaying the incident in his head, from the fall on the ladder to the screams of his first born, before rewinding slightly and thinking about his Aunt Hettie. What had happened to her since then? He hadn't heard from her and had no intention of tracking her down but she had a good fifteen years on him and was most likely feeling it if she hadn't checked out already. She had a penchant for doing stupid things, not limited to laughing at her nephew's misfortunes, and he wouldn't have been surprised if she'd been killed abseiling or bungee jumping over a river full of piranhas.

As it was, Hettie's fondness for laughing at other people's misfortune had led her to a life of solitude. She felt those around her needed to toughen up and felt absolutely no sympathy for what she considered their carelessness and this had driven many a potential partner away. Her best chance of happiness had been with a man she worked with in a sorting office when, six months in, he was carrying a tray full of hot drinks and carefully prepared snacks for the two of them to consume during a romantic film that he had no real interest in seeing. As he entered the front room he tripped on one of her shoes and the whole tray went into the air and landed on the back of his head, the coffee scalding his back and sticking his shirt to his skin. Before she considered that he might have done some damage her laughter filled the air and was comparable to a hammer drill scraping through unnoticed metalwork.

As he stood from his final position on the floor he noticed that she'd made no attempt to help him up so he remarked that her shoes were in a ridiculous position on the living room carpet and that she should learn to tidy things up after her. Taking this as the ultimate insult Hettie rose from her place on the sofa and launched a verbal attack so atrocious that her worst enemy wouldn't have expected it if they'd broken into her house and violently attacked her. Wishing for no further part in her miserable existence he donned his coat and shoes and made his way out of the door with the sound of her vile words following him down the road, confirming that he had made the right decision in wanting nothing more to do with her.

The next morning he'd resigned from his position, taken a month off with stress to serve his notice and left Hettie to tell everyone they'd worked with that he was too stupid to notice a pair of shoes right in front of his eyes. Most knew about her reputation and a few had even seen how heartless she could be and they struggled with themselves to keep quiet and let the situation run its course. The years passed inevitably and the final man in Hettie's life came and went before she turned fifty, after which her character became clear within her circles and she bitterly resigned herself to remaining a spinster. Dying alone in her house after a long but ultimately negligible life, Hettie cursed the people she met and spent time with for not seeing her restricted views of the world. As she drew her last breath, she uttered the words, "It's not me, it's you", soundlessly.

The image of Hettie dangling skinlessly over a river of carnivorous fish brought Alf back to real life with a jolt and he looked around, half expecting to find himself surrounded by the trees of the forest with wet feet. Instead he saw his more than restful wife facing towards the wall on her side next to him and an empty bowl with the remnants of the cereal milk settling in the bottom. The news had changed to some terrible show about people emigrating because they hated their neighbours and he watched a few seconds of it before wondering how these people made enough money to skip the country over a small row with someone who lived next door instead of moving to the next street across or putting up with them as he'd done for all those years. Alf and Mabel had rarely watched much TV during the daytime and he was sure he wasn't about to start so he tried to decide what he'd do with his day. Most decisions were made jointly and the knowledge that someone agreed on an idea was helpful in knowing whether it would be a good idea or not, however Alf knew he wouldn't have that privilege anymore. He certainly wasn't ready to tell anyone about Mabel's situation so he left her in bed and made his way to the living room to kill a couple of hours with some woodwork.

The birdhouse he'd been putting together was more than a little extravagant as he had plenty of time to commit to it and had considered all the elements he'd want from such an establishment if he'd been born with wings. It was almost complete, requiring a few more nails to keep the interior wall between the two bedrooms upright before the front could be carefully crafted from the twigs he'd gathered. As he was lining up the third nail with great care an inconsiderate outsider decided to phone, making him miss his target and split the entire wall in two. He rarely received calls so to say it was a surprise would have been an understatement, however his wonder turned to disdain when he realised he didn't have a replacement wall and would have to venture out to get more materials for it. His frustration was clearly audible to the caller, breaking the ice immediately between the two.

"What's wrong with you?" came the introduction in a familiar tone. His son never did say a simple 'hello'. Instead he was left explaining about the wall of the birdhouse and the fact he'd have to go out, his tone of voice clearly hopeful in an effort to persuade Wayne to do the deed for him. Alf was knocked back once more as Wayne steered the conversation back to his original motive for calling, to find out whether Alf had remembered the dinner reservations he had made for his wife three weeks previously. Alf was never noted for his memory and had regularly forgotten appointments that concerned his son and daughter so they'd taken to phoning him to make sure nobody could charge them for services he'd simply forgotten to use. Alf felt this was unnecessary, although on this occasion he had once again failed to remember the plans for that evening and was unable to cover up this latest failure in time.

Wayne sighed and asked if they were still going out as he was keen to show off his new beau, Alf suddenly remembering that he was meant to have returned his son's message by then. He apologised and suddenly remembered a bigger issue than forgetting the dinner in his recently deceased spouse. Alf couldn't leave her in the house on her own and clearly wasn't going to be taking her out for a meal so he told Wayne that he would be staying in and watching something on TV, to which he was told that the new couple would be over to dine with them since they were no longer due to go out. Alf froze with the phone to his ear, trying to determine a solution to stop their evening together from taking place at all. There was no way he'd be ready for company without at least getting Mabel out of the house yet this would involve calling someone of authority and he still wasn't ready to let her go. He tried to put them off, Wayne refusing to take no for an answer and even offering to take the food and cook. With that he hung up and Alf was sat listening to the dial tone with wide, terrified eyes.

His first task was to cancel the restaurant he was booked into so he pulled himself together and made the call, apologising for the late cancellation but assuring them it was out of his control. The young man who took the call was very understanding and that made Alf feel better about the situation before he remembered that he'd have to spend the evening keeping Wayne and his latest squeeze from going anywhere near their bedroom. He raced upstairs and looked around the landing to make sure there were no clues of her passing anywhere, taking his search into the opening to their room and around his side of the bed. True to her living form, his wife had remained tidy in death and the duvet prevented any initial smells from emanating around the house, her body still looking like it was no worse than in a deep doze.

His search for clues had left Alf lethargic and concerned. He knew it wouldn't be easy to keep his guests busy all night while continually excusing Mabel, however he knew it was best for his current situation. He had to think of a particularly good story for where she'd disappeared without Wayne becoming suspicious or trying to get hold of her. She rarely answered her mobile when she was alive but he and his son knew that if they rang it enough times the ringtone would drive her crazy and she would press buttons until it stopped complaining at her. He tried to think of a place she could have been that evening, despondently asking for her help as he did so.

"Just tell him I'm at Freya's house recommending a few books to her", she replied.

SEVEN

Alf had heard voices from inanimate life forms before. When he was in primary school he'd been asked to get some milk even though the sun was setting outside and he hated walking around in the dark. He tried to plead with his mother to send one of his older brothers but had been knocked back as they were all busy with other tasks she'd assigned them. On his way back from the shop he was walking quickly past a row of houses when he heard a bush say, "Get out of the way, son", and he jumped back, whipping his head in the direction of the sound and pointing to himself for confirmation.

The owner of the voice came forward from the bushes and Alf noticed a large tattoo on his forearm. Although he was wearing a coat his sleeves were rolled up and the topless dancer was in full view, causing great embarrassment to the young man as he tried to avert his gaze. A woman from the houses screamed which made Alf look across just in time to see her nude figure pulling the curtains closed and, all of a sudden, he felt trapped in a sea of unwelcome nakedness. He dropped his head into his hands and closed his eyes tightly, bracing himself as the man from the bushes knocked him with his binoculars and willing himself out of the situation.

Time seemed to pass so quickly at that point and, before he knew it, a police car had pulled up next to him and two officers had taken positions either side of where he was standing. He looked up with his mouth wide open, terrified he would be put in jail for witnessing both the adult tattoo and the body of the occupant from across the road. He pleaded his innocence, apologising over and over again until one of the officers jumped in and tried to console him. The woman from the house appeared in her doorway and saw the officers which made her dart across the street, glimpsing for traffic as she crossed over. She could hear his pleading tone and, seeing how young he was, considered that he wasn't a part of the pervert's plan, simply an innocent bystander who had clearly witnessed too much.

The woman offered the three of them into her house to get the situation in hand and she boiled the kettle for the officers, offering a fruit juice to Alf which was declined. He had tears running down his cheeks but had managed to control his earlier panic and was able to offer some two and three words sentences. The officers waited until he was calm before they asked him about his part in the affair and he assured them he was simply buying milk, an alibi that was confirmed by the discarded, broken bottle still lying beside where he'd dropped it sometime earlier. Alf told the officers that his mother would be infuriated by his late arrival and failure to deliver the goods, both of which they promised to sort in exchange for some details about the man in the bushes. He was able to recount the man's dark hair that was parted at the side and slightly chewed left ear before giving details of the tattoo which confirmed his identity to the woman.

Her reason for living in that particular house was as an escape from her husband who she had requested a divorce from. He had been overbearing and unfaithful several times, often phoning late from various locations and asking for a lift back home. She thought that would be the highlight of his impetuous behaviour until he came back with the tattoo, a fair representation of one of his conquests. She had asked him about it and he had simply said he'd liked the design, a suggestion she had believed until the woman turned up at her house with a view to maiming her for being the 'other woman'. He had returned home from work just in time to see the tattoo subject dragging her nails across his wife's face and had intervened, later telling her that it was lucky he'd arrived when he did. This was too much for her and she'd lost control, shouting abuse while reminding him that he'd put her in that position in the first place. The neighbours had called the police to the disturbance and they'd initially tried to arrest her for a breach of the peace until she managed to convince them that she was in danger from both her husband and his conquests and they'd finally assisted her in finding a new home.

The officers were noting the details of the case and were concerned that her new position had been compromised, a situation that had occurred within weeks of her moving in. She asked them to get her out of there and Alf couldn't believe what he was hearing about the abuse that had been put upon such a beautiful woman. She showed the officers scars from past fights in which he'd overpowered her and treated her to whatever he felt she deserved, details that landed deep within Alf's psyche and shaped his view on relationships well before he was ready to be a part of one. The officers realised that he was hearing more than he should have and decided to take him home, noting his details in case he should be needed in the future. The woman thanked him for his description and kissed him on the forehead before escorting the three of them to the front door. The officers informed her that they'd return and they guided the young man into their car to return him safely to his family.

On the way Alf reminded the officers that he needed to get some milk but that he'd spent all of the money he'd been given on the previous bottle. They supplemented his purchase and delivered him back, explaining what had happened to his mother to ensure he wouldn't be punished for witnessing the scene. He was often caught in daydreams and he knew he would never convince his mother of the truth so asked for their help in explaining which they were more than happy to do as it also meant they could confirm the details they held for him. As he made his way into the house the officers could see his muscles tense and he even started to walk in an odd way, almost dragging his feet along the path.

Alf's mother was there to greet him at the front door and immediately scolded him for being returned to the house in a police car. One of the officers jumped in to defend him but was soon argued down with the declaration that the neighbours would only have one thought when seeing a young boy returned in a vehicle that was visible to all around them. Alf said nothing as he knew from her tone that he was not likely to see a positive outcome and he simply thanked the officers for their help before he tentatively made his way into the living room to rest. His mother completed her berating of the officers and saw them out of the door before she turned her attention to her son, offering a tirade of abuse concerning the shame he'd brought on the family and even offering evidence of the fact as the neighbour in the opposite house was soaking in the view behind twitching curtains. He offered no more than an insincere apology, sure that her indifference to his sensitive side would earn him a tongue lashing if he spoke anymore, and she concluded her point by sending him to bed for the rest of the day.

He'd suffered a similar punishment before, however it usually occurred later on in the day when he'd had a chance to complete more than a short trip to the shop for milk required by the family. There was no way he would be able to sleep from early afternoon until the next morning and so he lay in bed cursing his stomach for wanting anything that day despite the fact it was connected to his mind and the latter had full knowledge of the situation. He took an occasional glimpse out of his bedroom window but was never there for more than a couple of minutes in case his mother visited his room or he attracted the attention of those who knew what it meant for him to be peering from that window in their house. It was the longest day of his life; though he was loathed to complain as it fitted with past punishments for similarly petty incidents.

The two officers had left the house with ringing in their ears and made their way back to the car in silence, both exchanging knowing glances as they opened the doors and climbed into the seats. They drove away without comment; afraid they would be heard by the abhorrent woman and reported for having an opinion. They both prayed they wouldn't need Alf in their investigation and only spoke of what had happened when they were safely on the road and out of harm's way. The officer who had bravely intervened spoke first, suggesting adjectives that best befitted the woman they'd interacted with so briefly. The second officer gave a nervous laugh and nodded along before pondering out loud what would become of the young man who had to put up with her every day of his life. During the silence that followed they both hoped for a brighter future as that was the least he deserved.

EIGHT

"...Fre...ya...", Alf stumbled, staring at the peaceful body of his only ever spouse.

He was numb from the neck down and couldn't take his eyes off her pale, colourless face as he heard her suggestion more clearly than he'd heard anything else over the past ten years. The suggestion that he was dreaming was the strongest sense although his dreams were generally of a more positive nature and the scenario in front of him hadn't ever occurred despite their age. Alf gathered his thoughts, realising that he had to answer the proposal to maintain his courteous nature. He could deal with the possibility of death when he better knew what his plan would be for the impending visitors.

"I can't think of the last time you spoke to Freya. Wayne is bound to know that and he'll know something's up the second her name is mentioned."

His pitch was confident and he put that down to the rationality he'd seemingly plucked from the air. The desire to lie beside his wife screaming her name and begging the Lord to give her back was nowhere to be seen but he knew that was a normal situation, particularly for someone of his disposition, and he expected the feeling to rush over him at any moment. Perhaps her gentle conversation was keeping it at bay.

"She's the only one of my friends you know, dear. If you can remember the name of another then feel free to use it but, as it is, I can only offer what you already know."

Alf's subconscious was suddenly providing a fantastic representation of his recently departed best friend yet he was nowhere near picking up on the fact. To his mind he was conversing with the very soul of Mabel, albeit in a higher volume and less fuzzy tone than they'd spoken for a long time.

He thought about her answer and tried to conjure up a name, any name, so that his son would be convinced of her temporary departure. Whenever they'd had people over for dinner in the past they'd both been present every time and it was going to take an A grade performance as it was without providing a name that aroused suspicions. Freya had stopped talking to Mabel following a disagreement between the two women about him despite the main theme of the argument being out of his control. He had the day to think about an alternative and put it on his mental to-do list.

Alf had seen enough crime scene programmes to know that the scent of his discovery would soon start to contaminate the surrounding air and so he went to work on the bedroom, opening the window and covering Mabel with the duvet both to aid his efforts and to stop her from potentially getting cold. He kissed her on the forehead after tidying the few items littering the floor and closed the door. His only hope was that nobody would get too close to their room which he knew was unlikely but not impossible. He was certain that he'd have to steer conversations away from her whereabouts as much as possible and try to keep conversation light as he had a tendency to continually think about issues on a loop rather than forgetting them until it was appropriate. This would most likely have seen him blurting out the situation and that was the last thing he needed to happen.

It took a few hours to clean the house as he was used to seeing it and he finally started to appreciate just how much Mabel did for him on a regular basis. He hadn't cleaned a toilet for over a decade and had taken it for granted that they would be clean when he came to use them. He silently thanked his wife for all of her hard work as he wiped surfaces with tears in his eyes and a feeling of emptiness that wouldn't leave him for a second. With the house gleaming he realised that he'd overworked himself and was exhausted by his efforts, trying to ignore the pain before deciding to return to the bedroom and taking a mutually acceptable film for them both to watch together before he had to entertain that evening.

Wayne was never one for punctuality and arrived a predictable thirty minutes late with his girlfriend, Isobel, in tow. He was his usual, disappointing self with his greasy ponytail attempting to cover the bald spot that graced a good proportion of his head. His brown leather jacket covered his sizeable midriff and, as he took it off, he showed yet more brown in a plain shirt and dark trousers. Alf went to ask if brown was in fashion, stopping himself just in time. He hugged his son and moved on to shake the hand of the jaw-droppingly stunning girl he'd brought along, curious as to her intentions but not able to find the right words.

As Isobel removed her faux fur, sleek coat and uncovered a tight, white dress that hugged her slim figure and perfect curves Alf couldn't help but gesture to Wayne, nodding his head in her general direction and shrugging his shoulders as if to say, "What is going on *here*?" She wasn't just out of his league, she was playing on a different continent; a different world, most would say. Wayne, as sharp as ever, didn't understand his father and smiled curiously while his father's eyes rolled in his head. To passersby it would almost certainly look like she was his sympathetic friend or sister, yet she held on to his arm and smiled as Wayne introduced the two of them. As she extended her hand and continued to grin Alf once again snatched words from his mouth and led his guests into the kitchen, trying to swallow the questions about where she'd left her golden retriever and white stick.

Remembering the situation with his wife, Alf's mind turned to more important matters as he suddenly tried to remember the name of the now elusive friend Mabel had once had and they'd agreed, in his mind, to use as a reason for her absence. Was it Frieda? He started to prepare the veg for their meal as this single name repeated itself to him over and over again, seemingly incorrect without him being in a position to state one way or the other. Frieda. Frieda. Fr…idea. His doubts were growing every time the name appeared and he almost forgot the knife in his hand that was creeping up towards his fingers. He stopped mid cut, concentrated on the final slices, then filled a pan with water and topped it up with his oddly sliced preparations. Frieda..?

"Where's Mum?"

There it was; the inevitable had occurred and he was stuck on the name of someone he'd more than likely met in his life but hadn't had the pleasure of remembering who she was or where she'd been. He turned to his bad hearing for a hurdle, asking Wayne to repeat the question before finding himself in exactly the same position he'd just been in. With no time to lose he started his sentence, repeating the name that had to remain with him.

"She's out…"

To his relief he was cut off before he could finish as Wayne's air of self importance took over the conversation.

"Typical, I was going to tell her our news."

Alf's curiosity finally took over as his relief subsided. The idea that Wayne had news was incredible as his life had generally been a bumbling of different jobs, different business ventures and the general loss of everything at weekends. Alf was sure he wouldn't want to tell his news twice but knew Mabel wasn't making an appearance any time soon so had to convince his son to spill all. By the time Alf had worn him down the veg was cooked and the meat that had been slow cooking for the day was just shy of completely burnt and therefore ready to serve. Why his son had been so stubborn he didn't know although he was glad he was about to find out.

"Isobel and I are engaged!" he shouted excitedly, at first hardly believing the words that were coming out of his own mouth.

Alf was immediately immobilised by this news and, instead of plying congratulations and shaking hands as he knew he should have, his mind went crazy trying to suggest reasons why this incredibly attractive young lady would want to spend the rest of her life with his dimwitted son. The air of silence went on for far too long before Alf's sense of normality and civility in situations kicked in and he finally gave his son the sentiments he was expecting. Isobel looked concerned, even a little hurt, making her future father-in-law feel ever so slightly guilty about his mistrust of her intentions. He couldn't shake it off, however.

Once the formalities were over and wary hugs were exchanged Wayne's mind turned to his mother once more. Her reliability was legendary and the likelihood of her being out when her children were visiting was minimal, especially as they'd been there for a little while by then. He was starting to feel his own suspicions creeping in and couldn't stop himself from enquiring.

"Out where, anyway?"

Alf's guard was down and he knew he couldn't blurt anything out straight away. He had to give himself time to recuperate as his head was spinning and the image of Mabel's ice cold form was still fresh in his mind. Her lifeless body was lying exactly as it would have been any other morning and that wasn't helping the situation at all. He silently called out to her for the alibi she'd provided earlier yet her voice was nowhere and he knew he had to rely on his own shaky memory to bring up the name that he wouldn't have believed if it had been provided to him. Still, he had to say something as the tension in the air was once again building to unbearable levels. Fortunately, given a little time to formulate his words, he was able to blurt out the word, "Freya's". Unfortunately Wayne's return was fast and curious.

"She hasn't seen Freya in years though. Not since she tried to…" That uncomfortable pause, as thick as ever, before he continued, "…with you."

Alf had absolutely no response for that. His now shattered brain quickly took him off to another place - as Wayne had said, years ago - when he was slightly more vulnerable. Perhaps it was a test of their relationship, maybe just a common blip. Either way, Freya hadn't helped in the slightest.

NINE

Freya's dog was often referred to as 'the rat' by most of Alf's family, Alf himself being the only exception. Freya had moved in to the house next door almost eight years before Mabel's demise and, had she been alive to convey an alibi to her husband herself, she would have chosen someone more topical and less horrendous to put forward. As it was, with his despair heightened and his sense of time diminished, he'd lost touch with her most contemporary associates and had opted for the last one he was aware she'd had contact with. His acknowledgement of her existence had caused tension in their marriage despite his refusal to return her advances.

He'd considered himself an old man even back then and, upon seeing a woman fifteen years his junior; he'd agreed inwardly that she was attractive but that he would never stand a chance with her if he'd wanted to. He was very much in love with Mabel which was highlighted by the length of their relationship and he had absolutely no intention of moving away from their marriage, though he was about to find out that some people can't leave others to be happy and her actions towards him, despite being completely her work, would serve to cause friction where he'd worked hard in the past to avoid it.

When he'd first seen her she was wearing a tight leather jacket and black, shiny trousers more suited to a twenty year old than the woman who'd paid for them. Her long, bleached blonde hair stroked right down her back as she walked and she clearly accentuated her walk in a desperate bid to attract a man. She was a smoker, made more obvious by the wrinkles meandering across from her eyes and her very lean, near athletic figure was clearly visible through her unlikely clothing.

Freya had been their neighbour for a week before she'd introduced herself and Mabel was curious as to whether she was simply busy or just plain rude. The few times they'd moved house gave them the need to get to know their new neighbours and they felt it appropriate for new people in the area to do the same, backed up by the fact that most of their neighbours had. When she finally got in touch to speak to the couple she spent the whole time talking to Alf, licking her lips and laughing at his ridiculous jokes. Freya was continuing to disrespect her yet it wasn't in her nature to pick her up on it and so she bit her tongue and shook hands like any civilised individual. Once Freya had gone, the couple had their first argument in years.

At first Alf was defensive of their new neighbour and he tried to convince his wife that she'd simply been friendly, although he had to resign himself to her way of thinking eventually. He hadn't noticed her flirty mannerisms and Mabel was furious that he could be so blind. To finish the discussion quickly he promised to be vigilant around her and assured her that he was still a one woman man before reminding her that Freya had offered to share books with her in a bid to show a positive side to the subject of their debate. In truth he was a little bemused as to what his wife had thought may happen yet he wasn't one for drawing out disputes of this nature and managed to predict how he would be feeling if Freya had been a gentleman caller who had acted in the same way towards Mabel in a show of empathy.

As predicted, the rat was let loose on every possible occasion and the repulsive woman was around to ask for Alf's help to round him up at least twice a day. It was clear that she knew how unreliable her dog was yet she persevered in her attempts to hold his attention and draw out his switch to the other side. In his mind he was simply being polite; however to his wife he was leering over her and trying to cash in his initial investment early for a better return. She had even tried to befriend Mabel in a transparent attempt to spend more time with him, spending regular hours talking about common interests while Freya tried to mask her sneaky glances. This thought ate away at her for a number of nights, moving into months, before she decided enough was enough and their petty arguments descended in to a full blown row. Unpredictably, Mabel threatened to move out.

As the heat died from their bitter exchange Alf could see the sincerity in her face and the tears she was fighting back glistening over her eyes. She explained that she hadn't asked for the world, just that her husband would stop chasing the girl next door who was herself an older woman and leave her to find her own irritating dog. As he swallowed to reply, his head full of possible excuses, he finally relented and agreed to explain to Freya that he would no longer spend his evenings chasing her mutt. As though planned, the doorbell rang and Alf was faced with the subject of his last discussion. He closed the door behind him and Mabel listened in as he rescinded his original offer to help.

Without warning her tongue plunged into his mouth and she held him close to her, moaning with apparent ecstasy as she breathed in his aftershave. Contrarily, in front of her unseeing face, Alf's eyes were wide open and he was trying desperately to push her away. Anybody viewing the exchange would have seen it as a one-sided affair and noticed the panic in Alf's expression, though Mabel was only listening in and the kiss, which lasted no more than five seconds before he managed to fend her off, sounded like it was enjoyed by both parties.

As he walked into his house, with his former partner in dog-finding now heartbroken yet reluctantly understanding, he noticed his wife's absence and walked up the stairs to see her packing a suitcase. As he got into the room he could hear her angry tears being sniffed back and sat on the bed to talk to her. She was clearly in no mood for excuses and so he bared his feelings and hoped for an encouraging response.

It was late in the evening by the time Mabel was suitably convinced of her husband's innocence and the two of them were far too fatigued to make anything of the night so they both made themselves a snack and took it to bed with them. Alf had admitted to feeling a little underappreciated but swore that he would never allow that feeling to come between the two of them and confirmed that it had been Freya who had tried to unite the two parties. After nibbling their respective suppers they climbed into bed and hugged tighter than they had in years. He couldn't help but suggest carnal relations yet his advances were thrown out due to the sheer exhaustion she was feeling.

Three days later, after a period without contact, the couple watched Freya as she loaded a van with enough to fill a small house and smiled as she drove across their road for the last time. The rat was barking on the front seat and continued to do so as she drove away, probably keeping up its single track routine for the entire journey. Mabel's face lit up as she noticed the joy her husband was expressing at her departure and apologised for ever doubting him, feeling the love build up between them both once more. It didn't feel like a victory though it was relieving to know that there would be no further sign of her.

Before too long Alf received a letter from Freya inviting him to stay at her new lodgings; but warning that the offer only covered him and not any other members of his family. She had moved over fifty miles away as she stated that she couldn't bear to see him being intimate with his wife, and despite not including the sentiment in her letter, had wanted him to move in with her to a location he couldn't easily go back from. Alf was certain of her intentions and he knew better than to keep the letter from his wife who agreed that she was plotting a last ditch attempt to lure him away before they threw the letter in the bin without even considering a reply. Freya waited for a couple of weeks and checked her postbox every day before realising that, contrary to Mabel's initial belief, she had lost.

    Wayne had visited a few times while Freya was in the neighbouring house and had tried to make light of the situation by joking to his father about his 'new belle', a comment that was quickly extinguished by his simmering mother. Seeing how strongly she'd felt about the woman gave him the correct impression about Freya's intentions and the jokes quickly subsided as, although he could be inappropriate at times, he was never knowingly malicious with it. As he helped his mother load the dishwasher one day he asked her what had happened and had been given no real information other than what Mabel would have done to her adversary given the opportunity. Remembering this conversation despite the length of time that had passed since meant that Wayne wondered how on earth his father could have provided such a ridiculous alibi for his mother and started to worry about what she was really doing.

TEN

"Dad...Dad...DAD..."

Wayne's impatience finally grated on his father as it snapped him back to reality. He suddenly realised what his son was likely to be thinking and quickly turned the situation around by suggesting there was a new Freya in their lives, one who was less keen on trying to separate the pair for her own benefit. Wayne was somewhat appeased by the suggestion, still thinking it unlikely but with less inclination to search the house. It had crossed his mind after he arrived that his father may have killed his mother given how many arguments they'd had in the past, reconsidering when he realised that all couples argue and they'd grown stronger after every battle.

They sat in silence as dinner was served and the peace continued as they all demolished their meals. Isobel couldn't stop herself from looking between the two men and wondering why there wasn't so much as a pleasantry exchanged between them, figuring that the missing figure from the table was likely to have been the catalyst for any conversation as Isobel had been for her family before she'd found her independence. The slurping of the gravy was a sound she could have done without yet she knew it would all be over as soon as they finished and made a promise to herself that she wouldn't make a fuss.

Without Mabel's ability to keep conversations flowing Alf tried desperately to think of ways to keep his guests entertained after the meal as they were both filling the void quite nicely and seemingly had no inclination to take a look around the rest of the house. Before too long Isobel was cooing at photos of her husband to be as a baby, a toddler and in his school uniform before they moved on to his more moody years as a teenager. Alf was still a little confused as to why this highly attractive girl could want to marry his son but he knew love was blind and he'd seen some particularly mismatched couples in his life. He'd also considered himself a mismatch for his own wife when they'd first started to see each other, although he had to admit that he looked considerably better than his son at the same point despite his perceptions.

The photo albums killed no more than twenty minutes and Alf was just about to suggest a board game when Wayne started to make his excuses to leave. Stuttering ever so slightly, Alf tried in vain to keep his son at the house yet knew it was unlikely as he was struggling with the most basic of conversation and the pair were growing visibly wearier before his eyes. Wayne insisted on using the upstairs facilities before he left despite the fact the downstairs washroom was a smaller version of the pristine bathroom upstairs and Alf started to panic at the thought of him meeting his mother in her condition. He knew he had to let his son go to reduce suspicion and, as Wayne climbed the stairs, he started to watch the clock in order for him to time his son's activity.

Conversation with just Alf and Isobel seemed much easier as the latter instigated a number of conversations designed around getting to know both of the new men in her life better. She offered nuggets of her own life in with the conversation, admitting she'd been a glamour model five years before and arousing Alf's curiosity even more. It may have been as simple as her wanting to settle down with a trustworthy man as Wayne was both consistent and loyal but it still seemed like a young princess had found her yeti in a yet-to-be-made Disney film. Beauty and the Beast sprung to mind, although his son would never be attractive enough to play the beast in his mind.

Fifteen agonisingly long minutes drew themselves out before Alf's eyes and he was just hearing about the experimenting his future daughter-in-law had done in college with her friends when he couldn't take the pressure any longer. He excused himself and climbed the stairs just in time to hear a relieving flush and inhale the last remaining remnants of Wayne's offering to the porcelain fixture. While expending his effort trying not to gag, Alf ushered Wayne back down the stairs and away from his bedroom, an act that made Wayne realise that his father was hiding something from him in the room. His face lit up with delight and he jovially tried to spring past the outstretched arms of his panicking pop as he asked what was really going on.

Isobel heard the disorder from the bottom of the stairs and climbed to get a better view. She was laughing to see them playing around when she arrived but noticed a look of real horror in Alf's face and deduced that he must have been planning a surprise for his wife that he knew her lump of a fiancé would accidentally ruin given his bounding nature. She allowed the activity to continue for a little while before relieving Alf of his duty and directing Wayne to the bottom of the stairs. He faked a turn as they got there but saw the severe look in his father's eyes as he followed them and knew that the game was over. Alf was sweating unnaturally and Wayne took that as a sign of victory on his part yet Isobel considered that he was actually furious with the situation and she insisted they leave straight away.

Watching the pair of them rushing their coats on made Alf realise that he still wanted their company and he apologised for being so belligerent despite the fact all in attendance knew the belligerence had come from Wayne. The two men were able to be civil as they said their goodbyes though Alf was fighting his urges to ask them to stay as he knew the desperation in his voice would have given away more than he would have liked. Instead he considered waving them off and phoning Jill, a decision that instantly brought calm to him as he knew it would stem the silence for a little longer.

As the car pulled away from the kerb, his son sat in the passenger seat with his arms crossed like a sulking toddler, Alf made his way to the phone and immediately went to lift the receiver. As he did so he realised that he didn't know exactly what he was going to say and thought that the call itself may have been a little suspicious. Anxiety started to rise within him and he put the phone straight back down before making his way up the stairs to consult his wife once more. He'd barely realised he was climbing the stairs with the mess of emotions taking over him yet he managed to get himself together by the time he reached the top step and practiced his opening dialogue as he'd done so often in the past. As it was, Mabel had seemingly heard everything.

"That pig-headed son of ours is still as vibrant as ever, then."

Mabel was always smart enough never to speak about people when they could potentially hear her and had never been considered anything other than an angel because of this, however they both knew that she gave her views when they were in private and those who deserved it got the sharp end of her otherwise still tongue. She knew that people rarely responded to criticism in an affirmative way and, even if their children were tearing her house up or indeed the parents were speaking out of turn, in telling them so she would have come across as a bitter or fussy woman. As it was she let them get on with it and tidied after them, remembering to cut their visits short in the future.

"You know our Wayne, ever the showman. He had to show off in front of his new fiancée. What she sees in him I don't know."

Mabel's body was as still as ever but she chuckled at the notion.

"You used to say that about us, dear. You asked me a hundred times a day what I ever saw in you and that was after ten years of marriage. If he marries her and they get divorced it's an expensive lesson learned. If they split now it's a cheap lesson learned. If they marry and stay together for the rest of their lives...perhaps they can be as happy as we are."

Hearing Mabel say 'are' rather than 'were' was a clear sign that Alf wasn't ready to let go, although he barely noticed her choice of words. He could only agree that she was right as he kissed her on the forehead and continued his internal concerns about his son's relationship. His choices were very simple and the analysis of the different outcomes more so, but as ever, he wanted to protect his son despite his age. To Alf, Wayne would always be that little lad who cheated at football and tried to use the money from board games in their local shop. Moving on seemed to be the hardest part of growing old.

Alf offered Mabel a cup of tea and, as he heard her positive reply, he instinctively went to put the kettle on. He could have stayed talking to his wife all day before realising that his call was necessary to warn his daughter of Wayne's mood. After all, Jill had been Wayne's ally in the same way Alf and Mabel had teamed up over the years, therefore her brother was certain to call when he arrived home. With two beverages neatly made he put Mabel's on her bedside table to go cold while he made the call to Jill.

ELEVEN

"How can you two be brother and sister?"

It was a common question for the siblings in school and it wasn't hard to work out why. Wayne was larger than any of their peers and had been labelled obese while Jill, who ate more than anybody she spent any time with socially, looked almost anorexic. If she hadn't had such a multitude of activities that clearly kept her so fit her parents may well have taken her to see a doctor but, as it was, they knew she was simply fit and healthy. Wayne was more than a little jealous though he knew he'd rather be overweight than have to put any effort into exercising.

"Simple, numbskull. We have the same parents."

Jill often had to stick up for her brother and this day was no exception. She was in her final school year and had to remind the bullies that, regardless of her absence for his last years of school, she would still be around to haunt them. As ever she'd spied her brother's distress from a window and had run out to his aid before things got physical as they had so often in the past. Jill despaired at the teachers' lack of intervention, knowing that it was better for her to be punished for getting involved than it was to drag her brother in front of their parents and try to convince them that it wasn't his fault as he was responsible for more than his fair share of mischief during his time there.

As Jill stood beside Wayne he visibly increased in size by puffing his chest out and bringing his ample arms up by shifting his shoulders. When he was in this position, primed and frightening, the other pupils knew to stay away as he had a fair punch on him. However they also knew that he would never use it until things got really bad and they were happy to torment him up to that point and watch him fly just as a teacher strolled in from whatever they pretended not to do at break times. Wayne had a very laid-back, unenthusiastic heart of gold and that was regularly his downfall when it came to other people.

Today's adventure had begun when a mutual enemy of both Jill and Wayne had stolen the bag from another pupil who wasn't nearly big enough to stick up for himself. Wayne had alerted a teacher who had blatantly brushed him off by insinuating Wayne would get in trouble for wasting his time. He could have pushed the teacher further and taken him outside, but with his level of luck, chances were high that the scuffle would have been over and there would have been an alarmingly low number of witnesses to back him up. With this in mind he waded into the disagreement, obtained the bag and returned it to the other lad who had simply snatched it and run off. Spoiling the fun of the bully seemed to be a punishable offence and, while it started with the usual name calling - "Moby Dick", "Everest Moobs" and "The Incredible Blub", the latter also a reference to the time he cried in a Biology lesson during the dissection of a frog - it was very close to ending with the usual blows by the time Jill managed to intervene.

Her presence invited a number of other names to the fray from the bully and his gang of four others, who felt it necessary to outnumber the duo before vanishing if someone of authority made their way towards the crowd. These insults again were unimaginative and repetitive, leaving Jill feeling unthreatened and calm. She countered with a retort about his stupidity by recounting the time he tried to argue with his Maths teacher about an answer he had come to that was hideously inaccurate but his gang laughed off the incident and the lad seemed unfazed outwardly, although there was a telltale flick of the eyes that Jill could guarantee was him revisiting the incident one last time.

With the insults expended the head of the gang decided it was time to start dealing the punches and he tried to go for Wayne's midriff, missing by a fraction and spinning around on the spot. As Wayne started to chuckle he threw another punch that landed squarely on his chest and winded him, dropping him to his knees. Jill stepped in to stop any more blows landing on her brother and was caught on the cheek by another of the lads who tried to control his pace, as he'd been in love with Jill since his first day in school. The establishment being what it was he felt it necessary to punch the girl of his dreams so as not to give away his secret; later that year she would turn him down as a date for a school disco and break his nose as revenge for his current attack.

As it was Jill simply glared at the lad who stopped dead, stood wide-eyed for a second and backed right off allowing her to get back to the centre of the fray. Wayne hadn't realised the punch had been so soft and was amazed to see his sister recovering so quickly and this inspired him to get back to his feet, wipe the tears from his eyes and stand beside her. The two of them felt an incredible force of unity and were ready for anything right up to the point the head of the gang came forward and lumped Wayne a second time, sending him back to the ground.

Jill could sense that the punch was due to swing towards her and she found herself in a great position to lift her bony elbow, bringing it down right on the back of the bully's skull. Having not expected such an attack he was then sent flying onto his male victim who avoided further discomfort by grabbing him and throwing him across the school yard. The lad landed with a thud and his throbbing head then hit the floor, adding to his agony. He was clearly done for and could only moan in distress while his stunned friends looked on, uncertain as to whether they should get involved again.

As ever in these situations the Headmaster was on hand to see the end of the fight and called on Jill and Wayne to follow him to his office. Having been tipped off about the scuffle he had missed the initial cause and the blows that had first been dealt and could only consider a punishment for those he'd seen in action. As the two of them were marched across the school other pupils started to glare at them and some chuckled at their misfortune having seen their tormentor dealing his attack and escaping retribution.

The Head sat the pair outside his office and closed the door, keeping them both in suspense for a few minutes. During that time they couldn't help but run through what had happened, exclaiming how unfair it was that they'd been caught retaliating when their enemy had clearly started the trouble. Their combined accounts were enough to convince the Head that they were innocent of any real involvement and, as he listened to their complaints, he decided upon his action to take. When he finally called them into his office they were both bright red from the energy of the fight and the potential injustice they were about to suffer, although both were willing to take the consequences as they knew better than to argue with authority.

As they listened, their Head discussed the issues with fighting and informed them both that they should have stood back from the situation and informed one of the teachers on duty that day. After a small protest from Wayne about the teacher he'd spoken to, during which he was sure to name and shame him, Jill asked him to calm down and the conversation continued. He was lenient with them as he knew they hadn't started the trouble and had generally good school records, although Wayne still felt a little aggrieved that he would be spending two lunchtimes in detention after a situation that was out of his control and, in all honesty, none of his business. The three of them agreed to the punishment, Jill being the main negotiator, and the Head made a note to speak to their bully and the teacher who had ignored the situation and allowed it to escalate. Both were reprimanded far worse than either of the children in front of him at that point and the bully was also warned off of causing any more trouble, particularly where Wayne and Jill were concerned.

That night they both recounted the situation to their parents and Wayne even managed to laugh when Jill reminded him of the fact he had been sent to the floor twice in one fight despite his size. Jill had always been a great calming influence on Wayne, and had she not been present for the fight, he may have ended up in a red mist situation, dealing out clumsy punches with his full weight behind them and causing some serious damage. The fact that he was able to laugh about the situation was clearly down to his sister's intervention; even their parents were aware of that.

TWELVE

"What's that big idiot done now?"

Although Jill would never deny her love for her brother she couldn't help but speak ill of him when he wasn't present at times. She was also more than a little aware that the altercation would have been a lot more to do with Wayne's manner than her father's. As she prepared to listen to the story of the evening she started to imagine the situation and half predicted what would come through the speaker of her phone without needing to hear the words. The one thing she hadn't counted on was the declaration of engagement that had been made at the table.

"Engaged? They've only been going out for ten bloody minutes!"

Jill had no idea how long they had actually been going out for and had failed to implement the inevitability of time passing when she made the statement. The engagement had actually come at a fairly average point in their relationship, although Jill's failure to see her brother for so long had made the gap seem so much shorter. Onlookers may have seen it as a denial of her own shortcomings yet she was never one to consider her responsibilities. Instead she reflected her feelings and continued on with Alf none the wiser as to whether the situation was out of the ordinary or not.

He knew the situation with his wife was nothing usual, however. He had a slight urge to tell Jill what had happened and to discuss the conversations that had taken place between his wife and him; but he knew his daughter was a tight bundle of rationality and would have called the police immediately, possibly also thinking he'd had a part to play in her death and trying to stall her removal for that very reason. Keeping this at the front of his mind he managed to bite his tongue until Jill made a decision to call Wayne and hung up the phone. He then made his way back up to the bedroom to tell Mabel of the ongoing saga between their two children that was possibly about to spiral out of control.

Fortunately for her father, Jill was an expert in calming Wayne down. She'd had to do it so many times while they were growing up and knew exactly what to say to stabilise him and reduce his mood. Unfortunately for her it meant being nice to him and feeding his ego for a few minutes. As she lifted the receiver she was certain she'd hear his voice, soon realising that he most likely hadn't yet made it back to answer her call. Half an hour later she tried again, finally hearing his gruff voice introducing himself with urgency. Jill spoke calmly, at first asking if he was alright and then feeding in subtle questions to get his side of the story.

She knew it had been his fault. Over the years his emotive nature had landed him in all sorts of trouble and he'd always tried to cover his tracks with implausible lies that buried him deeper and deeper. As he discussed the situation that had occurred with Alf he first tried to make out that his elderly father had lifted him out of the way and then changed the story to involve a stray dog biting his leg and forcing him to pull away from the bedroom. Why he tried such outrageous claims was beyond his sister yet she pressed on, keen to know whether Alf deserved any blame at all. Eventually she resigned herself to the fact that the occurrence was his fault and his alone before telling him that he should calm down and take a few minutes with his eyes closed and some deep breathing.

Isobel was in the room during the conversation and was re-painting her nails as she'd noticed a couple of chips at the end of her index and ring fingers on her left hand. As she observed her husband to be she saw him following the commands from the other end of the phone and became slightly jealous of the voice that had finally managed to calm him. She'd tried a number of techniques in the car, most of which were generally suited to children such as a promise of sweets and extra dessert; however she hadn't considered that a moment of quiet meditation would have done the trick. Eventually she realised that her envy was directed towards his sister and had been irrational, leading her simply to file the image of his slowly rising chest in her memory for the next time he became unbearably aggressive.

As he hung up the phone Wayne started to get tearful that he had treated his father in such a manner. With his voice cracking he relayed the conversation he'd had to his fiancée and she hugged him tightly, desperate to have some part in making him happy once more. As his tears dried on her designer cardigan he picked his head up and looked into her eyes, seeking some confirmation that she loved him and wasn't trying to get hold of the vast savings that he'd been stowing away since he'd first realised what money was really for. Without any response he'd had to come straight out and say, "Why do you love me, Is?"

Hearing this was no shock to her as he seemed to ask her once a week, however she gave her standard answer for the situation and reassured him that his good moods more than outweighed the bad. As his face morphed into a giant grin she pulled him closer to her chest and stroked his hair, further calming his breathing and making her feel that she'd done her bit to sedate him. The two of them hugged on the sofa for almost twenty minutes before he started to feel an empty space in his stomach and requested that she fill it. As the bread was buttered in the kitchen she could hear Wayne let go as he cried into his hands, dribble and mucous exiting his head en masse.

Meanwhile, in their bedroom, Alf was lying beside Mabel and he too had tears in his eyes. He could make out the back of her head with the duvet pulled right up to the top of her neck yet he was still unable to call anybody about her death. The fact that he was still having a conversation with her wasn't helping his decision. They were both so in tune during her life that he was almost telepathic after her demise, believing that every word she spoke had made its way from her lips to his ears as every other word had in the past. Losing her now would mean losing everything about her for the rest of his life.

As they lay together and discussed their children, reminiscing about the quarrels and battles the family had seen over the years, Alf found himself playing with Mabel's hair as he had done when they were younger. He'd stopped doing it well into their thirties and, though she'd missed the soothing nature of the act from time to time, she'd never thought of asking him to continue. As it was she now couldn't feel it, though she was blissfully unaware of this irony.

Alf had never been one for looking back at the past and spending time remembering funny or poignant incidents. He felt almost forced to make the journey back as his wife seemed incredibly good at bringing up events that had occurred and reminding him of how he'd felt, yet he knew he was in a position that required some action and sprung back to the present with the thought of what people would say about his hiding of her body up to now. A hot flush hit him and he started to sweat before putting the conundrum to his chatty spouse. This stopped her conversation immediately while Alf stood up and walked around to the other side of the bed, kneeling in front of her gently smiling face with its closed eyes.

"We need to go out."

Alf hadn't really thought it through but he knew he couldn't conceal Mabel any longer. He could only think of being sent to prison either for not declaring her state or, worse, being convicted of her death. Staying where they were left them open to further visits and having to leave her would be heart breaking. He wasn't completely sure how far they would make it though he knew he had to give it a go, even if the move turned into a dry run. 'Being sure you have the strength is half the battle', he thought to himself.

The first job was to convince his wife that it was a good idea. She'd had her own reservations about being found and was sure to back him up when he'd suggested keeping her under wraps but it was possible that she would now need some persuasion to move from the warm, comfortable bed that lay beneath her. This was a good chance for him to practice his powers of enticement as well as his non-motor assisted driving skills; he hadn't been in charge of a wheeled vehicle responsible for her wellbeing since her accident.

THIRTEEN

The witnesses that had been innocently walking through the main street had described the impact as 'sickening', yet Mabel knew nothing of it until she woke up in agony at the side of the road. As consciousness returned she could feel every muscle in her body ache and there was a stinging sensation running up her left arm and in both of her legs. She had no recollection of where she was or what she'd been doing, however she had a vague sense of a dream that had disturbed the sleep she was returning from. In the vision a yellow car, something small inhabited by two rowdy lads cheering and racing around, was coming towards her and she sensed she had to act quickly. As she tried to dive out of the way…that was when it all went black.

The hideous realisation that her nightmare had been true hit Mabel as she tried to get off the cold, hard floor. People had started to gather and that was the first image that she noticed as she prised her eyes open. A man in a dark blue suit was telling her to stay down, almost as though they were in a conflict and the enemy may still have a chance to attack. Her head was thumping and she wanted to tell the man to get away from her and stop yelling or at least to speak to her like a human being and not a Private yet she couldn't muster the strength. Before too long a younger man in a white vest took offence to his manner and hit him, sending him sprawling to the ground in the opposite direction. The crowd went crazy at this point until a smartly dressed woman called for silence, reminded them all of Mabel's position and stepped in to assist her.

Instinctively Mabel put an arm out to the woman for a hand up but the woman shook her head and advised her to stay where she was. This was very concerning as she'd had errands to run and was making good time but now it seemed apparent that she was in a bad way. Her thoughts were tortured with both the things she had to do and concern for her limbs which, given the correct amount of attention, sung out with acute displeasure. One of the spectators, a teenager or very young adult by the look of him, had his hand over his mouth as though he were about to vomit and was staring at her legs, correctly suggesting that they weren't both where they were meant to be.

The kind, smartly dressed woman continued speaking to Mabel and was asking her a number of simple questions that were frustrating her as she knew the answers should have been at the front of her mind. So far on her tarmac quiz she'd got the date, time and location wrong which had all been indicated by a less than discreet dropping of the woman's face. She knew she was running errands, she remembered Alf, Jill and Wayne and that she was due home before three o' clock but she was reluctant to put those answers forward while other questions were being delivered to her. Instead she lay and listened to the bits she didn't know and became agitated that her lack of correct answers was concerning the horde.

A sound of sirens disturbed the peace before too long and it made Mabel relax a touch to know professionals were on their way. Although the woman had been a great comfort to Mabel, disregarding her expert level quiz, she was highly aware that she was purely keeping her talking so she'd remain conscious and had done nothing to right her condition. As the two medics rushed from their vehicle towards her they guided the woman away from Mabel and she was never seen again, although she could be heard in the background as the trolley was placed in the back of the ambulance while the crowd grew ever larger.

Her stay in hospital was longer than she could ever have envisaged and meant numerous trips back and forth for Alf who was trying desperately to keep the house in one piece with his limited knowledge of how the cleaning gadgets worked. Jill was fortunately on hand to help him out but he knew he could never fully take on Mabel's role and was more than a little relieved when she was finally able to join him back at the house as she could guide him in her idiosyncrasies. Her leg had indeed been as badly broken as the close-to-vomiting teenager had suggested and so needed a good amount of physiotherapy before she was up and moving again, a task Alf was happily able to help with. In the meantime he was even happier treating her wheelchair like a racing car and, as they braved the town centre once more to tackle the regular errands, Mabel relished the opportunity to beep people out of the way as they whizzed past with her chariot.

Things took a slight turn for the worse one day as Alf was attempting to knock yet another minute off of their time trial by taking the curbs to the limits. However, in his haste, he hadn't noticed that one curb had been knocked by a careless driver and was jutting upwards slightly more than he was used to. As the wheel of the chair hit the curb Mabel felt the whole thing sliding and tried to hold on as the memory of her accident jolted back to disturb her formerly excited mind. She'd felt the way a child had in a car, barely aware that somebody was in control and could lose that control at any second without notice, yet she had been brought back to reality and her landing on the pavement was less than graceful. She screamed in pain as the reality of the situation hit her husband and his soul tore in half when he realised the gravity of what he'd done.

Feeling the guilt rush over him, Alf ran to the front of the chair where Mabel was sat upright having literally been bounced onto the floor below. She was holding her leg although her back was also experiencing a shooting pain and she was unsure of which bit hurt the most. A passing stranger saw the accident and bounded over to help lift Mabel back into her chair, assessing that she mainly had bumps and bruises and should be fine before declaring that he 'wasn't a doctor, mind'. Alf knew that they had to get her back to the hospital and carefully wheeled her home, both of them returning in silence and feeling particularly foolish.

The guilt haunting Alf was overwhelming him by the time they made it to the car at home and he was almost crying as he helped Mabel into the front seat so she pinched his cheek and told him that it was as much her fault as it was his. As she kissed him she saw the remorse in his face and gave him a smile that cracked his stony silence, inducing a subtle smile and a huge apology. The trip to hospital was lighter than the trip home had been but Mabel's pain wasn't easing much and she knew she had probably set her recovery back by a short while. As they checked into the Accident & Emergency department they were reluctant to give the real cause of the accident and simply blamed the pavement for her condition. The receptionist was horrified and suggested they sue the council to which Mabel agreed and they went to wait with slightly guilty expressions etched onto their faces.

They were more truthful with the doctor and, while he repeatedly looked at Alf with disgust in his eyes, he treated her cuts and bruises as best he could while advising on safer methods of wheelchair use. Alf felt like a small child being told off until his wife confessed her love of the speed and the thrill she needed following the massive change to her life she'd been through. The doctor was no more sympathetic, telling her that recovery is a huge part of an injury and that she should have just accepted her position until she was well again. As he turned to look at his notes Mabel stuck her tongue out and stretched it towards his back while Alf watched and nearly burst with laughter. As the doctor turned back her tongue disappeared and the doctor returned to his notes looking incredibly annoyed.

The journey back home was lighter still and Alf promised to keep looking after Mabel until she returned to fitness, which was to be around four months later. As they discussed the doctor who had lectured them both so sternly they laughed and dissected his life, concluding that he must have ceased his sexual activity decades previously. In truth they both knew he had been right yet they used his less than friendly nature to eliminate any last feelings of regret they had inside them. By the time they made it home they were already planning on ways to improve their speed across the dangerous pavements although both knew they would never repeat their actions.

FOURTEEN

"Out? Are you mad?"

Mabel's assessment of her husband's state of mind was more accurate than intended, however the look in his eyes was enough to confirm to all present and conscious that he was serious. He didn't have access to a wheelchair as he'd had following Mabel's accident but he did have the next best thing in the garden. With a single wheel it would prove to be more difficult to navigate but Alf's wheelbarrow hadn't let him down in all the years he'd owned it.

"If they find you they'll take you, and if they take you I'll lose you."

This was confirmation of what Alf had known all along; he definitely wasn't ready to give her up and felt that by moving her to another location he could hide his tracks better and keep their relationship alive despite her actual state of being deceased. He reiterated to Mabel that Wayne had very nearly discovered her; and Jill would no doubt be across in the next day or so and, between them, they were close to making the discovery. She was no more convinced after ten minutes of discussions so Alf told her to wait where she was and trotted down the stairs to his shed to prepare their getaway vehicle.

Her total silence had eluded Alf and, even as he made his way outside, he could hear her voice inside his head pleading with him to reconsider. A wheelchair would have been a better option but he had limited access and even less time to spare. The lock slipped off the shed easily and he was surprised at how little wrestling he had to do to remove the barrow from the back of the outbuilding. This was testament to the fact that Wayne hadn't borrowed anything for a short while as he had an odd tendency to move everything into the doorway to find what he needed and then kick it back in as far as he could to enable him to get out again. Alf had hoped this was a trait of youngsters and that he would eventually grow out of it but his faith had been in vain and he still found himself battling with the rakes and hosepipe from time to time even after his son had moved out.

With the wheelbarrow in position they were ready to go, or so Alf had thought. Suddenly his stomach started to growl at him and he realised that, should they be gone for a short while, he would need some provisions to keep them both alive. He grabbed some sundries from the kitchen including a loaf of bread and what was left of the crisps after Wayne had snuck in and filled his pockets yet again, pondering whether he should take some cutlery and the small camping stove to ensure a little variety in their outdoor meals. Mabel was starting to get particularly irate at this point, growling about the use of the barrow despite the fact Alf had wiped most of the concrete from it with his hand and so he grabbed what he could and made his way back up the stairs to calm his beloved.

As he was doing so a car pulled up outside the house and came to a stop suddenly, the handbrake taking most of the force of braking. As it rose the ratchet clicked loudly and alerted the occupants of the street to the cars arrival including the driver's parents who were now preparing to leave with haste. Alf looked up and caught a glimpse of his daughter, hardly believing she'd had enough time to drive to the house following their earlier phone conversation. However, he considered that he'd lost track of time as he lay next to Mabel and that had given her the opportunity to speak with Wayne and decide to tell them both face to face what had happened. This was a fairly typical strategy for Jill as it meant she could offer sincerity with her discussion to ensure they would take her side as they had so often in the past, yet another possible cause for Wayne's bullishness and selfish nature.

Pulling up to the door Jill offered a little more time by checking her phone for messages and noticing there was one from her colleague Roy. Jill had turned him down for dates more times than she'd turned up for work yet she was still bombarded with notes, flowers and gritty chocolate that she wouldn't have dared to eat if she was seeing the guy. For some reason he couldn't accept that he had no chance and Jill was contemplating reporting his actions to the management as her mother was bundled into the bucket end of the family barrow under protest. Realising she had more important things to attend to Jill put her phone away; removed Roy from her mind entirely and rang the bell. She looked around as she waited, noticing a few neighbours were out cutting their lawns and smiling to those she knew.

Calm came over her as she stood waiting, expecting her parents to be a little flustered. She knew that by tapping in to her inner serenity she would be able to deal with the situation better and come out on the other side looking like the glue that bonded them all together or, at the very least, looking better than Wayne. That wasn't hard with the way he acted at times but she knew she had to work harder with each incident just to maintain her reputation, a fact that wasn't fair yet seemed to correlate with the rest of the world.

In contrast, on the other side of the door, Alf was sweaty and tired with wide eyes and a head that darted around like the prey of a wild animal. He'd carried his wife from the bedroom to the bottom of the stairs where their vehicle rested and was now ready to burst out of the back door, out of sight of the rest of the neighbourhood and on a quick road to the woods. There were plenty of hiding places beneath the trees and rocks and Alf had devised a plan to keep them both safe while he figured out what he was going to do about the situation in the long term. He hadn't had room for blankets to keep them warm at night, although he planned to return for them once Mabel was safely out of view if the distance wasn't too much for him. This was a decision he would have to make towards the end of the journey. The only issue now was the sharpness of the figure at the door despite the fact she was not technically in the way.

Mabel made the decision to go for it. Her exact words were, "If you're going to do it then just do it now", a realistic interpretation of what she would have said during her living years. Alf nodded in agreement and co-operation before charging for the back door and bursting into the garden, quietly enough so as not to alert Jill but dramatically enough that two of their gnomes appeared to faint with disbelief. They were well on their way to freedom; sure they'd eluded their visitor.

At that point Jill was starting to worry about the lack of response from the house. She was sure they'd be in as it hadn't been long since she'd phoned and her parents were not well known for their spontaneous trips out anymore. There had been the Dartmoor incident and that crossed her mind, though it had been so long ago that she instantly dismissed the idea of a repeat performance. She took her phone back out of her bag and rang the house in case her knocks hadn't been heard and was surprised at just how long she was stood listening to the ringing from inside with no reply.

Finally she gave up and took to banging continuously on the door and shouting her parent's names, causing her hand to tingle as she did so but not enough for her to stop. For most this would have been a point of panic yet Jill was more concerned for her own embarrassment, knowing that she was attracting the attention of everyone who was close or passing. Her twisted face glowed red as the banging continued and her screams became indistinguishable noise before too long, all of which was heard by the intended targets of the commotion.

As the yells soaked into their ears the escaping duo were left motionless and staring at a barrier they hadn't considered a few seconds beforehand. In front of them, surrounding the entire garden was a four foot concrete wall complete with bushes on top and the distinct lack of an obvious escape route. Alf's mind was looking forward to a short break as he darted for the woods but now knew that it would have to work double time to conquer this obstacle. He barely knew where to start, although he studied every inch of the wall in the hope there was something he may have forgotten. He then cursed himself for failing to plot an effective escape route as he sighed loudly. It was the only break from the noise coming from the front door which continued incessantly and this provided an opportunity for Mabel to project her view of the situation.

"You numpty."

FIFTEEN

Alf and Mabel never referred to it as 'an incident', though Jill and Wayne were happy to disagree with this. The house was emptier than it had been for a long time now that their offspring had moved out and Alf had managed to convince his wife that they could look forward to long nights together without the need to consider anybody else before finally realising that they also had a chance to go on holiday alone, something they hadn't done for three decades.

Mabel took out the map on the Thursday night and they both plotted a number of possible locations for an unplanned excursion from the secluded to the extravagant, including Blackpool, London and Aberdovey. They could barely contain their excitement as they wrote down things they'd have to remember and knowingly pushed out things they'd packed for their children in the past. Wayne had pigheadedly refused to pack his own suitcase on every occasion and their battle of wills with him before a holiday meant they were better off giving up than putting up with his sulking for the following week. Jill voiced her opinion that she shouldn't be made to do what her brother had gotten away with and so it happened, every year, that four lots of clothing and essentials would be packed by the two furthest ageing members of the household.

As dresses and trousers flew across the bedroom the two of them hadn't really decided where they were going, almost uncaring as to where their location would ultimately be. They had a long list of places they wanted to visit and suggested that they could do them all eventually, allowing themselves time to digest which were most important to them both. With their cases packed, the necessities list double checked and a cup of tea in hand they got back to their provisional locations and studied it in more depth before deciding that Dartmoor would be the best consideration as it was the height of Summer, they had access to a camper van that belonged to Alf's uncle and they'd avoided camping vehemently when they had children to consider. Now was their time to explore something they'd never achieved before.

As they pulled off the drive and towards the horizon Alf shot Mabel a cheeky smile and they glided at a moderate speed towards their location. The scenery they took in was beyond breathtaking and they were both able to soak up the country air on the journey, feeling like every strain and worry was draining out of them, no doubt ready to be picked back up on the way home. That last thought was struck from their consciousness as the roads reduced to single lane tracks and they navigated their way through drivers who were irate at their innocent lack of reversing skill and others who were happy to allow them to pass.

Finally their campsite came into view and, although the sign at the main gate was worn down and lacked care, the rest of the site was well strimmed and expertly maintained by a team of professional gardeners. They had electric via a hook up that was soft on the eye and were looking forward to getting in touch with their inner children at the games rooms, a place they had never ventured into without their own parent's supervision. This was set to be a return to more carefree times but without the watchful eye of those in authority; they were finally at the top of the hierarchy.

As these thoughts came and went and the fees for their stay were handed over, adverse events were unfolding for Wayne. He'd entered a poker tournament that had been suggested to him after an illogical trip to a betting shop where he'd placed bets on horses he liked the sound of ('Sticky

Treacle' and 'Barbie Queue' being just two of them). Time passed quickly while he was studying his opponents and, before he knew it, he owed over three thousand pounds to gentlemen he'd known for less than an hour. He thought he'd been doing really well as his first hand had five ascending cards of the same suit – the five, six, seven, eight and nine of diamonds, an occurrence where most would have suggested that the cards had not been shuffled correctly, if at all – however, it didn't take much to convince Wayne that they were actually a *descending* hand that was completely worthless, hence he should surrender all of his placed bets immediately. His eagerness to learn the game saw him owing the ludicrous amount before he even considered his actions and, as the crowd of hardened men started to realise that he didn't have more than twenty pounds on him, they decided that three thousand would be enough for him to find in the short term with the threat of missing fingers hanging over his head.

With this information made public they threw the now panicking young man onto the street and made ticking sounds to imitate the imaginary clock that hung above him, the ever decreasing window only seen by himself and a group he was hoping to call his friends by the end of the evening. His only hope was to get in touch with his sister who by this time was living half an hour away by bus or taxi. He had no choice but to hitch a lift, his wallet having been seized as a down-payment for the outstanding debt.

As he emerged from the third car he'd had to flag down, the first two only offering short journeys that barely got him out of the town he'd spent the day in, he felt the guilt and humiliation rising up from within him as he realised that he was visiting Jill for the solution to a huge problem rather than as a social visit that might only include tea and a chat. He knew this would bear an even larger debt that would take even longer to pay back despite the fact he'd get to keep all of his digits. Nevertheless he hung around at her door for ten minutes before internalising his pride, breathing deeply and knocking loudly.

Bereft of information, Jill was both suspicious and unsure how to act on seeing her brother at her doorstep. She prepared herself for what was about to come out of his mouth and knew only that it would be bad news, particularly judging by the state of his clothes and the stony look on his face. He'd never considered himself particularly fortunate to have a sister like Jill who was willing to take care of his problems in the way that she did and, under questioning, he'd have to admit that he took her for granted most of the time. This was yet another opportunity for her to get him back on track and she only hoped he learned from this mistake and never gave in to gambling again. By the time Alf was running around his garden trying to escape from the hero of this situation, Wayne's gambling losses had amounted to nought to her relief.

Jill's first instinct was to speak to her parents in the hope of securing finance either from their savings or a loan that they would have been more eligible for than her or Wayne. She took Wayne straight to her car and drove over, her anxiety subsiding at the sight of their car on the drive. As she walked up to the front door she never considered that they weren't in and spent over ten minutes tapping, and then banging, on the front door. The neighbours were aroused and some walked over to ask for details, walking around the house in an attempt to spot the inhabitants. As the tension returned Jill started to imagine what may have happened to her parents that meant their car was intact, their house unaltered and yet their ability to answer the door was hindered.

Finally she snapped and ordered everyone to the front of the house. By now the image of her parent's murdered corpses was so strong in her mind that she couldn't convince herself it wasn't accurate and she picked up the most appropriate decoration from Mabel's rockery to throw at a window. The crash echoed around the neighbourhood as Jill climbed in and started to venture round the property. She heard the concerned chatter of the people outside, blocking it as best she could as she studied the evidence of the rooms and drew no real conclusion.

Satisfied that her parents were alive, or at least had been dragged to the woods to be hacked to pieces, Jill searched for a solution to her original problem. She'd heard Alf discussing his distrust for the banks yet knew he was a fervent saver and concluded that he must have had a big stash somewhere to hand. A few disturbed drawers and cupboards later and Wayne was finally in the clear as Jill had found over four thousand pounds in total. She took what they needed and returned downstairs where Wayne was already patching up the broken window with the help of an onlooker from further down the street. Having no way to get hold of the absent couple meant the pair had to escape to pay the unnecessarily high debt before tying up the loose ends when their parents re-emerged.

On their return Alf and Mabel were chuckling like reignited school lovers. Their trip away was just what they needed, even if the return meant cleaning up broken glass and wondering why they'd been burgled by people who didn't want their stuff and had repaired the damaged they'd caused. One confused phone call to their daughter cleared everything up and Alf cursed himself for not realising that his money had been disturbed. His next call was to Wayne who promised to pay every penny of the fund back and finally made good on his guarantee over two years later, as predicted by his father.

SIXTEEN

"Thank you, dear."

    His reply was loaded with sarcasm which proved that he wasn't concentrating, the getaway being the most important thing on his mind. He'd enjoyed the occasional sarcastic quip in the past but rarely used it on his wife, knowing that if she'd put forward an exclamation that he hadn't liked the sound of then it was probably for good reason and he was in the wrong. In this instance he was halfway between wondering how he could ever have forgotten the wall around his garden and realising that it was due to the fact he'd hired a gardener to do all of the horticulture over two years previously, putting the entire section out of his consciousness as it was only Mabel who tended to use it for recreational purposes.

    He started to visualise the easiest options, or at least what he'd thought were easy options. The first was to bounce the wheelbarrow from the ground to the chairs, from the chairs to the table and finally on to the top of the wall and through the bushes. To confirm whether this was a viable option he tried to bounce the wheelbarrow a little off the ground, finding his test to be a complete disaster. The whole thing refused to move due to a combination of Alf's age, Mabel's mass in the bucket and the overall ridiculousness of the suggestion. He then looked around for ramps to butt against the wall, a better idea that may have had a place in the situation had he any spare wood or logs the right length to complete the bridge. Unfortunately, as time passed, he found nothing that could be of any use.

    At the front of the house a crowd had gathered to add to Jill's humiliation. She knew she had no control over whether her parents answered the door or not but her certainty of their location made her think they may have gone temporarily deaf or insane or even both. Before too long she was handling a number of questions about their whereabouts from people who were talking for the sake of it rather than offering any really helpful suggestions. Their utterances such as, "Do you think they've gone down to the shops?" and, "Could they have gone to the beach?" were about as helpful as "How do you think they get rockets up that high? I mean, without researching it. Your best guess?", and Jill was having to remain civil while losing her patience quite quickly. Her only plan at this stage was to ring Wayne to find out if they'd mentioned going out anywhere and, if so, how long they were due to be out for.

As she dialled she had a strong feeling they were close enough to answer but were refusing for some reason. She was concerned that they'd had enough from their children and wanted some time alone, considering that if it was the case she would happily leave and give them some space. All she needed was confirmation that they were alright as she would never forgive herself if they were both lying motionless on the other side and she could have helped, maybe even prevented…the worst. The ringing stopped and was replaced by the sulky voice of her brother, a tone she'd heard so many times before and didn't give a second thought to.

Jill told herself that she'd keep the conversation short and got straight to the point, asking if he knew why they weren't answering and if he knew where they may be at this point. He started to go back over the story of what had happened and was cut off by her matter of fact voice which suggested she thought something was wrong with them. He was upset and still a little angry yet they *were* his parents and he had every right to feel concerned for their wellbeing. He responded appropriately, telling her everything he knew and offering to go back to the house. She didn't know whether his presence would be helpful or not, although a familiar face among the growing crowd was always going to be preferable. She took him up on his offer and waited for his arrival, telling those closest that all was in hand and she had help on the way. The neighbours refused to take the hint and continued looking around and shrugging, irritating her further and making the wait until her brother arrived seem even longer.

As the car pulled up to the kerb Jill caught sight of Isobel in the driving seat and started to wonder why she was stringing Wayne along. She was absolutely stunning and Jill submitted that she was probably just a little jealous while holding on to her belief that girls like her didn't usually go for types like her brother. Perhaps she had a fetish for carelessness or enjoyed watching a grown man strop about like a teenager when he was out of cereal; either way, realistically there was nothing she could do about it. She smiled as the doors opened and turned her attention back to the real issue of the hour. Why was she being ignored by her own parents?

Wayne noticed her smiling and it eased his concern a touch. It meant they probably weren't lying dead on the mat by the door at least and insinuated that she knew they were alright. He smiled back, turning to his fiancée who seemed relaxed about the fact that they'd been pulled away from their time together. If this had been her parents there would have been vocalised anger from her, making him wonder if she actually liked his parents more than her own. It was true that they were more laid back and had let the two of them get on with their lives whereas his future in-laws tended to interfere more yet, in his experience, girlfriends refused to like anyone else's parents more than their own. This thought made him smile even more and his grin shone through the crowd like a beacon, furrowing brows and bringing forward tuts of disapproval. The fact that they were rubbernecking didn't seem to be an issue but Wayne's apparently cheery attitude towards his parent's disappearance was.

He made his way through the unfriendly faces, noticing his oral muscles wane with each person he passed. Isobel was right behind him and they both arrived at the door together, making eye contact with Jill and asking for an assessment of the situation before putting their thoughts forward. They didn't actually have any thoughts initially; however there was no reason for them to confirm this fact as they stood confidently listening and forming proposals as they went.

In the garden Alf was putting together a plan of his own with the help of his recently departed soulmate. He took time to scan the garden and allowed himself to relax, particularly when the racket from the front door temporarily ceased suggesting they were finally alone once more. He took himself back to the times he'd spent in the garden, the battles he'd had with the weeds and the structures of the place and how he'd conquered them both. Or had he?

The weather recently had been very agreeable and had prompted many to go into their gardens to sunbathe and catch up on their planting and trimming. Mabel had made it out less and less over the years but even she had broken the curse of the indoor lifestyle and taken a day to read a book in the garden. Everything around them was dry and the plants were really starting to look beautiful around the whole landscape due to the work of their gardener, particularly in one place.

As soon as Alf caught sight of the area in question his chest loosened and his eyes lit up. It was dark and grey beneath yet the flowers surrounding it hid this fact from those who weren't aware of the truth. The moisture that came anywhere near the space was soaked into the concrete and meant that only hardy plant life could survive there. The wall that surrounded the area had always been an issue and nothing that Alf had put in place had ever been good enough to sustain such a simple construction. It had taken up so much of his life that he was genuinely planning to put a request in for it all back if he ever made it to the pearly gates.

He beamed as he considered the possibility of escape through this sodden and overcompensated region, reaching a point where certainty entered his deteriorating mind. He would need to clear the greenery from the area with a knife first but knew that it wouldn't take more than a few minutes given the quality of the machete he kept safely tucked away in the shed. He looked down upon the face of his wife as his lit up and let out his idea in a very contained manner.

"Crumbly wall?" he suggested.

Mabel replied with vigour.

"Crumbly wall!"

SEVENTEEN

Finances had always been an issue for Alf as the children grew up as he was a hard worker but also unskilled, meaning any redundancies normally went his way first. This had led him to a varied career which saw him working for a firm an hour away from his house that produced drill bits. His only job was to take the completed bits and sharpen them for up to ten hours a day. Although mundane he continued with Jill and Wayne in mind, encouraging them both to work hard lest they land a similar job to him.

While at the company he became an acquaintance and almost a friend of a workmate he knew as Gnarly. Being a six-foot-two monster meant that he advertised himself well as a hard worker who was more than capable of construction which was highlighted by his tales of what he'd achieved and the fact that he was muscle bound and had plenty of stories regarding time spent at the gym. Alf felt a little inadequate around him at times, cunningly disguising his envy as admiration without truly knowing that he was doing so.

At the time a van had reversed into the corner of his wall and ripped a large hole in it before taking off at an incredible speed that left the owners with the responsibility of patching the damage. Mabel had run out of the house on hearing the initial noise of the impact but had missed the driver's registration, cursing him quietly under her breath as she looked around for witnesses. As ever there were none to be seen, although the gossip of Mabel running into the street with curlers in her hair and a dressing gown on went suspiciously far given the circumstances.

The incident came up during a particularly complaint-riddled tea break at the drill bit production company and

Gnarly had been listening intently to what Alf was saying and looking more interested that he ever had before. He possessed a natural ability for acquiring tools and materials for building and decorating and had offered to help rebuild the wall for a minimal fee, one that should have seemed too low even if he'd known about how the resources would be acquired. As it was cash in hand he couldn't refuse and their agreement to work together on the rebuild had been the point at which they'd very nearly become friends.

Mabel was rightfully anxious about the possibility of her husband getting involved in a repair job of that size and was suspicious about the price they'd been quoted, however with no other possible way of getting the work completed she reluctantly agreed and prepared herself for two weekends of dusty floors, concrete filled sinks and watching her beautiful garden being trampled beyond recognition. Alf made the mistake of suggesting it was a positive outcome as it gave her an opportunity to plan and implement a brand new garden although his wife could only envisage weekends of back breaking labour to be a hindrance.

Despite being an accomplice to the terrible work Alf had never paid much attention and, had he bothered, would never really have understood what was going on in front of his eyes. The time passed in a blur and he was happiest during the times he made the tea as he felt some sense of achievement and had also been able to leave Gnarly to work his magic. As corners were cut and holes were filled over rather than in Alf was blissfully unaware and was even starting to get concerned that he was paying too little to the workman. He echoed his thoughts one evening to his wife who had reminded him that any surplus funds would be going towards her new, unintended garden and he knew that a change in conversation was necessary.

Having been consciously absent from what had actually been done to the wall meant Alf was in for a nasty surprise during the winter of that year. He'd moved on from the drill manufacturing industry into injection moulded toolboxes as the company was closer to home and even paid a little extra, meaning their funds had increased with a reduced effort on his part. The job itself was just as repetitive and lacking in ultimate achievement but it meant he had a little more time with his family. He also had more time to watch the rain penetrating his brand new wall, concerning him more every time a fresh grey patch appeared along the middle and induced cracks into the cement.

When gaping holes started to appear in the wall he was duty bound to do some repair work, trusting nobody with the project after being burned so badly with the initial construction. He also still had limited funds despite the pay rise so was unable to employ a reputable builder, a move that would have saved him a lot of work over the coming months. After spending a week of his hard earned holiday adding patches to the existing framework Alf was thrilled to see the wall coming back to life and starting to look as it had after Gnarly had finished with it. Two weeks and one rain storm later, Alf and Mabel sat watching the grey patches emerging from the fresh concrete like beautiful yet smug butterflies, a sign of things to come.

Whenever guests came they would admire the beauty of the plants selected to brighten up the garden, skimming over the corner of shame that hung over the occupants and refused to even hide when visitors came round. It became known as the crumbly wall as the children grew up, always knowing their father to be a runner up in the battle against the inadequate structure. He could never just let it go; however, returning the wall to its rightful state at the start of every summer when the weather was bearable enough to do so and watching it degrade over the following months.

Inevitably age took its toll on the couple and they had to give up their battles of the garden, leaving the care of the plants in the hands of a young Spanish gardener named Eduardo. He was studying horticulture at a local college and was keen to get some experience, his leaflet wafting in front of Alf at just the right moment as his knees were starting to swell from a morning planting begonias. A short discussion with Mabel was all that was needed before the call was placed and they found themselves staring at yet another muscular figure willing to help with their garden. Eduardo was far less threatening, remaining in their lives past his college course as he found himself plenty of employment opportunities close to where they lived and he felt a great deal of gratitude that they had allowed him to experiment with their garden so early on in his studies.

This lack of relationship with his garden meant that he put all of his concerns out of his mind and left the maintenance of the solid structures indefinitely, forgetting about the ambitious conflict with his old foe. He never thought he'd be pleased to view the shameful boundary, let alone smile at its decline; however Eduardo's skill evolved to such an extent that he was able to incorporate the wall into a display that made it seem like he'd deliberately selected such an atrocious piece of architecture for that very purpose. Their most distant neighbour, Glenda, enjoyed almost monthly visits to their property just to soak in the negative aspects of the crumbly wall and took great delight in telling others about it right up until her visits offered her a chance to view the gardener's superb achievement. Mabel often thought she'd never stop inviting herself around and berating her husband yet this proved to be the final occasion and the family could detect a very strong feeling of disgust as she excused herself from their property.

Eduardo received pleas from Glenda in the following weeks for him to perform similar miracles at her property but he politely refused, taking more satisfaction from letting her down than he had from most of his work. He knew that the structure would never be solid and could be destroyed easily by anybody who put any force behind it but the aesthetics were the most important feature as the only use it had was to mark the boundary of the property. He planted a few perennials to ensure his work would endure a long period of time yet also incorporated some less hardy plants to protect his future at the house. Alf was a very laid back employer and regularly made him laugh, something he wasn't used to in his other positions. More importantly Eduardo had introduced Alf to motorbike racing and they were both enthusiastic about watching the stages together during his years in their employment, a bond that only ceased when the gardener finally moved back to Spain to be closer to his family.

EIGHTEEN

Alf started to make engine noises with his mouth. This wasn't normal for him yet he hadn't felt this level of excitement for an incredibly long time. He'd felt frustration, pride, concern and incredible jubilation at the actions of his children yet he'd not had an adventure for as long as he could remember. He felt almost childlike, sneaking out of his house while a massive group of people tried to discover his whereabouts though unsure whether he would make it in time. Even if he did, making it to his hideout would be another task required before he could relax. The adrenaline was flowing around him at an incredible speed and had been extremely helpful during the short period of hacking he'd performed to clear his getaway route of greenery.

In his mind, Mabel was not enjoying the shower of spit raining down on her face. He'd noticed it travelling from his lips through his vision but hadn't really considered where it would land until she vocalised her position. Alf apologised indifferently, never removing his gaze from the wall of shame that was destined to become their escape hatch. It didn't occur to him that he wasn't really listening to the voice at that point and he'd effectively ignored his wife, although it wasn't for the first time.

As he accelerated away, twisting his grip on the wheelbarrow in what he considered to be a realistic motorbike fashion, he only had eyes for the wall, particularly at the point he wanted to hit. The centre of the crumbly wall was just to the left of the corner and was therefore no more than a few blocks in width. Even so, Mabel was concerned that a charge towards the wall wasn't the best way to complete their escape, shouting his name as loudly as she could until he finally realised why their peace had been shattered. He drew up to the wall and parked the wheelbarrow sideways with a few inches to spare, trying to work out what the issue could be. He finally paid some attention to Mabel as she suggested kicking the wall down and then barrelling out of the garden, a tactic that seemed obvious once he'd heard it from someone else. He put his boot through the wall and found it wasn't quite as brittle as he'd thought, conjuring images of his wife flying over the wall if he'd continued with his original plan.

It only took a minute to create an adequate sized exit in the barrier, the concrete flying into the street as the blocks shattered and their parts tumbled to the grass verge beside the garden, after which Alf beamed at his first ever victory over the wall. He was reminded of the pandemonium at the front door by his silent wife and ran back to the wheelbarrow, dropping the engine noises and concentrating on where he was going next. He could only hope that the intrusions would be as minimal as possible as there was no real explanation for what he was doing that would have appeased any passersby.

Jill was unaware that he had left by the time the police arrived, the driver of the car having to shoo an unprecedented amount of people for such a call out of the way. The two PCs were sure this would be a standard shout, envisaging the elderly couple in front of the TV with their hearing aids out or returning from a stroll in the park where they'd gone to get away from the nagging of their family. Parking the car, PC Drayson cursed himself for his indifferent attitude when he saw the look on Jill's face. She was completely pale, almost shaking and looked absolutely petrified in complete contrast to her normal, uncompromising demeanour. The crowd were no doubt adding to her condition yet he'd known Jill for a number of years and had never seen her look even remotely like she did at that point.

Drayson's partner was an old school officer who had moved to the area from the Metropolitan force and had spent most of his career chasing drug dealers and petty criminals around the busy streets of London. Having decided he'd had a few too many close calls, PC Graham put in for a transfer and never looked back. He'd found out the hard way that he was not built for running as he stood barely five foot from the ground and was fairly stocky. He'd complimented his ability with regular jogs twice a week to keep up to date with his fitness yet found the harsh reality of passing time to be too much. The country was perfect for him, particularly when he was assured that most of his work would be performed from a car. A call to a missing man and his missing wife was just what he'd hoped for as he signed his name on the transfer request letter.

Drayson took the lead due to his familiarity with the family and approached Jill at the same point that Graham was leaving the car. She was distraught and found it hard to talk as she'd been certain her parents would be in and so had started to envisage her father lying on the floor after his ordeal with Wayne. It seemed the convenience of their ever presence had now turned into a reason for concern and Drayson knew there was little he could do about it. After determining that Alf was contacted just an hour or so beforehand he saw no reason to break in and attempted to allay her fears by suggesting a number of places they both could have gone. Jill remained adamant that there was a problem so Graham offered to look through the windows to see if he could spot either of the occupants, finding nothing after fifteen minutes of searching.

Isobel attempted to help the situation but was politely asked to keep her thoughts to herself by her future sister-in-law after which Wayne found himself a use by comforting his clearly concerned fiancée. She'd heard enough about the family for long enough to know there was almost definitely an issue yet a lack of evidence meant that the officers couldn't act. Finally Drayson decided that the crowd was becoming an issue and advised them to disperse, inwardly admitting that it should have been his first action upon arrival. Something was definitely in the air and this made him curious. He offered to take Jill around the town in the squad car to give them more scope for finding the elusive pair as Graham, himself and Jill would give them three pairs of eyes and a chance to look at each spot simultaneously. She had no choice but to agree, leaving Wayne and Isobel at the house to call should their parents return. As this was being arranged the recently disseminated crowd watched from their windows, unable to pry themselves away from the most exciting action the road had seen for quite some time.

The trio spent over an hour scouring the area, avoiding the woods as they were so vast and would have needed a bigger team to search. Every possibility was considered from the snooker room to the village hall where Mabel often cleaned as a volunteer, though both were locked and bereft of life signs. The officers quickly ran out of ideas and offered to take Jill back to her parent's house, advising her to go straight home and wait for news of their return. They knew it was unlikely anything was awry and, as such, had to wait another day before they could act on her concerns. As they pulled up Jill could just about see the wall around the garden and noticed the bits of concrete littering the road, cursing the idiotic thing for ruining her father's relationship with gardening.

As she exited the car her first thought was to pass on her new found calm to her silently waiting brother. Drayson had that effect on her and could have transformed her from a blood thirsty Rottweiler into a timid Labrador in the time it takes to boil a kettle for which she was grateful. She showed this by taking his advice and disbanding the waiting family, watching Isobel driving the two of them off before she folded herself into her car and gently accelerated towards a well earned meal. PC Drayson wrote up the incident while he sat in his car, the top of his head barely missing the roof lining as his legs protruded from the sides of his seat. He and Graham had received a considerable amount of abuse from the youngsters in town due to their vast height differences but the truth was they made a terrific team as their personalities complimented each other perfectly with Drayson's serene outlook and Graham's ability for solid, swift action.

By the time they made their way back into town Alf was already in the woods. He'd had to overcome several dogs that were yapping for a taste of the widower's passenger and had hidden behind low walls whenever he came close to anyone who might have seen them. Despite his frame of mind he knew there was no explaining what he was doing and anyone catching sight of them would have phoned the police immediately. He had to keep going and complete his task to allow him more time to think about how he would cope without Mabel as, for the time being, he didn't have to.

His final site for the evening was an opening too small to have been a quarry but too large to have occurred naturally, at least to his family's opinion. They'd discussed it on many an occasion over the years, considering that it may have been the possible site for a small construction at one point that was disrupted and never completed. There he found a messy tarpaulin, plenty of rocks to hold it in place, twigs and logs for a sustainable fire and a hole in the wall big enough to shelter them both for a short while. He wasn't sure how long he could withstand the pressure of life outdoors but he knew it was his only option. With Mabel by his side comfort was less of a priority.

NINETEEN

"PC Drayson, sir."

Drayson stood to attention awaiting his new sergeant's response. As he did so Sergeant Holton looked his paperwork up and down before becoming distracted by the stillness and silence of his new colleague. He was fresh out of the wrapper; after initial training he'd completed six months with Powys Constabulary and had been transferred upon his previous sergeant's satisfaction of his capabilities. It seemed Drayson was one for the country life and Sergeant Holton knew he would make a good officer, if only he could learn to…

"Relax a little; I'm not assessing you for immobility. I'm Sergeant Holton."

Drayson tried to drop his shoulders and move his legs apart, perhaps even bend one a little. Unfortunately his ability to take it easy had not yet kicked in and he looked uptight despite trying to follow what had sounded like a direct order to him. He took his new sergeant's hand and shook it stiffly three times before his discomfort grew to gargantuan levels and he felt an urgent need to let go.

"I know sir; I saw so on your door."

Holton had to hold back a chuckle. His instinct was to apply sarcasm here, perhaps asking the constable if he was looking to make detective, but he knew his new recruit would be much less receptive to this than his other officers at this point. He took a breath to allow the condescending quips to escape his body and the two of them went into a discussion about aspirations, workloads and leaving Wales. Drayson's accent had rather given him away and, although it wasn't as broad as a citizen of Holyhead it was certainly noticeable in comparison to Holton's Yorkshire twang.

Drayson's first week was a week of nights, a matter that didn't concern him too much as it meant he could concentrate on the job rather than being distracted by the local sights. He made a note to take a good wander around the local area within the next week or two, mainly so that he could determine shortcuts, hiding places, dens made by local hooligans and areas for possible fly tipping. To say he was focused was an understatement but Holton knew it would wear off as soon as he got into the flow of life in his new jurisdiction. Sure enough, it did.

Drayson wasn't so convinced it would to begin with as one of his very first incidents involved a drunken teenager who was acting aggressively in the park following her very first session with cider. He was sure her parents had no clue she was there and it didn't look like there was a big group of them as often happened with teenage drinking incidents. What he didn't know was that she had become intoxicated to a level that made her scary to others and her normal bossy attitude had multiplied tenfold, forcing those around her to seek shelter instead of joining her in drinking. Rather than finding somewhere safe to watch from they all decided to make their way home and left her to it. One of the residents who lived beside the park had phoned to complain after the girl asked her terrier what it was looking at and started to growl at the petrified mongrel.

As he approached the girl she looked up and caught sight of the car initially, finding the officer and his partner for the night slowly creeping towards her position. She smirked at the thought of two officers cowering as they moved towards her and started to gesture that Drayson may have been there to apply for his position on the sex offenders register. He responded calmly, masking the intense fear he was actually harbouring. He'd seen drunken teenagers before, crowds of the little hooligans, but none so aggressive towards an officer of the law as this one. He took point as his partner followed, both of them keeping their eyes on the offender as they stalked across the grass.

"What's your name, sweet?"

His voice carried across the still air, echoing slightly in the distance. The teenager took another swig of her very cheap, apple bereft booze and sneered across at the two of them. She seemed completely unconcerned with their presence and almost found it agreeable that they were there, a reaction Drayson found considerably disconcerting for the type of area he was residing in.

"It rhymes with Old Bill", she retorted, cursing herself for not coming up with a witty reply that didn't give her name away; after all, it didn't take a baby name book to find all of the possibilities with such a clue.

"Must be Jill then? Am I right?"

Her stupidity forced her to stop talking; still believing she could walk away with a caution. She could see now why people drank as it helped her to stand up to the police and would probably serve as a vital tool in helping her to become powerful at school. The only issue was that she couldn't afford the ridiculous price for the awful stuff despite the fact that it was just apple juice with alcohol added at some point.

In the time it took her to construct this thought the two officers were practically beside her and she had to act quickly to get away from their grasp. Deciding to flee south towards the main road she threw her bottle behind her and flung herself down the hill, tripping over a raised drain cover in the process and landing face first into the relatively soft grass. Drayson acted quickly to secure her before leading her along the path back to the car, weaving across the width of the tarmac as they went. He could sense that she wasn't used to this feeling and was concerned mostly with having to clean vomit from the back seat when he made it back to the station. Fortunately Jill's stomach was way ahead of him and emptied its contents onto the wall beside them, the smell of stale apples with steak and kidney pie hitting the officers without apology.

Jill spent most of the ride home with her face pressed against the glass as Drayson's partner gave a serious and long lecture about the effects of substance abuse, every word passing up to and over Jill's head with no chance of penetrating into her mind. Her final thought before she passed out included a colloquialism for defecation and the face of her father giving her exactly the same lecture she was missing out on in the car.

The next morning Jill could finally have empathy for her father when he'd asked them to be quiet as children due to a nasty hangover. Alf was never a big drinker yet he tended to enjoy himself when he was invited out for special occasions and he always suffered for it the next day. Jill and Wayne had once thought it humorous to play up to the situation, making as much noise as their energy levels would let them and taunting him by calling him an old man and making 'Awwwww' noises. Alf had never forgotten this, relishing the opportunity to exact revenge on his daughter. Rather than banging around and screaming in her ear as she had once done to him, however, he gave her a long list of chores to perform and reminded her of the amount of taxpayers' money she had wasted with her feral visit to the park the night before.

The neighbours had all seen the police car pulling up to the drive and had let their curiosity loose on Alf a bit at a time as they saw him during the week, seemingly judging his parenting as he explained how out of character Jill had acted on that isolated occasion. He took little notice of their false concern, reminding them all that they had more than likely partaken in their own similar incidents during their childhood. One of the more elderly residents had given more advice than she had been invited to yet Mabel had witnessed her smoking a giant marijuana joint while she was topless in the company of several men during their wilder days, something Mabel wouldn't have dreamed of pursuing. When Alf relayed her preaching to his wife she couldn't help but raise her eyebrows and filled him in on the old bat's activities in her youth. Alf raised a smile, banged two saucepans together and shouted "What a hypocrite, our lass. A *hypocrite*!" at the top of his voice.

Jill lay on the kitchen table with an ice pack on her head praying for death. She managed to give her father a look to encourage his own demise if possible, closing her eyes after a few brief moments when she failed to achieve her goal. Every part of her body ached, her temples throbbed and her chest was tight where she'd rejected most of the cheap cider, the false apple taste bitter on her tongue the second time around. In that moment Jill finally realised why most people don't use alcohol to cure their problems, swearing she would never drink again. Ever.

TWENTY

Her mind was working much harder than usual for the time of night which meant that the small joint of meat and roast potatoes she had initially been looking forward to had nearly been burnt beyond saving as she imagined her father trapped somewhere, shouting for help yet receiving no reply. She knew eating was a priority to keep her energy levels high, after which she chose a red wine with a mediocre film to take her mind away from the worry. She was certain she wouldn't know anything that night unless Alf chose to call, an unlikely scenario given that he most likely didn't know about their panic. The wine seemed to be doing the trick and Jill made a note of the details from the label to ensure she would pick it up again. These days she stuck to grape based drinks as the cider aisle in the supermarket made her feel sick for reasons she couldn't place.

    An hour into the film she was brought back to reality by the sound of the phone ringing, sending her immediately to her feet as she ran towards the noise. Picking up, she managed a quick, "Hello?" before the flat voice of her brother settled her overactive heart. He seemed incredibly upset, an emotion that was normally tarnished with self righteousness and a sense of injustice, both of which were absent from his tone of voice. He felt that Alf's disappearance was his fault and explained that he'd tried to convey his feelings to Isobel but she'd had been of little help before she'd taken herself off to bed. It seemed amazingly early to Jill although Wayne assured her that it hadn't been unusual. She was something of an early riser, the opposite of her future husband, and as such made up for the lack of sleep in the morning with more in the evening. He'd had no issue with this up to this point and had simply phoned Jill to try and extract some further sympathy.

Jill was all too happy to take his side, trying subtly to convince him that he was making a mistake in marrying her. In truth she simply felt that Isobel was out of his league, trying to push him towards someone who was less attractive to spare his feelings. He retorted by assuring her that he was prepared for her departure, enjoying the time they spent together and the looks they got as they walked through town hand in hand. He suggested her ease in doing so was a good sign that she was happy to stay and Jill found it hard to argue with the point, instead offering a delicate word of caution and changing the subject.

Inevitably the conversation swung to the whereabouts of their parents with both parties offering comforting suggestions as to where they may have been. She reminded him of the Dartmoor incident and they were both able to laugh at how foolish he'd been and found themselves reminiscing for longer than they had in recent months, both needing to hear the voice of the other as a reminder that, in time, they would need each other more than ever. Quietly they both hoped that it would be a good few years down the line before such a circumstance would arise.

Wayne spent the conversation with one eye on the clock, ever aware that he'd made the call and would foot the bill if their dialogue continued for more than sixty minutes. Both were uncomfortable with long goodbyes and he knew that if he started to wrap up the call at about the fifty-five minute mark he'd stay within his free call allowance and so he implemented this plan, the two of them losing connection at fifty eight minutes. He smiled at himself to know that not only had he been reassured by his sister and made to feel so much better, it hadn't cost him a penny. That thought triggered his overactive stomach and he made his way into the kitchen to make a fried bacon and egg sandwich. As he placed the frying pan on the side he noticed his future wife's phone sat charging on the breakfast bar.

The kitchen was completely silent; the only movement was from the electrons passing across the element of his hob and, likewise, those entering the charging socket of the mobile phone in front of him. He'd never had a reason to be jealous before as Isobel only ever phoned her mother once a week and any meetings she had that weren't to do with her choir or drama groups carried an invitation for his presence. One thing that had crossed his mind was the fact that he couldn't be with her all of the time as she worked, meaning she had every opportunity to be unfaithful at her place of employment. A little voice suggested that any act of defiance against their relationship would surely be accompanied by messages from her beau that would be kept on the phone and, the minute that thought entered his head, it became a priority.

He was knowingly trying to bat the temptation away, focusing his concentration on the choice between ketchup, brown sauce or barbeque relish on his less than healthy choice of supper. However, a subconscious voice was nagging him to take a peek, a quick peek, nothing more than a miniscule peek just to be sure there was nothing untoward on the phone. Having never checked it before meant his fiancée would have the ultimate trust in him, suggesting she would be free in her mind to leave it so close to him regardless of whether it contained evidence or not and it was this apparent trust that finally led Wayne to crack. As his bacon sizzled in the pan and soaked up the lard he was using to cook with he extended his arms and picked up the phone, entering the 'mylovelywayne' passcode necessary to put life into the device.

He headed straight for the text message section and scrolled through those that contained his name, that of his sister and also those titled 'Mum'. Before too long he came across a bank of three with the name of a colleague, Ray, and begged himself not to look any further. By dismissing the possible content of the messages he knew he could continue the life he had that had seemed so impossible, giving himself to Isobel with only a small possibility that he was sharing her with another man. He was certain he could trick his mind into forgetting the existence of the messages and continue as he was, openly flouting the love of his life as she happily consented to public displays of affection occasionally involving her tongue in his mouth while they shared a swing at the park. This triggered a darker thought as he conjured an image of Ray, a man he'd never met, kissing Isobel at work before they'd shared their own kiss on the swing and he vividly pictured Ray's saliva coating the lips of his beloved. The anger built up inside him and he was finally able to convince himself that, not only was she having an affair, she was using Wayne as a cash machine and living rent-free in his house as well as parading him around town for her colleagues to potentially catch sight of and laugh.

The bacon spat across the room, seemingly furious that the ring below it was operating at its highest setting and the bumbling fool had refused to turn it, the golden brown colour of the meat rapidly turning to a dark brown and finally to black. With no more lard for it to hide in the heat finally linked the pan and the contents, causing smoke to belch out as it made the most of the freedom it had been granted. The smoke alarm sucked in a good amount of its eternal enemy, unable to act due to the fact Wayne had taken the battery out on the first day of his time in the house during a particularly long chip production session. Had he left it in the high pitch would have snapped him back to reality, causing him to drop the phone and end the battle that was raging just a few metres from his current position. As it was the smoke had crept upstairs to disturb the sleeping blonde haired beauty who had unwittingly caused the situation and suggested she nip downstairs to return the kitchen to its former state.

As she reached the bottom of the stairs she was unsurprised to find the pan sizzling on the hob trying to spontaneously combust, however she was drawn to the silhouette of the chef with a phone in his hand that could only have been hers as it was connected to the wall via a lead where she'd left it. She felt betrayed as she watched him staring blankly at the screen, seemingly unaware that he was surrounded on all sides by a thick, black fog that was quite happily trying to asphyxiate them both. He didn't notice her arrival, only waking from his state at the sound of her voice.

"What on earth is going on, Wayne?"

He froze on the spot and attempted to justify the situation inside his head. There he was, phone in hand, listening to the white noise from the kitchen that was emanating for some reason. Had he started to make a sandwich? Somehow he knew that was the least of his worries.

TWENTY ONE

The keys banged under her fingers, each one taking the pounding they deserved as Isobel attempted to complete her work on time that morning. She loved office work and was a little gloomy that her current position was only temporary as she was well liked and reciprocated those feelings to her colleagues, however the machine she had to work with was slower than a tortoise hitching a ride from a snail in a salt mine. The banging was meant to be a warning to the inanimate pest that worse was yet to come, although it didn't seem to heed the warnings at all.

As her cursor stopped flashing for the fourteenth time a clapping rose from the other end of the office and everyone looked up in hope, wondering whether the business was doing well enough to grant them all a small rise in their salaries or even a tiny one-off bonus. As ever this was not the case, however optimism was in short supply and the workers felt their dreams were all they had to cling to at times.

The clapping was coming from the head of the department, Richard Johnson, who had spent most of his life trying to disguise the fairly obvious fact that he had two different euphemisms for the same sexual organ as his shortened Christian name and surname. His best friend in school had told him that Dick Johnson could be shortened to DJ, a handle he used for a long time before approaching his first management position. His nickname seemed to become less acceptable the further he went through an organisation and he was forced to find a way to block the sniggers from his staff and even his own bosses from time to time.

Today was about introducing a new employee and he'd been satisfied with the way this gentleman had barely broken a smirk when he mentioned his name, thinking of no better reason to take him on despite his apparent lack of experience in their field. He had plenty of qualifications and had once co-managed a bank in one of his previous positions, leaving on the grounds that sales had overtaken customer service and left him in a position he felt unwilling to continue with. This had impressed at interview, although DJ was hoping he would be able to combine the two practices to make the company more successful than it was.

Ray smiled as his position was announced across the office comprising six separate desks in an open plan fashion around the outside of the room. Isobel was just to the right of the door, partly obscured by a photocopier that enabled her to feel hidden whenever people entered or left the room. She leaned slightly backwards to get a good view of her new colleague and nearly fell off her chair when she'd caught a good enough glance. Ray took this as a sign that she'd overstretched on purpose, perhaps through the shock of how attractive he was, and smirked in the same way he had when Dick had introduced him. Isobel dropped back on to the wheels of her chair and apologised, clocking the expression on the new employee's face and wondering what on earth he was thinking about her.

The whole introduction lasted a matter of seconds but it allowed her five year old computer to catch up with her speed of work and she breathed a sigh of relief to know that she could carry on. The problem had inspired her to save the document and this released the feeling of stress that had appeared when she considered she may have lost her work from that morning. A quick chew on her pen focused her mind and she began tapping away at the keys in front of her only to be disturbed by Mr Full-of-himself seconds later.

"I don't mean to be rude but you're by far the sexiest animal in the room."

Isobel didn't look up immediately as she was trying to decide whether he'd actually said that monstrous line or whether she was simply imagining it would be something he'd say judging by the ridiculous grin spread across his face. She grimaced and opened her eyes widely, her appearance mirroring that of a person being robbed as she turned her head to look at him. He didn't flinch as he received the peculiar look, instead taking a minute to think about how fantastic he must have looked to her. She knew he was going to cause an issue yet couldn't bring herself to be outrightly discourteous to him straight away; had she done so the next few weeks may not have occurred. Instead she smiled politely and excused herself, blaming an intolerable workload for her unwillingness to converse.

During the first week Isobel returned to her desk from errands, breaks and meetings to find small notes littering her work area, the first of which started with cheesy lines such as, 'Are you a fan of Barry White? If so we could be *soul* mates'. However as time went on the content of the notes became more and more graphic and her aversion to discussing the content with him escalated the tone of the messages to the point that she felt it necessary to report him to her boss. The note she went in with read 'I'd pay for a minute in your company…as long as I could choose the outfit'.

After a brief discussion with their boss Ray was called into the office and asked for his views on the incident. To Isobel's mind he should have been sacked on the spot as there was plenty of evidence to confirm her complaints yet he made it out of the office with just a warning and gave her a look of death as he left to return to his desk. How he'd got her mobile number she would never know and, had she found out, she'd never have believed that her best friend in the office would have been the one who would have done it, innocently believing he was organising a surprise party for Isobel.

Originally he'd bombarded her phone with abuse, advising her to 'sleep with one eye open' and describing what he'd do to her if he met her in a dark alley at some point. He was reported to the police, although she only kept the three worst messages from the bundle to stop her inbox looking like they were having an affair with a stream of disgusting and outrightly perverse ideas. This apparently wasn't enough for a conviction and she didn't think to ask for an injunction, the latter finally unnecessary after a few tough weeks of lingering looks and despair.

It transpired that Isobel wasn't the only woman Ray was tormenting. A cashier in their local supermarket had found him attractive enough to message him on the phone number he'd passed across to her one lunchtime and she'd been caught in his sights as a target for filthy messages. She too was the settling down type and had no interest in the acts he was describing, eventually telling him to keep his thoughts to himself and leave her alone for good. Denying her request, he continued for another two weeks before she hatched an idea to get rid of him forever by agreeing to a date with him.

They met at a chain restaurant and both ordered steak, his reason being to prove his masculinity as he ordered it rare and wanted her to see the blood dripping from his mouth as he dined, her reason being the sharper knife that would save her a lot of effort. As he tucked in to a giant serving of his ultra rare serving she watched his grinning lips silently before plunging the knife into his leg and twisting, half anxious about the ramifications of her actions and half certain that she would hear no more from him. As the serrated edge tore his skin apart and ripped the muscles adjacent to his thigh bone she warned him to stay away from her and to never send another message to another woman again, finally retrieving the knife from his pouring leg and dropping it on the table in front of her. She left swiftly as their fellow diners attended to his wound and called for help, taking his side in the dispute as his date had imagined they would given their lack of information.

Ray was unable to use his left leg properly after that night, choosing to walk with a hospital stick after countless hours of physiotherapy. He left his job as it was so close to the supermarket and, although he hadn't reported his attacker for fear her collection of messages would further incriminate him, the thought of meeting her again filled him with dread. He forgot about Isobel completely, finding a new life in another town where the women weren't quite so negative about his forward approach.

The incident was kept secret from Wayne as she knew he had a jealous nature and their entire relationship was based on her reiterating that she was with him for love and, regardless of how others described his appearance, she found him to be attractive, witty and charming with a very low chance of leaving her when she needed him due to his obvious faithfulness. She figured her constant affirmation of the authenticity of her love for him was a small price to pay for an actual soulmate who didn't rely on cheesy lines and constant gifts to keep their relationship alive. His reaction to the situation would have been to blame himself and to suggest she leave him for this other guy despite having never met the rat, an absurd solution she would never have agreed to. Instead she moved forward with the help of her best friend, who never quite shook the guilt of giving away her information, and left her significant other safely in the dark.

TWENTY TWO

"You've got some messages from a guy called Ray, Is."

Isobel rolled her eyes and sighed quietly, immediately regretting the gesture when she considered the duality of its meaning. Inwardly there was a grimace before she explained her annoyance at the fact that she'd had to keep Ray's messages and they'd been found as opposed to feeling disdain for Wayne feeling the way he did. In truth Isobel couldn't believe she had to go through these motions with him yet she knew it was necessary to ensure he knew she was committed and faithful to him regardless of what others tried to insinuate.

She ushered him over to the table, holding his hand from the moment she reached him and continuing to do so as they were seated. They sat opposite each other and Isobel looked deep into Wayne's eyes before starting to talk. Giving him every detail of the incident, from that very first smug look he shot across the office to his eventual disgraceful departure, she hoped he would realise that the messages were purely one way and so obviously detached from the type of communication she had with her fiancé that there was absolutely no chance of them being anything more than a pervert's fantasy. Wayne's self esteem prevented him from seeing the situation for what it was and, as such, his frown directed unwanted tears that flowed down his face onto each of his legs in turn. He took in the information about the police reports yet still convinced himself that it could be a cover story.

She asked about the content of the text message, predictably hearing about her former colleague's confidence about the size of his genitals and what he may have done should she wish to meet him somewhere quiet. He even had the impertinence to suggest she buy them both coffees, a line that wouldn't have worked even if she was single. She'd almost forgotten what he'd written, shuddering at the thought that he'd been anywhere near her during his brief employment with the company.

Disregarding the message she reiterated her feelings for the sulking, unnecessarily heartbroken man in front of her and attempted to coerce him into divulging his feelings about the situation so that she could deal with them separately. He continued to frown at the floor, only looking up occasionally to catch her eye and hopefully inflict a feeling of guilt onto her. Isobel would never have picked this up as she knew she had nothing to feel guilty for yet she continued to hold his hand and offered gestures of peace, reminding the grown man in front of her that she no longer worked with the brainless fool in question.

After a minute of silence, the two of them both looking at each other simultaneously for the first time during the conversation, Wayne restated his concerns that Isobel should never have been in love with him. He offered apprehensions about his appearance, which were generally reasons for abuse from people he spent time with and even gangs of teenagers looking for fights, before telling her that she was far too good for him and needed to find someone she could really be happy with, throwing in his low self worth as though it was an issue she should have been surprised about. She smiled at this and a tear sprang from her right eye as she poured out her feelings for him, giving every reason she could as to why she'd picked him from the scores of men she could have decided to settle down with.

Wayne wasn't used to praise or hearing that he had positive attributes and became embarrassed as he heard about his selfless nature, incredibly good dress sense and his motivation for a better world. He was certainly too lazy to make any real changes yet seemed to have ideas on how to improve things like no-one else and at least had the decency to write to powerful people in the hope that they would be implemented. He often concentrated on his appearance and threw in his worries at this point, hearing that he wasn't ugly and had actually acquired a few female fans of his own. Isobel had been reluctant to mention that the women in question were from the same salon as her and were generally much older than the two of them yet this fact seemed to provide a small boost to his ego, a welcome result at this point in the conversation.

It was obvious that he wasn't completely satisfied at her reasoning for having the texts on her phone yet she knew it was important to keep them for the time being and pointed out the age of the messages as evidence that he was no longer keeping in touch. They were bound to have more discussions of this nature while they were together, however she was keen to ensure that he knew exactly how she felt about him and was happy to repeat this as much as he needed. It was sure to grow tiresome, a risk she was willing to take in the battle to keep the man she loved and to be with him regardless. As soon as they came to a point in the debate that no further questions were forthcoming she started his sandwich from scratch and made sure he was at least well fed.

As he put his plate on the side Isobel looked deep into his eyes and promised to remind him of why they were together, hoping to implant a permanent reminder by submitting to his every request. She knew that would probably mean dressing up as Supergirl before performing a striptease and preparing herself for the final act as a missionary might yet she was keen to show him that there was more to physical affection than satisfying his visual needs and, as such, sat him on the bed and blindfolded him. This may have seemed like an exercise in trust to some; however it was purely intended as a way to rob him of his most worn down sense and to ignite the use of those he squandered so regularly. Her part as the dominant mistress also served to heighten the roleplay, ensuring his short term fulfilment and hopefully planting the seed of her devotion to him as intended.

While Wayne closed his eyes to sleep off his latest emotional episode, Jill was still barely holding on to consciousness and relentlessly pushing images of her parent's possible whereabouts to the back of her mind. As she dozed on the sofa images of her fantasy partners came floating in before her, offering a number of services she could never have performed herself. She had often dreamed of a sports star falling for her as she adored watching the muscular physique of those who excelled in demanding activities and could imagine being swept off her feet by an Olympian or, at worst, one of the swimmers she occasionally shared the pool with who regularly put her ten slow laps to shame in her own opinion.

Recently she had found herself fantasising about politicians, putting herself in an imaginary situation where she would have to give insight into current events and suggest ways to improve the lives of so many with incredibly tight budgets. Failing to do so, her party leader would then call her into their office and berate her faltering skill before having to apologise in ways she would never choose to share should such a conversation arise in real life. As good as the fantasies were Jill was often surprised to see the figures she conjured up, particularly given her attraction to athletes and elite track personalities. She never considered that she could find herself dreaming of Harriet Harman in the same way she imagined Jessica Ennis-Hill.

With the fantasy continuing, Jill found herself being ushered onto a small wall outside the parliament building to be formally punished in front of her peers for her ill-advised views when, just as the cane was being brought to the fleshy bulge of her upper thighs, the wall started to crumble beneath her. She couldn't stop herself from descending with the blockwork, seeing the concrete that had held it all together burst from the seams and cover the walkway in front of her. She became worried that she might fall further forward and into the Thames, preparing herself for an almighty swim using all of her experience. As she dropped the foundation finally gave way and she felt herself fall, the jolt waking her immediately from a fairly deep slumber. Most of the dreams she'd envisaged throughout her life had faded into nothing, the images of her subconscious mind becoming nothing more than a blank page as she opened her eyes. This time was different, however, since every small detail was there to be recalled. The debate, the object of her desire, the parliament building, even…

"The crumbly wall", she gasped.

TWENTY THREE

Jill's last year of college had been a demanding time as she battled exams, parental concerns about her whereabouts and the temptation to use drugs alongside her peers. Her previous experiences with alcohol had led her to believe the latter would be a very bad idea and so she had managed to keep herself away, putting all of her energy into the one area of her life that she could feel comfortable with and rely on her certainty to guide her through. She'd never told her parents about her sexuality as she knew her father had an antiquated view on same sex relationships although, judging by the two DVDs she'd found under their bed when she'd been around eight, it seemed likely it was only male to male contact that he had any strong negative feelings about.

Regardless, when Jill started to see her best friend Amanda in a new light she kept her feelings to herself and made a bid to muddle through anything she was unsure of. It had begun after cross country running one afternoon, the two of them finding that they were the last to get changed in the locker room and hurriedly throwing on socks and shirts in a bid to get to their next lesson. As Amanda looked up she caught Jill's eye, who had become entranced by the simple action of her bra being fastened and pulled into place. Amanda had never thought her friend could view her in such a light yet the glance was so long and obvious that the intention was unmasked immediately. Jill's eyes widened as she found she'd been caught and she blushed, apologising profusely as she directed her head away from the beauty before her.

Amanda took a moment to consider her own feelings, coming to the conclusion that it would be mutually beneficial for the two of them to discuss whether a relationship would be possible. She thought that an open discussion in the middle of a room that could be occupied at any moment would be outrageously stupid and so she suggested they meet at Amanda's house that night to talk openly and honestly about the situation. They'd known each other long enough to be sure that confidence was guaranteed and Jill agreed, finding the possibility slightly intimidating despite keeping the usual brave face that had almost deserted her momentarily.

That night Jill suggested it would be best if her and Amanda spent the night together so that they could revise for their upcoming exams and her parents were ecstatic to think that she was going to so much trouble to get the best possible results. As she arrived Amanda's mother opened the door and let her in, offering a hot beverage and supplying information on the arrival of their dinner. Before they sat down for the meal Amanda suggested they start studying immediately having so much course material to get through and they almost tripped in their haste to climb the stairs, the two girls beaming with anticipation at the mere thought of being alone together. This instilled confidence in Jill and further removed some of the doubts she had initially experienced about whether her friend was likely to return her desire.

As intended they initially discussed what had happened in the locker room, Jill again apologising before admitting to her feelings of attraction for Amanda. They'd been firm friends for around a year, Amanda being cast off from a group of popular girls who had been her friends since the start of secondary school. She'd had a disagreement with the implied head of the group and had left under a dark cloud, vowing never to return to the shallow and ruthless crowd. Jill had been more of a loner, moving between different groups of friends while never having a permanent place of her own. As she'd spotted Amanda crying on a bench beside the athletics track on the main field she'd decided to console her having never really conversed in the past and therefore holding no grudges. Jill had noticed her as a part of the group, inwardly believing that she was an ill fit due to the sharp and exclusive nature of the girls. Amanda was clearly more emotional and all inclusive, perhaps shielding herself from the group by becoming a part of it.

As Jill remembered their initial encounter and had put forward the fact that she'd lusted after Amanda for so long her friend put her arm around her to confirm her mutual attraction. Jill was still a little guarded, aware that any move she made could be misinterpreted if it wasn't reciprocated. As she held back Amanda noticed her stiff posture and told her to relax, smiling as she leant forward to cement their feelings physically. Inevitably they were called to dinner at that point, the two of them promising to pick up where they left off when they returned.

Later that night they asked for total peace as they had a lot to get through and Amanda's parents agreed without question, bidding a good night to their daughter and her studious friend. They'd been pleased when Amanda had changed friendship groups as she really settled at home and became more attuned to her parent's wishes for her. Jill seemed to be very positive and complete, the kind of person to keep Amanda on the straight and narrow when it came to relationships and school work. They smiled at each other as they heard their daughter's bedroom door closing and didn't hear a peep from the other side for the rest of the evening.

As they were considering how good Jill was for their daughter she was removing Amanda's top in between deep, sensual kissing. Their lack of previous sexual experience meant that this brought embarrassment to both of the girls and they decided to continue to explore with the safety of a duvet over them both. The lights were extinguished and they used their limited imaginations to complete what would become an experimental phase for Amanda but a life affirming act of confirmation for Jill. As they lay exhausted beside each other Amanda's parents experienced the climax of their romantic comedy and decided on a quick malty drink before they retired for a night of undisturbed sleep.

Jill met Amanda four more times before their secret relationship ended, each encounter matching those they'd previously completed. By the time their final connection occurred Amanda was starting to worry that people had found out about them both and couldn't shake her concern at being harassed or belittled for her choice of partner. Though she felt very strongly for Jill she decided to call it off, leaving her partner heartbroken and inwardly depressed for the weeks following. Fortunately for her the course came to an end fairly soon after the relationship and she was able to find a steady partner who was completely convinced about her feelings.

Jill's new companion taught her a lot about the physical side for future relationships, although she was still keen to keep her activities out of the sight of her parents and, as such, they didn't find out the truth about their daughter until she was in her late twenties. By this time she was less concerned about how they would react and, by their own admission, her lack of boyfriends was a good sign of her true feelings. They were perhaps more accepting of this information later on as Jill was certain they'd react adversely if she'd let them know as soon as she was sure.

As time progressed she found herself dating a lot and seeing girls on a casual basis but none of her potential matches seemed to want to introduce permanence beyond the first few encounters. She initially put this down to a world unaccepting of her chosen way of life before starting to feel more concern about the sheer volume of dates that turned her down as time progressed. The truth was somewhere in between yet it was impossible for her to ever realise this and meant that she often overcompensated on dates by trying to reinvent herself. Finally she gave up and committed to a life of sin, enjoying the temporary debauchery that kept her inner happiness alive. Although the ultimate goal was always for her to settle down and deep down she knew this, there was a part of her that realised she was more likely to find a partner who was a good fit by meeting as many people as possible and making herself available as much as her schedule permitted and she came to find that this would turn out to be correct.

TWENTY FOUR

Sid thought he had seen everything in his seven years on earth yet he was astounded by what was presented to him as he roamed the woods near his home looking for jars he could fire stones at from his slingshot. There, in an opening, was an old man lying on the floor with an old woman in a wheelbarrow beside him. He picked up a stick and gave the man a poke, becoming concerned at the lack of movement from the subject. He stood silently for thirty seconds to ponder his next experiment before he reached out with the index finger of his right hand and touched the protruding side of the man's body, finding it to be cold to the touch. *Very* cold.

He'd been camping before and had even seen other adults camping in various fields around the town but he had never found anybody camping in these woods with just a tarpaulin to cover them. It wasn't even a good tarpaulin as the holes were big enough for cats to fall through meaning that rain would have absolutely no problem. He looked around for help as he felt out of his depth, finding nobody else even stirring in the vicinity. Despite his lack of survival equipment Alf had picked an excellent spot to hide from passersby and that had probably kept him away from prying eyes. Anybody finding them in that state would have called the police immediately, unless it was a seven year old boy coming back from the bottom of town with his sweets. The fear was rising in Sid's mind and he knew he had to do something, deciding that a good firm poke would be advisable before he searched for assistance.

As his finger stabbed into the fleshy midriff the unconscious man sprang to life and yelled, initially alarmed about the pain that was shooting through his ice cold body until he opened his eyes to a small boy with a baseball cap and short jacket staring at him with wide, manic eyes. The reason for the boy's appearance was clearly robbery in his state of mind and he reached for a large branch that he'd kept nearby to warn off animals that might have caught his wife's scent, swinging with all his might and almost catching the boy's head. Sid witnessed the weapon brushing past him and that was enough to send him over the edge, his flight decision taking hold and wrenching him towards the clearing. He screamed as he ran, bringing Alf round completely to realise what it was that he had just done. Worse still was the fact that they'd been discovered and would probably have to move on, although Alf was keen to eat some of their provisions first.

He offered Mabel a snack and was treated to her trademark sigh before realising that she'd consumed her last meal some time before. He grumbled a response before piling a packet of cheese and onion crisps between two slices of bread and opening a small carton of milk to wash it down with. He hadn't realised just how hungry he was and managed another two slices of bread before his stomach began to settle. He finished the milk and sat down beside the wheelbarrow to decide where their next move should be. He looked around their current location, one of the places PC Drayson had discovered on his first ever trip around the area and not too far from where he'd picked up Jill following her drunken antics, wishing they could stay a little longer as he was fairly comfortable and the good weather had meant the ground was still dry.

As Alf was surveying his surroundings, Jill and Drayson were investigating the giant hole in the garden wall. Neither of them could work out why it would have come down in the way it had, Jill's experience of the gentle way it had dropped every year suggesting that something was amiss. Both thought that the debris strewn across the road suggested a purposeful break out from the inside and Drayson was sure the pair would have used it as an escape route but was still at a loss as to why. With no sign of them in the house Jill concluded that he could be right and put forward the suggestion that they may have become frightened by the earlier crowd, fleeing to safety somewhere before deciding to return at a later point. The pair knew that they should have reappeared by now and started to become concerned that they'd had an accident somewhere and were unable to move, therefore waiting for help. Drayson knew that missing persons could not be declared as such before twenty-four hours had passed; and called in to the station to suggest he take a sweep of the area, creating the impression of abnormality but keeping details to a minimum so that he did not go against the orders that were in place.

Jill told Drayson how grateful she was, the officer assuring her that the hard work was yet to come. He knew that they'd have been found by now if they were in or around the town, suggesting they must have been on the outskirts somewhere. Being such a large area meant they could be searching for a long time yet a team would never be assembled until a full day had passed, something Drayson was not inclined to wait for. Jill called Wayne and Isobel to acquire their help after which Drayson took Jill to a few locations to start their search.

Wayne and Isobel arrived promptly afterwards and Drayson thought it best for them to work in teams of two, giving a spare radio to Isobel and ensuring she didn't use it unless the pair were found so as not to give away their defiant plans to the rest of the force. Finding them was his first priority and he knew he could deal with his superiors after the discovery of the missing parents. He also knew not to give the radio to Wayne as he was sure to put on his best truck driver's voice and shout things like 'ten four' down the receiver. Drayson would have been right.

During their search Wayne and Isobel came up dry, looking well into the evening for a sign of the absent parents. Drayson and Jill were similarly fruitless, although they did come across a tarpaulin in the woods with a bread bag and half a packet of crisps beside it. Jill inwardly commented about the laziness of some people and questioned why they couldn't have taken it home with them; oblivious to the problems Alf was having storing packets in the wheelbarrow even with a low wind. He was concerned about situating their effects underneath Mabel as he worried for her comfort yet placing items on top of her made them dangerously unpredictable and he'd already lost a jar of yeast extract in this way, a luxury he was really looking forward to.

As the sun began to set Drayson felt mixed emotions of incredible concern and terrific relief as he could now allow Jill to call in a team to help in their search. Asking Jill to call it in meant that he could join the search and suggested he'd been performing routine rounds for the day, keeping him out of trouble for disobeying distinct regulations. His association with the family meant he could never ignore their pleas and, given that Alf and Mabel had been missing for the best part of thirty hours by this point, he knew they would be requiring medical assistance regardless of what state they were in. He was particularly concerned about the drop in temperature that was set to occur once the sun had settled beyond the horizon although he kept this from Jill to reduce her concern as much as possible.

Before too long a cloud of officers had descended on the town; bringing dogs, dirt bikes and even a helicopter with them to search the nearby area. The operation had been taken firmly out of Drayson's hands unknowingly, with the officer happy to be a small part of a very large team. The participants were briefed, during which a number of members of the public joined the officers and they spent the night scouring the woods and fields surrounding the tight knit community.

Sid was interviewed later that evening, giving the information about Alf's previous whereabouts and stating that the two of them were both 'sleepy but alive and well'. This was a relief to Jill and gave the officers hope as they had their last known position and knew the dogs could pick up the scent of the couple without any problems. The head of the operation was quietly confident, keeping his optimism hidden as he'd experienced situations like this before and had seen other officers jumping the gun too early and giving false hope to the family. He remained in the giant trailer they were using as a base and sat waiting, willing them both to return so he could be hailed as a hero.

TWENTY FIVE

The unknown whereabouts of Alf and Mabel wasn't the first time the family had utilised the police to find a missing person as Wayne had disappeared well before Drayson's arrival when he was just four years old. His stubbornness was showing through well before this, yet Mabel was reaching the end of her tether, asking Alf to employ some of his harder side to combat the tension that was growing during this episode. She'd only requested that he finish his vegetables for a change, using tactics such as the aeroplane and the train to encourage his imagination to no avail.

Had Mabel succeeded she was sure she could have gone on to get him to eat a healthy diet rather than the constant stream of crisps and sugary yogurts that seemed to be the only things he'd willingly put in his mouth. She'd succumbed to his temper so many times in the past that she knew changes had to be made and decided that she wouldn't be moved on this issue. Alf seemed a little clueless as to what he was meant to do and called Wayne a 'spoiled little fool', pouring petrol on to the fire and standing well back when his screaming began.

Having exhausted himself ten minutes later, with his parents at a suitable distance in the living room watching an episode of a soap to calm them both down, he decided that it was time he took life by the scruff of the neck and walked out of the unlocked back door to the promise of a more relaxed and comfortable habitat. He knew that the neighbours were likely to take him straight back to the house and so he hid himself temporarily beneath Alf's car, watching as an endless flurry of people passed him unwittingly. Despite the flow he knew he just had to wait and settled in for the long game, falling asleep within twenty minutes as his eyes started to feel heavy.

Jill was the first to notice his absence as she'd broken his favourite toy aeroplane and was keen to frame her brother, leaving her in the clear. When she was unable to locate him she hid the evidence and alerted her parents, swearing to return to the scene when he turned up. The three of them spent over an hour calling his name and searching the house, checking all three of the locations he used for hide and seek before turning to more specialist areas used by Jill and their friends. Finally they looked in every possible location, logically combing the house for any sign of him. Mabel was frantic before too long and Alf told her to continue searching inside while he checked the garden.

As Alf shuffled the bushes and listened out for signs of distress their former local officer, PC Harland, noticed his anxiety and offered to help with his issues. When Alf told him that their son was missing he smirked slightly and Alf watched his dark moustache twitch before he was told not to worry. Harland stated that most cases of missing children resulted in them being found fairly quickly and he was sure he would be back on his rounds before too long as he scoured the perimeter of the garden and then checked the outside of the wall. He came within inches of the sleeping lad, casting his eyes across the grass between the car and the wall before moving on.

A short while later Harland was on the radio to his colleague and feeling a touch embarrassed about his overconfidence during his first conversation with the missing lad's father. To avoid raising suspicion he asked for a little help with a possible domestic situation, keeping the rest of the station on high alert just in case but stressing that further back up was not currently required. His partner was a young female officer with long blonde hair that she was required to keep tied in a bun, although that didn't stop half of the town from imagining her letting her hair down and biting her lip. Fortunately she was extremely professional and never let the knowing looks and whispered comments penetrate her thick skin, often retorting in a way that humiliated the culprit before she left with a roll of the eyes.

The two officers initiated a search of the immediate area with Mabel staying at the house in case the young Wayne returned from wherever he had disappeared. Jill was made to feel like an adult when she was told she could search alone and this pleased her immensely despite her concern for her brother's safety. She was still fairly reluctant to move too far from her house and started to search the neighbours' gardens while the officers and Alf moved their efforts out of sight. Jill suddenly felt very alone as she watched them move on and her mind cast an image of a dark stranger who may have been responsible for the kidnap of her brother. Unbeknown to her, Mabel was watching her every move from the house.

Searching for a lost brother turned out to be incredibly hard work and Jill was starting to wane well within the hour, although her concern never diminished. She decided to have a short rest and sat beside the car, sighing loudly as she did so. Two elderly neighbours walked past and asked if she was alright to which she nodded and asked them to keep a look out for a young man in a stripy top with long shorts on and to send him home if they caught sight of him. They willingly agreed and wished her the best in the search for him before ambling along the road once more. Seeing the concern on their faces made her even more anxious to see him again and she breathed in as deeply as she could to exhale his name at full volume, waking him from his slumber and causing him to bang his head on the exhaust of the car.

Jill heard a very definite clunk and turned her head beneath the car to see Wayne rubbing his forehead with his eyes tightly closed. A smile adorned her face for the first time she could remember that day and she slid underneath to give him a huge hug, something he neither expected nor particularly wanted. He pushed her back and she laughed hysterically to know he was alright. As she emerged from the bottom of the vehicle she told Wayne how much trouble he was in and they were both met by Mabel who had seen her daughter disappear beside the wall. Expecting a reprimand though not really caring, Wayne looked up at his mother and was pleasantly surprised to receive yet another unsolicited hug. He was quietly pleased that this was the outcome and the shock led him to proclaim his love for Mabel which was reciprocated immediately.

As the two of them walked into the house beside their mother she advised them both to talk to her about their feelings if they ever felt unhappy or unloved for any reason, assuring them both that her sole reason for existing was to ensure their happiness was maintained. This sentiment partnered with her relief for the reappearance of Wayne made Jill cry and she hugged Mabel tightly before they all crossed the boundary into the house. Mabel then rang their local police station to advise them that the officers could return and put the kettle on in anticipation of their arrival.

Her heart had finally stopped beating excessively and she turned the radio on to listen to some soothing music to help further with this. By the time she'd turned the dial her peace was shattered as Wayne walked in with a broken toy, demanding to know what had occurred to leave it in so many pieces. Mabel called Jill downstairs and had to interrogate her before she would release the truth about the plane. She did so with slumped shoulders, knowing that she would be punished for what was essentially an accident. Her apologetic nature was critical in the decision made by her mother and she was thrilled to know that she just had to apologise sincerely to her brother and give him a hug to appease her. Wayne wasn't quite so impressed with this outcome, although the promise of a replacement was enough to stop him from complaining too much.

As Alf and the officers arrived home they knew not to make too much of a fuss regarding Wayne's disappearance as Mabel had been there long enough to have dealt with the situation. She reiterated the hassle he'd caused and told him that he'd forced them to get the police involved, to which he had to give his own apology before they set off a cup of coffee heavier. As Wayne watched them walking down the path he imagined having to go to jail if he ever disappeared in that manner again and it was enough to put him off for a long while. As this thought came to a natural end he breathed a long sigh that was followed by a bellowing of incredible volume from Alf.

"Who's broken Wayne's bloomin' plane?"

TWENTY SIX

Having to press on was a bit of an inconvenience but the arrival of Sid meant a certainty that their whereabouts was compromised and it was only a matter of time before they would be discovered. Alf had a few ideas about their next resting ground, although none of them were particularly cosy or well hidden. During breakfast he discussed them with his wife and, between them, they decided on the abandoned fire station behind the housing estate at the top of the town. It meant walking near the houses, however making it there would allow them more security as it was well out of the way, never visited and the structure was still fairly intact.

As he licked the last of the marmalade from his fingers and made his favourite morning meal joke, "Marmalous", he surveyed the area and decided it would not be necessary to clean up to any great degree as there were idle beer cans strewn around and he had encountered problems with wrappers in the breeze on the way to their location. The tarpaulin had been spread across the area and the rocks were randomly strewn so he was never likely to be too fussy about their final locations as he was in no state to be dragging rocks backwards and forwards to where he thought they'd come from. He still had a few items of food left so had no worries about securing more for the time being and his final thought was his affirmation that nobody would imagine they'd been there should they come across the site soon.

As he picked up the handles of the barrow he took another quick look around and was pleased with his assessment. He'd often seen litter and the remnants of fires as he'd walked the path beside it, berating those who didn't respect the beauty of the area. He'd been able to cover the small circle of ash that his fire had created and couldn't see any reason why others couldn't have done so themselves in the past with a little mud and the use of their shoes.

The difference between his current location and his intended destination meant that he was required to walk down towards the town, and then up a fairly steep hill running parallel to the main street. He'd initially made it to the woods through the housing estate beside his cul-de-sac, although the adrenaline had been flowing at the time and he hadn't considered how careful he'd had to be with the mode of transport he'd chosen to use. Now that he'd had time to compose himself he realised how lucky they'd been not to be spotted and he quietly thanked whoever was looking after him for their fortune.

As he descended towards the town he thought about his children, particularly how close they'd been with their mother over the years. He knew he would eventually have to give this game up and break the news to them both yet he was still reluctant to let her go so suddenly. Mabel crept in on his thoughts and told him not to worry as, with her by his side, they could achieve anything although he couldn't shake his instinct that something wasn't right. Having spent the last night sleeping alone on the floor while his wife slept a few feet away from him made him feel empty and despondent; knowing but denying that he would have to repeat this from that point on. Her cold body was too much for him to bear and made the facts seem too real so he refrained from hugging her without noticing that his embraces would never be reciprocated again. He acknowledged her latest interjection and they made good time on the journey down considering the circumstances.

The second leg was set to be a lot more difficult due to the incline and Alf stopped momentarily to study his opponent.

He hadn't climbed the hill since he was much younger and even avoided it when the family went for walks around the town, choosing the longer but less arduous routes every time. A lack of experience was keeping him from pushing on, although Mabel assured him that he would only have to do the journey once and at the top of the hill lay a resting place with so much potential that he wouldn't be able to contain himself. He smiled at this and silently agreed, shifting his weight forwards and onto the handles of the wheelbarrow before giving an almighty shove and setting them on their way.

The hill seemed as long as it was steep and he found himself having to stop every now and then to catch his breath, soaking up his sweat with his filthy shirt and composing himself before moving on as far as he could. It was still early in the day and he needn't have worried about passersby but he kept looking around just in case as there was no way to explain what he was doing. Even if he claimed Mabel was unwell and needed to get home, her position in the bucket of the vehicle suggested otherwise. Alf had notice her slip backwards at the start of the hill, feeling that she was more balanced and therefore more helpful in his efforts if he left her as she was. He put all thoughts of other people out of his mind to concentrate on the task at hand, realising before he knew it that the housing estate was coming into view and his journey was about to get a lot easier.

There was a concrete lane around the back of the estate that was used by dog walkers and Alf knew that he had less chance of being spotted if he avoided both that route and people's homes where he could. He picked up a little speed as he walked around the front, the reduced incline an incentive to spur him on. As the old fire station came into view he thought to himself that it looked more dilapidated than he'd anticipated but the fact that it was a three storey building meant that, should the roof be in a poor state, he'd still have two floors and ceilings above him to keep the rain out and a touch of the warmth in.

As the blockwork came into focus he came face to face with the moss growing from the cement and found that more than half of the windows had been broken either by the wind or rowdy teenagers. Cans were strewn across the foot of the building and, as he made his way through the rotten, wooden front door, he realised he wasn't the first to use the building as a shelter, the floorboards exhibiting evidence of a small fire from previous dwellers. He was starting to have second thoughts about using the space, his weary limbs proclaiming otherwise. Mabel even suggested moving on the next day, the support coming at just the right moment and allowing him to collapse in a heap beside a rusty, steel desk.

It had taken them a couple of hours to get to their destination yet it was still early in the day and, as the wind picked up outside the building, Alf became concerned that they might get bored. Almost as soon as the thought hit the room he smiled, remembering the near miss they'd had involving the local fire department and feeling his mortality rise up once more. Mabel told him to supress his thoughts, however it was too late. Alf was drifting into a deep sleep, spurred on by his aching muscles as his wife asked him to stay conscious with her. The voice receded as his eyes closed and he saw images of the flames in front of him as he slipped into a deep, satisfying nap.

When he woke the wind had calmed and a shower had obviously passed judging by the amount of water settled on the ground outside. He became concerned about the cold air penetrating the building and engulfing them so he looked around for anything that would be useful and came across a couple of dusty fire blankets that had clearly been considered surplus to requirements. They weren't ideal and had become stiff where they'd been sat for a little too long but he figured they were better than nothing and stowed them by the wheelbarrow ready for the evening. He nibbled on a few biscuits and apologised to his wife for abandoning her with his surprise siesta to which she forgave him and asked about his dream.

Alf hadn't questioned how his wife knew that he had dreamt, he simply gave her some sketchy details so as not to dislodge the memories of the frightening events of their past once more and brushed the crumbs from his jumper before asking how she felt. It was never uncommon for him to ask and then ignore the answer so, as she passed on some vague details about her now defunct bodily systems, he glazed over and prepared himself for an appropriate answer. Finally he let the words pass through his lips and sighed with relief, knowing they would be safe for a few hours at least. Nobody seemed to be passing and he was sure he hadn't been seen, meaning he would likely be in for a long night under a dusty blanket. He prepared Mabel with this news and they continued talking, covering his fall and her car accident as they had so many times in the past.

TWENTY SEVEN

Alf's dream about the fire would have been more intense and realistic if he'd had enough stored energy for his mind to put himself back into the situation. As it was he simply saw visions of what had happened and remained aware that he was in no danger from the recollections. It had all started at about two in the morning and he may never have woken in time had he been on the tablets he'd been on six weeks previously to get him through the pain of his peritonitis.

Fortunately he smelled burning and woke to investigate the smoke, believing at first that he'd fallen asleep at a disco. He woke Mabel before disappearing into the thick fog, filtering the acrid air through a woolly jumper he'd picked up from the floor beside his bed. Before venturing too far he considered the worst possible scenario and realised that he had to protect his family, waking Jill in the next bedroom and lowering her and Mabel out of the window after sending Jill's mattress and bedding out to give them both something soft to land on. As they reached the bottom, both of them looked up at Alf who was keen to get back into the house to find Wayne.

Within seconds Alf found himself engulfed in smoke and he could feel the heat rising from beneath him. The floor was becoming increasingly unstable but his only concern was the whereabouts of his son and he managed to get to the third and final bedroom in the house only to find that the missing occupant wasn't there. Alf gasped as he searched the room, realising that the smoke had not yet filtered in through the door due to the position on the far side of the house. He shouted for Wayne and heard a faint whimper from the bathroom next to his location. He filled his lungs with fresh oxygen and battled back into the hallway to make his entrance into the room that had echoed his son's cries.

As the door opened Alf noticed the smoke pouring in from beside the bath while Wayne sat beside the toilet, stroking the hair of his sister's doll. Alf had no reason to question the situation and thought only of their escape, realising that the window of the room was too small for them both and that they would have to go through the hallway once more. Alf hoped that the stairs would be accessible, however as he came to the top he saw the flames licking the bannisters on both sides and knew he had just minutes before he'd be trapped in the house completely. He guided Wayne towards his sister's room and gestured for him to shuffle out of the window so that he could lower him down.

Wayne hadn't realised that there was a soft landing waiting for him at the bottom of the drop and he began pleading with his father not to make him go, fearing for his ability to walk afterwards. Alf saw no reason for this display of concern and, having failed to brief his son once more, he told him that they would both die if he didn't move more quickly. Considering two broken legs an improvement on death Wayne finally took the plunge and braced himself for a hard landing, only to hit the soft ground and bounce out of his safety equipment. The moment his head hit the grass to the side of the mattress he burst into tears of relief, watched by his mother and sister who were simply overjoyed to think that he was safe.

Alf saw the rest of his family safely gather at the far end of the garden and his relief caused a tear to escape his right eye before he started to feel concern that there was no-one left to lower him out of the window and he would have to jump onto a mattress designed for the comfort of children. He hated heights as it was and had never attempted a jump like this before, looking back occasionally to see if the flames had started to enter the room by that point. He was fairly certain that the floor would give way before the fire became apparent and so faced his fear by sitting on the windowsill and gently rocking back and forth to get his momentum up. Mabel saw this from the ground and shouted for him to jump before calling him a stupid fool, a description he brought up in a later argument in an attempt to win the discussion. Unfortunately for him, Mabel simply told him he was a stupid fool during that exchange as well, leaving him somewhat perplexed and speechless.

Alf couldn't bring himself to throw his body from the house and rocked forward with enough energy to displace him from the windowsill. As he dropped his weight seemed to shift away from the target, leaving Mabel and Jill to believe he would hit the grass with a heavy force as Wayne cowered in the corner while still stroking the hair of the doll. As it happened, Alf's luck was in when it came to landing on the temporary crash mat and the lack of any sideways force meant that he simply bounced gently on the site once before coming to almost a complete stop. He looked up at the night sky and wondered if the stars were circling his head or whether they were the decorations of the solar system.

A number of neighbours had seen the fire tracing the outside of the house and called the fire brigade before making their way towards the house to get their facts straight. Whether they would have enough to pass on to friends and family who had nothing to do with the area was anybody's guess, however by surveying the scene of the fire they were more likely to get a higher feed of information and this was too much for most of the neighbours to resist. As the fire engines screamed through the crowds Alf and Mabel hugged their children tightly and watched the flames engulf their worldly possessions.

    The fire chief attempted to interview Alf at the scene, aware that the family were exhausted and cold yet needing to get the information from him as soon as possible. The interjection of the crowd made the whole situation tense and difficult until one of the neighbours, a good friend of Mabel's, offered for the family to stay in her two bedroomed bungalow across the road from their own house. The fire chief followed them across and finally managed to get what he needed to complete his reports before they all made themselves comfortable in the living room of the bungalow and got some essential rest.

    The family seemed to have shared the same dream during the night and woke with great relief to find they were safe and well despite their location being unfamiliar. The events of the past night returned to them fairly quickly and they raced to get their clothes on with vain hope that their house would remain standing and there would be a different explanation for their presence in a nearby property. As they made it to the front garden and stood in a semi-circle around the front of their house all of them stared silently at the charred remains and went through every single irreplaceable item they owned in their minds. So many years of articles obtained through so many different means were instantly lost and the reality of this struck them all with a heavy blow. Mabel consoled Wayne who was thinking more about his Brett 'The Hitman' Hart action figure, than he was his certificate for most improved pupil in his second year of primary school; while Jill applied an importance on every single item she had owned and grieved inwardly for them all despite saying nothing and giving little indication of her thoughts.

Alf remembered the smell of the fire and the intense heat for years after the event. The family were offered accommodation in a nearby holiday home, paid for by the insurance, and their possessions were initially replaced by friendly neighbours and their families until a cheque from the insurance company arrived. Life eventually returned to normal and the day was a distant memory before too long, especially after the cause of the fire was established. Although the insurers were satisfied with the conclusion of an electrical fault, Wayne's fascination with Mabel's candles soon came to light within the confines of the family home. As Wayne apologised to his parents and followed this with an explanation they were unsure as to what their next course of action should have been. Their house had been repaired by this point and they considered it best to keep the truth contained in case they were asked to return anything or more serious consequences arose. The first action Alf took was to lock the candles in the garage well out of the reach of his children and to lecture Wayne on his apparent pyromania.

TWENTY EIGHT

The site in the woods was exactly as Alf and Mabel had left it by the time the police dogs arrived there. They'd been gone for just over two hours, a good portion of which had involved Alf pushing the wheelbarrow and extracting all of the collective will he possibly could from the surrounding area. As the lead dog was sniffing around the tarpaulin the absent couple were safely tucked away in the old fire station.

Jill had stuck with Drayson and followed him down to the woods while Wayne and Isobel remained at the house in the hope they'd return. As the site came into view Drayson remembered the times he'd wandered the area, ever vigilant but quietly nostalgic. As the other officers made notes about the scene and looked for evidence of the couple being nearby he simply stood back and reassured Jill that her parents would be found. Both were expecting them both to be alive following Sid's revelation and Drayson felt no reason to tiptoe around the scenario, although he was obliged to use phrases such as, "…will do the best we can to get them home safely."

Jill was exhausted and was failing to hide it from those who could see her. She'd had little sleep and had been disturbed by dreams of what may have happened to them both yet she was now more annoyed that they seemed to be playing a town-wide version of hide and seek. What her father was playing at she didn't know, however she was keen to find out. Something didn't add up; he'd been all but predictable in the past, set in his routine and very rarely erratic so this behaviour was extremely out of character. These thoughts circled her consciousness until Drayson broke her concentration.

"Penny for your thoughts?"

Jill was stunned back to life, hearing the words and taking a few seconds to process them. She felt her thoughts were priceless, particularly as they related to the activities and whereabouts of her parents. All other issues had dissolved; the blocked sink upstairs that she'd tried to sort but had nearly ripped the pipes off the wall and had needed to call a plumber who was due to turn up later that day, the smell coming from the downstairs cupboard that she couldn't place or find the cause of despite it being a rather old and decaying fish her brother had put there as a surprise for her on his last visit, and even the garden that was overgrowing, causing the neighbours to tut and shake their heads as they walked past. She'd promised herself never to let the garden get into too bad a state as she knew it was visible to all and, regardless of how the inside looked, only a few people visited yet many seemed to pass by and cast judgement on her untendered plants.

Drayson smiled at Jill, waiting patiently for a reply that would take a long time to arrive. He watched as she craned her neck to the sky, looked up at the clouds for a short while and finally placed her hands over her face and drew them down, rubbing her eyes as she went and pulling her bottom lip right down like a child trying to impress an uncle with their silly face. Finally she looked towards him and her expressionless, drawn features said it all. They sat down on nearby concrete posts that had been installed to keep vehicles out of the park by the council and watched the other officers work the scene from their distant positions.

Drayson knew the importance of keeping family members calm through updates and discussions during stressful situations yet a new recruit who was helping in the search looked up from his location and sighed, unseen by the veteran from his seated position. A colleague of his looked up and saw the young man shaking his head with a grin on his face, almost chuckling at what he was witnessing. Inquisitively his colleague asked what had tickled him and was furious with the reply.

"Drayson's getting lucky tonight. Look at him, lazy so-and-so. All while we're down here doing this work on his behalf."

They both looked up to where Drayson was sitting briefly until the older PC turned back to his ignorant partner and explained about the importance of reducing tension within those who had links to missing persons. He'd worked with Drayson for over six years and the two of them knew each other well so the delivery of his speech was littered with contempt for what the young man had insinuated, instantly changing his expression from cynical to absolute shock. He suddenly realised that he'd overstepped the mark in trying to come between the colleagues and apologised profusely, stuttering as he did so and feeling his face burn with embarrassment at the thought of a reprimand for his suggestion. Fortunately for him he would later receive some silent scorn, however the PC was not one for escalating trivial situations such as this and the two of them kept their exchange to themselves.

Jill knew she could trust the man sat to her left and offered a few small suggestions about how she was feeling, keeping most of her emotions to herself as she knew that, ultimately, they would be no help in the search. Drayson knew not to push her yet hinted that she may feel better if she shared all of her thoughts, causing her to shed a single tear and pull her mouth in to stem the flow. He suggested it would be a good idea for her to let it out yet she was stubborn and didn't want to play the part of the tearful relative causing a scene during the pursuit. She felt she had to stay strong as she had so many times in the past as she'd watched Wayne expel the waterworks at every opportunity to get others onto his side. This had skewed her beliefs on the release of emotion through crying and left her almost unable to cry during the times when she had needed to most.

Pulling herself together she looked at Drayson and relented, telling him that she couldn't believe all that was happening and had even doubted the statement of the young lad who'd been the last to see them. She declared that something didn't add up and, as such, she was unable to relax despite the apparent knowledge that they were both alive and well. Her father had been logical and often stood back from situations to explore the bigger picture so the image of him running off with her mother to escape yet another argument with Wayne was too much to believe. He could neither agree nor disagree as, although he'd known the family for a long time, he had never spent much time in their company and couldn't use his experience to come to a conclusion. Instead he took all she was saying on board and tried to reassure her, eventually disbelieving the encouragement he was offering. She was right; this situation would have been unusual for so many families, especially those that had been in touch and settled their differences already.

As this thought spanned his mind a whistle blew and the team congregated around the site, to which Drayson and Jill stood up to join them. The head of the operation gave his confirmation that the couple had been at the site and the dogs were keen to trace a scent that seemed to carry on down towards the town. Jill listened intently to the information being presented in the hope that something being said would trigger a clue as to their whereabouts but it all seemed so routine and clinical. She spoke to Drayson about the site before they left and he suggested that they'd probably spent the night there, using the tarpaulin as cover. The two of them cursed themselves inwardly for not spotting the signs on their initial visit to the site before disregarding their past actions and concentrating on the present. Drayson was concerned about the low amount of food containers and wrappers, giving his main concern of malnutrition to the chief as they left but keeping it from the other officers and Jill to prevent it becoming a widespread concern. He was inclined to agree, simply suggesting that they move quickly to follow the scent regardless of the fact that the team was prepared for this tactic already.

Once the officers were ahead of her, Jill looked back and imagined the two of them cuddled together to share their body heat during the clear, cool night. She smiled at the thought of them both still in love after so many years, hoping they would have plenty of time left to enjoy each other's company. This thought made her shed another tear and she allowed it to flow finally, realising that she was allowing herself to feel blessed for having two parents who worked together and had done for so many years to create two fairly well balanced offspring. They weren't perfect and had plenty of arguments and problems yet she couldn't help but be grateful for what they'd achieved as a couple. She hoped one day to find the right partner and raise a child of her own.

TWENTY NINE

His cries rang through the maternity ward, aggravating the toxin fuelled mind of his father and inducing little sympathy from his waking mother. The nurses could see the parent's disdain, knowing they could do little about it initially. They would file a report on the unnaturally acidic responses to the baby for the appropriate authorities to follow up, though there were no signs of genuine neglect at that point and so they tried to help out where possible if only to keep the poor child happy and away from his supposed kin.

He charmed all who came on to the ward, earning the nickname 'cheeky' due to the flushed nature of his face and ears. However, he could only cry when attention came from his parents due to their short, sharp attitudes towards him and the paltry amount of time they dedicated to him in between watching the TV on full blast to drown him out and nipping to the toilet to sneak drinks and the occasional hit. Had they been in hospital any longer the nurses would have detected the substances on their breath and called them in straight away yet they could only be certain that the lad's father was half cut most of the time due to the fact his other half drank spirits laced with mixers. The drug use was well concealed and never appeared physically during the day and night that they were visitors.

On their return home they barely noticed the tiny package that now graced their squalid home and only tidied for fear that the community health visitor would write them up and damage their reputation, something they had taken years to build up through the concealing of narcotic and alcohol abuse. He was more than any parent could ask for; healthy, bright and not adverse to long periods of sleep, only really fussing when he was dirty or hungry, an inherited feature from his father. He had a tidy mop of hair on the very top of his head that was dark brown, a prominent feature of the lad's biological father and not something that the man who'd brought him home picked up on. In fact, the truth would remain hidden for another four years until it became the subject of an argument leading to the woman's death by her partner's claw hammer. Secrets and shiftiness were trademarks of hers until the facts were needed to create tension and, unfortunately for her, the parentage of the young man would be the final secret she would ever keep. By this time his father was completely off the scene and the remaining step-parent found that he couldn't bear to look at the boy, giving up almost half a decade of bonding to seek out a new family before his arrest for murder.

In the meantime his childhood consisted of avoiding needles and cans while trying to make toys from objects lying around, including takeaway menus, cutlery and milk cartons. He'd never seen a football, yet he'd observed his temporary father kicking a carton at his mother and had decided to make a game of it by taking the packaging into the garden and dribbling it around the outside. The forks made superb space craft as seen during the rare documentaries that were on in the background during arguments while the menus served as cards for a makeshift game of trumps with his only teddy, a rough bear that still smelled of the bin it had been hijacked from. It had been cleaned after housing a nest of ants yet the odour was persistent and the boy's father was sure to check it at least twice after it had been refreshed to ensure the insects would not reside in it again.

When visitors were expected he was cleaned up and their own residence was passable. Their lack of attention left no bruises to cover up which gave them less work to do in both respects and they were pleased about this, while their offspring seemed to become more comfortable with his own company, expecting nothing from his providers and subduing his excitement whenever a treat came his way. They became reluctant to use around him and his mother's reduced drug use meant he wasn't dependent when he was born, although his father's moods during extended periods of alcoholism were always an issue that made him wary. He learned not to ask questions, resulting in a stunted vocabulary and a stifled understanding following supressed curiosity, putting his energy into more creative activities instead. He learned about the difficulty of permanence in the house following his activities as all of his efforts were labelled rubbish to be disposed of and either destroyed or lost at some point. He grew used to the need for starting from scratch at the beginning of every day and knew no frustration because of it, patiently constructing all that was necessary for his imagination as it became needed.

On the day of his mother's murder he was spending time with a neighbour who often babysat him overnight. Frances lived next door to the family and had first become concerned as soon as he became an inhabitant of the street as she heard every word of every argument and even winced when bottles were smashed. She vowed to help in any way she could, feeling the boy deserved some respite regardless of her already bursting schedule. She'd heard the raised voices and had rescued him before the truth about his mother's affair was brought to light. The horrific screams were heard from the next house and she knew that it was too late and far too dangerous to intervene, deciding to stop at the police station before taking him to a local deli for some ice-cream and a seat away from the mayhem. He knew nothing of the fight as he was concentrating so hard on the game he was playing, particularly as it was the one chance he had to play with Frances' chess set. Without knowing the rules of the game he'd used the pieces as soldiers and, respectfully, took them into battle against each other in a way that kept them intact. If nothing else he'd discovered that it was best not to damage the property of others, particularly if he wanted to receive further invites to use the equipment.

He learned of the death of his mother and the escape of his apparent father through two police officers who tried to use euphemisms to explain the situation. With so little comprehension of double meanings they were forced to give more detail and were surprised at how mellow the child was on receiving this information. He was told that he would have to live with Frances for a short while before being found a permanent home and the relief etched on his face confirmed the hard life he'd endured up to that point.

It was longer than he'd anticipated before he said his final goodbyes to Frances and moved in with his new family. He was excited at the prospect of having two mothers and had met them already on day trips and visits to measure their compatibility. Frances found it hard to see him leave although she knew she was unable to take care of him due to her declining health. Despite a good nature, his incredibly high energy levels left her almost paralysed of an evening through exhaustion. His new parents would be able to keep up with him and provide the love and attention he deserved and that final thought brought a smile to her face as she watched the car transporting the young man over the horizon and towards his destiny.

As the car pulled on to the drive he awaited his instructions, an act that was misconstrued as shyness. In truth he had always politely waited for the next course of action as this reduced the likelihood of being shouted at during his time with his biological family. Silence was a necessary solution that he adopted and he found it hard to convert from this state of mind given that it was normal to him from such a young age. It required a lot of coercing from his new family to bring him out of himself, after which he was still extremely quiet and considerate. This meant he needed more time to adapt to situations which, fortunately for him, he was finally allowed.

Every night he was tucked into bed and read a bedtime story involving fantasy characters he'd never been introduced to before. As he started to dream about the adventures he'd just heard his two mothers would close the door, watching his gentle slumber as they did so and smiling to each other as they thought about the completeness of their family at last. They knew he had been initially unloved and couldn't believe anybody would feel that way towards such a handsome and intelligent young man. They both talked for hours about what the future may bring and how they would help him to achieve the life for himself that he truly deserved. Moreover, Jill finally had her wish; Charlotte, her beautiful wife and Alfie, a perfect son.

It had taken her years to get over the death of Mabel and, by this point, even her father had passed on. His passing was a comfort to her, however, as he'd pined for his wife during the last years of his life and, to her belief, they were finally together once more.

THIRTY

"Where the 'eck are they?"

Wayne was becoming frantic about the disappearance of his parents and he wasn't one to hide such an emotion. Sitting in Alf's chair he continually scanned the three windows that were in his sight and his ears were finely tuned to every noise that occurred. Isobel was with him but had no idea what to say to calm him down. She was certain both of them were alright and had tried this as an opening line only to be presented with the counter argument that they may not be. There was little to say to this and so she'd decided to keep quiet and allowed him to work through his emotions, encouraging him to use her as a sounding board should he require one.

After a few hours of staring out of the windows opposite those Wayne had covered she became a little restless, realising that she'd never been to the house before and had a fantastic opportunity to look at the ornaments surrounding the living room. She stood up and scanned the shelves in the wall unit, studying the old photos of Wayne and his sister as children before noticing the photo of Alf beside his beloved Austin Seven parked next to the beach with his top off, a tan and a huge grin on his face. She tried to hide her attraction to the younger Alf as Wayne could get very jealous during the most peculiar situations and her mild fascination with a gentleman long gone who happened to be his father was just the right occasion. He was never violent towards her yet his temper was something to behold and Isobel was constantly looking for ways to calm it as their relationship grew.

Leaving a handsome and topless future father-in-law behind, she continued perusing the assortment of bells, thimbles and china animals that adorned the cupboard-like space, smiling at a small black dog that caught her eye. It had the most forlorn and loving expression, almost begging to be held or fed, and she couldn't help but let out a small laugh at the sight. As she did so Wayne jerked back to life and looked towards her with an expression of confusion across his features. Isobel apologised faintly and he realised that, although they were looking out for his parents, they were hardly likely to sneak past the house. He knew that they were both in the situation together and decided to pay his partner some much needed attention.

He began with the story of the small dog and how Mabel had discovered it while the four of them were on holiday in Southampton. She'd fallen in love with the miniature right at the end of their holiday and Alf didn't have enough money to buy it and acquire fuel to get them home so Jill and Wayne had offered to partake in some fundraising to give their mother a reminder of their trip away. Alf told them that it was unnecessary, suggesting they make the most of the time they had left.

Isobel was fascinated by the tale and couldn't believe he had gone so far to make Mabel happy. She listened intently as he described how they'd gone into a local pub and offered to clean cars, telling the landlord why they needed the money. He'd warmed to their story and was astonished by their determination, giving them access to his and two other cars that belonged to regular customers. He duly paid up after the task was complete despite the fact his standards hadn't quite been met, deciding to complete the job himself as he'd been so touched by their efforts.

After hearing the story Isobel seemed keen to know about the other decorations and, given the right audience,

Wayne was glad he'd been asked. In truth she'd realised how much calmer he'd been while he was telling the story and used it as a way to take his mind off of the situation. He could do no more than be there if they did return and so this became a welcome distraction for them both. As they reached the middle of the top shelf a PC entered the house to check for any sign of the missing couple, leaving them both after receiving no news as he could see that they were both enjoying their time together.

Isobel blushed when they came to the photo of Alf on the shelf, particularly after Wayne described his father as 'handsome in his day'. He was keen to talk about the car as they'd spent a lot of time away in the old Austin and it brought back a few happy memories despite the number of times he'd had to push it after yet another breakdown during his childhood. He'd never understood why Alf had chosen to buy a mustard yellow car, a fact that had lined him and his sister up for further verbal abuse from their peers during their schooldays. They hadn't minded too much as it had been easy to deal with yet a black car wouldn't have brought them half of the unwelcome attention they'd encountered.

Predictably Wayne became overcome with hunger as he reminisced about pushing the car and invited his fiancée for some lunch in the kitchen of the house, an offer she could barely refuse. He'd become used to preparing meals to suit their very different requirements with Isobel tending towards salads and lean meat while Wayne opted for the combinations of sausage, bacon and egg where possible. He realised he was out of luck as he scanned the fridge, finding plenty of greens and low fat, plastic-like cheese but nothing that really suited his palate. Isobel knew the selection in front of him was a broad reminder of those he was missing and offered to drive to the chip shop to appease his appetite. He was never one to decline such an invitation and soon found himself alone in the house awaiting her return.

It had been years since he'd been in the house on his own and he realised that he could snoop around to look for clues, an excuse he would offer to anybody that might disturb him. As it was he simply couldn't help himself when it came to empty houses and he liked to look around to see what people felt was necessary to hide from their regular guests. His curiosity was mildly hindered by the knowledge that his parents may return imminently yet he had his excuse in place and proceeded with modest caution, thoughts of his old army commando toys crossing his mind as he did so.

He perused the spare room first leaving nothing undisturbed as he did so. Mabel had always been particular when it came to presentation and there was no way she would have left a retired toy soldier lying around or, as he checked, under the duvet of the bed, though he couldn't help but disturb her handiwork. He tried to iron out the creases with his clumsy hands as he replaced the covering, ploughing wavy lines into the surface and creating more of a mess the more he tried to undo his actions. Before long he gave up, figuring Mabel would blame Alf for it when they returned and leaving him completely blame free as had happened so often after he'd moved out.

Turning his attention to the other rooms of that level Wayne caught a whiff of something he'd never come across before. It was indescribable and pungent as it seemingly seeped through the crack in the master bedroom door. He took a few quick, sharp breaths and gurned at the odour that made it through his thick nostril hair, his mind working overtime to match a description to the smell but drawing a blank. He inhaled enough to fill his lungs in one long breath and almost choked on the air that obliged, his coughs loud enough to be heard by anybody who was beside the house at the time.

As Wayne tried to determine the unfamiliar scent the front door creaked open slowly, making a noise that stopped his involuntary shuddering. He forgot about the smell instantly and held big gasps of air in his cheeks to induce silence as he imagined the possibility of who was opening the door. It could have been almost anybody but he knew, given the circumstances, it was only likely to be one of three candidates. The first image that entered his mind was Alf returning and putting his keys on the hook as he had done so many times in the past. He could clearly envisage his father passing over the mat and kicking off his shoes having ushered the policeman outside away. He then considered it more likely to be the policeman himself, perhaps bringing news of where his parents had been over the past day or so. He listened intently for the first syllables to leave the new occupant's mouth, silently hoping he would hear one of his parents.

THIRTY ONE

Isobel was excruciatingly tired. If she'd sat down for more than a few seconds she'd have passed out and not seen another second of the day despite the fact it was only seven in the evening. She was considered a bit of a night owl and her two friends, Rachel and Heidi, could see that the situation had taken its toll on her but they were reluctant to allow her to let it beat her.

"Forget about him, he's a pri..."

Rachel never swore, considering it an art form to be saved for very special occasions such as leaving your job dramatically or embarrassing men in pubs who felt it was their right to grab you and smile cheekily. Apparently it was still considered assault to retaliate using the methods she found worthy of such an incident and so she took her time and formed each word of warning carefully, finishing with a description so cutting she was always left alone afterwards. To her mind Isobel's useless boyfriend was befitting of such yet Heidi disagreed.

"...at. A worthless prat".

Rachel swung her head around at this tame description, her auburn hair creating an umbrella effect as her face contorted beneath it. She couldn't believe she'd been cut off at such a point, realising as she met her friend's eyes that Heidi had recently been dating someone who was so much more than just a prat and conceding that the blonde's rationale was justified. Heidi could feel the air move beside her and turned her head to meet the eyes of Rachel, knowing exactly what she would see as their faces met. Heidi shot a knowing smile and they both returned to the girl who was crying in front of them, keen to convince her that he was a part of her past and that the only way to move forward was to dance rhythmically at a club.

Isobel's biggest concern was alcohol. Although she was by no means under a spell she knew that a few bottles of cider and a handful of shots would be on the cards, just enough to cloud her judgement and to make her search out the most rugged and seemingly compatible male in the establishment. What she really needed was somebody who would consider her needs and contribute to her goal aspirations without being too dependent himself. She needed a partner, deciding that she had to stop relying on physical appearance and to spend time searching for the right guy. There was no way she would allow her two friends to know this, however.

As they walked into the club half an hour later a channel of men and women parted, their heads turning to take in the beauty of these three occupants. That they spent time together was no coincidence; each found each other of little threat when it came to matters of the heart as they were all level on all attributes. Their views were conjoined and they had never fought in all their years of friendship regardless of external influences. If anyone had tried to come between them they would have been disassociated before they had a chance to realise what was going on.

Following their magnificent entrance the three amigos made it to the bar and ordered a drink each before surveying the scene ahead of them. There were the usual cliques littering the establishment with the most beautiful people occupying the centre of the dancefloor and the brave yet insecure trying to move into the same space before abandoning their attempts due to the looks and energy coming together to assure them of their place. Isobel found some of the interlopers cute and would happily have voted for a more even playing field, realising that the clique she'd been placed in would have found this hilarious. She had always followed trends and admitted she was never the first to try anything, blushing as she thought of the ruminant nature of her existence.

With a couple of drinks inside them Rachel and Heidi made their way to the dancefloor to join their kind, leaving Isobel at the bar though certain she would join them after another drink or so. Her isolation made her survey the scene more closely and she could see two short, older men trying to dance with young girls who must have been half their age. They were clearly struggling to get anywhere and the girls were blatantly laughing at them, giving them obvious signals that took a little while to sink in. As they finally left to join their sullen friends at the sides of the room Isobel started to resent being part of the popular crowd and decided to make a stand. Popular men were as arrogant as those girls and had given her nothing but trouble so she felt it was time to give one of the unpopular men the night of his life. The arrogance in this thought was lost on Isobel yet her willingness to act was more important to her cause.

As she looked around she noticed a bigger guy, about her age, who was balding on the top yet sported a slicked back ponytail of red hair. He had no intention of trying his luck on the dancefloor and was almost sneering at the men who had run screaming from the gyrating females as he slowly made his way through a pint of bitter. He hadn't dressed for the occasion and wore a blue fleece that was open just enough to show off his faded, plain black T shirt. Isobel found herself instantly attracted to him but couldn't put her finger on why; he was the opposite of everyone she had ever dated yet struck her as the type of man she could bet the rest of her life on. She made it her mission to have a quick conversation with him and decided that if his attitude didn't fit what she was looking for then she would retire to the dancefloor safe in the knowledge that he deserved to be on his own at the side of the room watching the happiness of others.

Isobel introduced herself and was pleasantly surprised when Wayne reciprocated, his face lighting up with disbelief that held an air of caution due to the odds being so greatly stacked against the situation. Nobody had ever spoken to him in a club, no ladies particularly, and her appearance as one of the beautiful people masked a deeper longing that intrigued him. They talked for the best part of an hour, their only interruption being her two friends rudely attempting to get her away from him, and she left without saying goodbye to either of them to get some unhealthy food with her new, interesting companion.

Their conversation highlighted just how compatible they were as Wayne was incredibly knowledgeable in certain areas and Isobel felt she'd missed out on a good education because so many people offered to do things for her. She'd thought her associates had just been incredibly kind yet she soon learned that most of them had other intentions and had discarded them quickly which left her guarded and untrusting for long periods of time, a cycle that had never really been broken. Isobel felt that Wayne may have been the person to break that cycle as he was warm and genuine, although he clearly had his concerns about her intentions. It took a lot of work to settle his apprehensions, something she wasn't used to, but the challenge meant that she would have a soulmate who worked with her and contributed to her life rather than a fool who drained her until she could stand no more.

Concern would be a theme for their relationship as people would often stare at them in the street and Isobel had to deal with meatheads flexing their muscles to her and asking why she was with someone of Wayne's stature, to which she would constantly defend their relationship. This made Wayne more and more insecure, in turn causing them to debate their situation as Wayne advised her to leave for someone more suitable. Their discussions were redundant as they both wanted the same thing and were conflicting as a result of interference yet neither could see this until they both decided that the best advert for their affections was to get engaged. This didn't stop the intrusion but it helped Wayne to feel more secure and, after convincing themselves that they weren't rushing into it, Wayne purchased the ring best suited to his budget that looked like it had cost a lot more. This finally made him grateful for online auction sites as it meant that Isobel had genuine diamonds for a fraction of the price.

  Her engagement somehow served to ostracise her from her former friends, after which she realised that they were not out to suit her best intentions and had probably kept her close to them to boost their chances of success. Looking back she knew that her happiness was the only element she really needed and, in Wayne, she had found the partner she was looking for. Her next quest was to convince her future sister-in-law that her intentions were honourable.

THIRTY TWO

Alf was woken suddenly by a dry, throaty sneeze and he looked around to see who it may have belonged to, trying to gauge where he was and why his nose was so itchy. He soon remembered that he'd thrown the dusty blankets over himself and his wife just a few hours ago and the talc-like debris had obviously irritated his own nose as he couldn't see anyone else joining them. He rubbed his eyes carefully and yawned deeply, certain he hadn't had enough sleep to rest him properly.

"Mabel, are you awake?"

He hadn't finished rubbing his eyes when he asked but her lack of response made him look up the second he did. A few seconds passed before his face adopted a quizzical look and he called for her again, listening intently to both his wife in the room and whoever may have been walking past outside. Finally the nearby residents were forgotten and, for a short moment, the old fire station ceased ageing and crumbling slowly around them. Their space was silent and seemingly not accepting the effects of time as it had previously.

Alf rose from his place on the floor and allowed his blanket to slide off him as he gently meandered up to the wheelbarrow his wife lay in. Her voice was conspicuously absent and Alf took her hand into his as he studied her body. Her hair was still wiry, coiled and soft like tiny springs, and it was an even grey colour all over though her roots were starting to fade where they'd held a little tint. This was the same for her eyebrows and lashes, a subtle change that felt like finality and gave Alf a lump in his throat. Her eyes were closed but her mouth was slightly open as though Mabel were sleeping with a cold as she had so many times during their life. He dropped his eyes to her hand, freezing in his despite the blanket having covered it a few seconds before, and he noticed the scars and marks of a woman who'd been busy with her family and was undoubtedly always on the go.

Beneath her thumb was a half-moon a few millimetres in length that had been accidentally inflicted by her never-ceasing vegetable peeler. There were several similar, straighter scars from knives and burns from pans that had long since rusted and been replaced and Alf was positive that he hadn't been around when most of them had occurred due to work or family commitments. He reflected on how many of them had been achieved and tried to smile as he realised how lucky they all were to have such an individual in their lives, stopping short of the facial gesture as the butterflies hit his stomach.

He looked down her arm towards her covered torso, remembering the times they'd made love and the passion that had erupted between them, sometimes even after a heated debate or full blown argument. They regularly listened to friends complaining of a lack of intimacy in their own relationships as they stifled smirks of satisfaction, enjoying the mutual knowledge of their fulfilment. Alf started to wish his memory would let him down at that point so that he could forget the last time they'd shared their feelings physically yet he recalled the events so well that he could actually smell Mabel's perfume in the air, cursing himself as he did so.

Nothing moved as the couple were joined; the water settled within the confines of the building and resisted gravity while the insects and nearby wildlife stayed soundlessly out of sight. There was electricity in the air that went completely unnoticed along with the stillness of the breeze, the only significant factor in the room being the two inhabitants. Alf remained oblivious, looking only at his former bride and finally realising what anybody would have been certain of given more than half a second in her company. Mabel wasn't asleep. Worse still, there was absolutely nothing that he or anyone else could do for her.

As he drew his lips into his mouth to suppress his emotions a single tear escaped from his static left eye. It traced a path down his cheek and landed between him and the wheelbarrow, a vehicle he soon realised was wholly inappropriate for the situation they were both in. He was exhausted, his limbs ached and there was absolutely no chance of him lifting Mabel back out of the wheelbarrow though he couldn't help but try as soon as he knew that she should have remained in their bed that morning. He was still reluctant to hand her over to anybody as he wanted to spend more time in her company, perhaps in the hope that her voice would return and he could continue their conversation, but he knew that what he had done was completely wrong.

This thought struck his conscience at the same time the dogs caught his scent hanging strongly around the abandoned building in front of them. The handlers led the way with Drayson and Jill following just behind them and the nature of the dog's activity gave them hope that the missing couple would be found alive and well, simply hiding from a family row that had unsettled them temporarily. Jill was keen to dive into the building and search around for herself before realising that she was obliged to leave it to those trained to deal with such situations. She was also concerned about the safety of the building as it was in the worst state of any she had ever entered before.

"Is anyone in there?"

One of the officers tried to trace their position through sound before they all entered in a bid to confirm that their actions would prove fruitful. Alf heard the call and looked up in silence, a gentle panic starting to form within him. He was conflicted about his current position; being found meant that they would no longer have to run and, even if they had the strength to do so, they couldn't escape the crowd that was forming outside, however it also meant that Alf would have to face the consequences of them taking his wife and they were sure to remove her immediately, a situation he still didn't feel ready for. He looked down at Mabel and opened his mouth to ask her for advice before quickly deciding against it for fear of being heard. Instead he clamped his jaw tightly and turned his head back to the main door, his eyes as wide as they would go.

Drayson looked at the colleague who'd shouted with a confident expression that suggested he needed an answer as to whether they may have been in the building. The returned gesture was a nod, to which he looked at Jill in a bid to prepare her for the worst. He calmly explained that, if they found anything, the officers would move inside and act according to whatever they found meaning she would be none the wiser for a few minutes. This took her by surprise as she was desperate for an answer and her urge to charge the door was increasing by the second. Her trust for Drayson's judgement was the only thing keeping her outside and she agreed to let everybody do what they needed to do before she acted, knowing that it would be the hardest thing she'd ever achieved.

Alf's mind was working overtime as the crowd stopped outside. He had to arrange himself in the right place for when he was found and tried to decide whether it would be best for them to see him or Mabel first. He ducked behind the wheelbarrow initially, figuring they were trained to see bodies and so would receive the bad news first before he jumped out as a potential good news item. He then remembered how he'd felt when he saw the most beautiful woman he'd ever laid eyes on lying emotionless next to him, never to breathe again, and stood up to shift to the front of the room. There he sat on the floor, lay backwards and waited for the inevitable. His final plan was to hold up his hands, explain the situation regarding Mabel and finally show her to the officers before handing himself in.

One final question crossed his mind before the first intruder made it over the threshold, kicking his imagination over to possible punishments for a crime he couldn't even name. Was he going to jail? He hadn't killed Mabel, nor had he aided her death. This wasn't kidnap since she wasn't unwilling as such and his reasons had been righteous, at least to his unusual mind. He made it a point to ask as soon as he got his reasoning out of the way before he finally caught a glimpse of the first shadow entering his fortress.

THIRTY THREE

Mabel spun on the spot and her dress lifted from the bottom, the red polka dots breaking up the main white colour of the body. Her long hair lifted in time with the dress and continued to flow across her beaming face as she stopped, perusing Alf's face for a reaction. He sat silently on the bed and almost seemed to be looking through her, causing her smile to drop instantly to a comical frown. She crossed her arms and let out a big, "Hmmmmph", bringing him round from his daydream. He shook his head and focused on her face, unsure whether she was trying to emphasise her disdain with such a dramatic expression or whether she was simply pulling the look for comic effect. He hoped for the latter and shook his head rapidly from side to side like a cartoon animal that was recovering from a massive blow to the head.

"Wow-wee!"

He wolf whistled nervously as he checked for a sign of just how much trouble he was in and was pleasantly surprised when Mabel lifted one eyebrow and put her finger to her chin. He'd seen this look of mock scorn before and knew that he simply had to pay attention for a couple of minutes to get himself out of trouble. He pushed his thoughts right to the back of his mind and smiled, showing his teeth to prove that it wasn't a lazy 'I'm sort-of watching' half-smile as Mabel pretended to clear her throat.

"Let's try that again, shall we?"

Once again Mabel beamed and turned on the spot, allowing her dress to ride up and her hair to stroke across her features as she came to a halt. Alf took in the view of the girl in front of him, someone who'd promised to dedicate herself solely to him and to never wander, while realising just how lucky he was. He'd used up his standard retort to her twirl and now had to conjure up something more gentlemanly to prove that he was deserving of the attention she regularly emitted to him. The smile never left his lips as he went to utter the words that would cause her to blush.

"You look delectable, my darling."

The plan worked. Mabel's cheeks turned red enough to warm the room as her beaming smile widened and he knew that they were in for a good night. They had been dating for eighteen months and the thought of children had not yet entered either of their minds, instead there was simply the thought of each other. The local community hall was putting on a dance to try to curb the problem of loitering by their peers and the two of them had been keen to go since the advertisements were first posted around the town, both to show off their moves and the fact that they were so in love.

As they descended the stairs Mabel's stepfather looked up briefly from his paper and shot Alf a serious look. He wasn't sure if his future stepfather-in-law meant anything by it and Mabel's mother assured him that he need pay no attention yet it made Alf nervous and that was more than enough to make sure he would treat Mabel like a lady for the duration of the evening, although that had been the plan all along. Mabel laughed at her stepfather and shook her head with a grin that should have been a good indication as to the true feeling behind the gesture but Alf remained cautious.

Mabel made her way to the centre of the living room and gave the same twirl she had rehearsed to her partner for the night, drawing excited expressions from both of her parents and soaking up the attention as she explained how Alf had originally reacted. Mabel's mother shot a look of false disappointment, knowing that in reality he was simply nervous and was trying to avoid confrontation for the entire time he was present in the house. The young Mabel knew that he would become more open once they had left and were walking towards the hall but she couldn't resist teasing him in front of her adoring parents. Alf smiled nervously and made the excuse that he hadn't known how to react, backing himself into a corner and realising he just had to take their comments with a pinch of salt. Mabel interrupted his flustering with a delicate peck on his nose which her stepfather warned should be the limit of their affections that evening before focussing a serious glare towards the quivering youngster. Alf finally realised that the best way to retort was with silence as he helped his girlfriend into her jacket and waited patiently as she said her goodbyes.

The walk to the dance was fairly uneventful, although Alf tried to explain his actions and was soon cut off by Mabel. She explained that the three of them had been joking and had enjoyed his stuttering and backtracking, however he had no reason for concern now that they had left the house. After that night he feared going back despite the assurance that he was most welcome in Mabel's house, although that was far from his mind at that point. He could already envisage showing off the most beautiful girl in the room and declaring their love for each other through their moves, watching the faces of the others as they wondered how someone so plain could land a catch like his. Mabel had never seen him in such a way, finding him interesting and attractive, but she knew he would never accept such a compliment and would rather reassure him often than live without him.

As they approached the hall Alf spotted Reggie, an older lad who had tormented him throughout their school years. It had been on and off, Reggie being the type of bully who moved between victims and kept as many plates spinning as he could, however the effect had been consistent for Alf and he was concerned that his nervousness would show as they drew closer. Mabel felt his hand tense up and kissed him on the cheek, reminding him that they weren't in school anymore and that he needed to move on but getting the distinct impression that he may not have been able to.

"'Alf-wit, nice to see you made it!"

Sure enough, Reggie hadn't moved on either. Mabel felt a little sad that there had been no progression between the two of them as they were all now free of the confines of the school and had other interests to keep them busy, Reggie's choice clearly still being the bullying of those he considered weaker than himself. She advised Alf to stay clear of him for the evening and to keep his cool and he managed to hear the words without really taking them in, something he perfected over their years together. As they entered the dance hall Reggie stepped to one side declaring, "Ladies first", and tapped Mabel's behind as she passed through the door. She failed to notice the subtle gesture but it was right in front of Alf's gaze and he started to steam with jealousy.

After Reggie had let himself in Alf followed on, finding Mabel and retreating to the comfort of a table with four chairs surrounding it. Alf recalled what had just happened and Mabel once again stressed his need to let it go before she started singing along to the track that was playing. She directed the love-filled lyrics towards her date and he smiled as she did so, ever wary of his nemesis in the room. She was pleased to see him perk up and offered her hand for him to lead her to the dance floor where they both started to move, bereft of any company but not shy enough to concern themselves with the fact.

After two songs other couples started to join them and, sure enough, Reggie invited a local single girl to accompany him. They danced innocently towards the centre of the floor yet Reggie was unable to stop himself seizing an opportunity to snatch Mabel away as soon as they drew near. The girl he'd left looked firmly in his direction and threw her hands into the air as she marched off in search of a more reliable date while Alf looked over and tried to establish whether Mabel had incited the pairing or if she was being kidnapped, the latter being the only option that would make him take action. As soon as she opened her eyes and saw that her partner had been edged out she pushed Reggie away and he went crashing to the ground having been caught off guard. No-one had ever managed to push him around, although he wasn't one to retaliate against a lady. Instead he turned to Alf and suggested he restrain his partner with a leash as he rose to his feet once more.

Being a man of honour, at least in his mind, he snapped at this comment and went for Reggie with a right hook that swung just in front of the tyrant's face. He watched his punch miss the intended target and returned with wide eyes to catch a glimpse of a fist coming towards him. He had time to utter, "Oh sh…" before he felt it land and lost his balance immediately, sprawling to the floor with his eye throbbing and catching his leg on a nearby table. Both injuries sent powerful pain signals out and he lay beneath his attacker with little sense of what he was meant to do at this point, too afraid to get up in case another punch flew in his direction. Instead he remained grounded and hoped he could find a method of escape once he could see without blurriness once more.

Reggie was disappointed to see Mabel dropping to Alf's aid and asked the people around them why the weakling got the girl when he'd so dominantly floored his opponent. They looked at him with disdain and suggested he leave before he was reported to the police, a suggestion that made him chuckle until he realised just how many people were looking his way to confirm the action. He tried to quip about the irregular loyalty of the crowd before heading straight for the door and leaving them to watch over their fallen comrade as he gingerly made his way to a sitting position. He felt foolish having missed such a giant target but was pleased to see so many people on his side, particularly with the concerned yet relieved look on Mabel's face.

They both left the hall after a few more songs as Alf's eye was starting to swell and they both agreed that an icepack would be needed before too long. Mabel walked Alf home and recounted the tale to his parents, omitting the fact that he had thrown the first punch and instead distorting the truth to suggest he had been the victim of a surprise attack. Alf's father, a very strict man with no sense of compassion for his injured son, laughed at his lack of fighting skills and was still taunting his son as Mabel left. Alf saw her to the door, managing to escape the jeers just long enough to thank her for her help that night. She kissed him on the cheek and beamed to see him blush, leaving him with his thoughts as she made her way back to her own parent's house. Not long after that night Alf and Mabel were engaged and planned on moving in together after the wedding.

THIRTY FOUR

It was in fact the third candidate who'd entered Wayne's parent's house and, as the unfamiliar odour of decline clung to the air around him, Isobel shouted to him at the top of the stairs and he breathed a sigh of relief. He'd been punished as a child for snooping around in the bedrooms when his parents were temporarily away from the house; it had only been a grounding but was enough for him to feel guilt at the prospect of being caught again. He'd also remembered the fight he'd had with Alf the last time they were both there and this image flashed across his mind before he made the descent to his fiancée. Had Alf been hiding something before? Was that why they had fought? What *was* that smell? The promise of hot fish and chips was too much and he promised to return after he'd eaten, prioritising in the only way he knew.

 Isobel started to talk about how rude the staff had been in the shop when she noticed Wayne's confused and guilty look passing right through her. It was mistaken for concern and Isobel stopped talking, offering words of encouragement as she watched him pile big forkfuls of the mixed up dinner into his mouth and listening to him swirling it around as he chewed. He looked close to tears, probably only stemmed by the fact he was filling himself with comfort food. Isobel was being torn apart inside, wishing he would smile as he heard that he shouldn't worry, but she felt her words were so inadequate. Continuing with her own meal Isobel was relieved to hear the phone ring before encountering the same images that Wayne had during his time at the top of the stairs. She silently prayed that it was Alf with a wacky story about why the two of them had been absent for so long.

 "Wayne, listen to me…we've found your parents."

Wayne clung unbearably to the phone as PC Drayson gave the good news, bad news scenario of the couple that had been discovered at the old fire station. They were concerned about Alf's condition and were taking him to hospital to have him looked over while Drayson attempted to paint the picture as it was and not give the young man too much hope. He was sure Alf would pull through, however he knew it would rely largely on how quickly they could get him the assistance he required. Finally he discussed the events Mabel had been through since Alf had woken up next to her and offered his condolences before agreeing to meet them both in the foyer of the hospital. Before he hung up Wayne asked about Jill and was devastated to learn that she was emotionally charged, a condition he hadn't seen her in for a number of years.

Wayne relayed the message to Isobel, stuttering after he'd finished describing his father's condition with the knowledge of what he was about to communicate. He finally managed to spit the words out before collapsing into a heap of tears and wailing while the love of his life scooped him into her arms and consoled him. She knew the next step was to get him into the car and drive him to see his sister and father before they all went to visit Mabel for the final time.

The journey was exceptionally quiet with the white noise of the tyres on the road outside the only sound they experienced. Wayne always liked to have the radio on in the car as he generally needed something melodic to occupy him; however he clearly needed the time to reminisce about his mother and to contemplate the fate of his father, the latter of whom would certainly need plenty of attention. He couldn't imagine what kind of state Alf would be in when they arrived yet he attempted to consider it to satisfy his own concerns.

Regrets were surfacing over the fact that he could have asked the constable exactly what Alf's condition had been but he knew that the phone wasn't really the right medium for relaying such information and so he frustratingly anticipated their arrival impatiently. Isobel had been crying yet her driving was as impeccable as ever, her main focus being her broken fiancé in the passenger seat who had been through so much already without the situation that was awaiting them at their local establishment of sickness.

Pulling into the car park, Isobel realised that she had forgotten her purse and would be unable to provide the extortionate funds charged by the local authority to those who least needed to waste time subsidising the tarmac beneath their vehicles. She cursed the situation out loud to alert her passenger, knowing well enough that he wouldn't have enough on him to cover the issue. He suggested she park in the thirty minute slots and move the car once they'd seen Jill as she was sure to have sufficient funds and she thanked him for his advice before he went silently back into his trance once more. Isobel was concerned for his mental wellbeing, knowing that she would have to be there for him in a way she'd not experienced before and that this was a good opportunity for them to realise the strength of their relationship.

They entered the hospital arm in arm and Wayne continued to look at the floor with no regard for their surroundings. He was thinking about the times his mother had lifted his spirits and protected him from outside elements, including the time Alf had given him food poisoning and nearly sent him to school, while realising that he would never be able to thank her properly for all she had done. Alf wasn't an ogre by any means and they got on just fine, however

Mabel had always been a necessary referee at times and to live without her input was going to be a challenge.

Isobel expended her effort looking for Wayne's parents while he seemed to ignore their position, a scenario that the reception staff had seen all too often. Assuming that grief had stricken Wayne to the point of numbness, the young greeter empathised and took care to direct them in an accommodating manner. As they walked towards their destination the girl went back to her duties and, within seconds, had all but forgotten the couple who had needed her assistance. Many of the other patients they encountered on the short journey to Alf's bedside gave no consideration as to why Wayne was walking with his head bowed to the floor yet most of them would have been horrified to hear his story, such was the nature of the place they were in.

Arriving at the ward that housed their reason for visiting Isobel once again took charge and spoke to the nurses on the desk. The one who looked least busy was a tall, young looking man dressed in light blue scrubs. Despite his availability he still had to finish with the screen he was looking for and, once he was done, he apologised for the delay. Wayne was in a petrified stupor by this point yet the nurse hadn't yet picked up on this and attempted to speak to him as he was stood in his eye line. Isobel flagged his attention and explained their reason for visiting, after which the nurse advised them to follow him into a side room before they were allowed to continue. This caused a disturbance in Wayne's demeanour which snapped him out of his trance as he contemplated the worst information that could be due. The nurse did nothing to alleviate Wayne's concern before they all walked off together and Isobel knew that he was struggling so she took his hand and smiled at him to insinuate that all was well.

The couple were led into a small consulting room with a bed and two chairs, the latter of which were occupied by the visitors. Wayne had hated hospitals since he was a child as he was phobic of blood and couldn't stop himself imagining what went on beyond the walls he could see. In this instance he hadn't paid much attention to their surroundings, however this new room housed a number of implements used to pierce and cut the body which almost brought him back to his usual state, the image of Alf being the one distraction that he could cling to. His eyes widened as he looked around yet Isobel was concentrating solely on the nurse who'd led them into the room and she was digesting every word that came out of his mouth. Wayne's nervous fascination with their surroundings came to an abrupt halt as he realised that he was missing the conversation and he told himself to put everything out of his mind at least until they were done with the conversation. He focused and looked at the nurse, finally hearing what was being said.

THIRTY FIVE

"I think he's really ill."

Alf rolled his eyes as he heard the diagnosis, sure that his son was playing up. He was halfway through putting his coat on and knew he had to make it to work or face being sacked as the company employing him was in big trouble. The last thing he needed were the tummy troubles of an eight year old boy, however he had to be more tactful when putting this to his wife as he hated leaving the house on an argument.

Mabel had been working part time in a bakery and was quite happy for them to let her go as she was looking for a more permanent, secretarial position. On the other hand it was important to her to help Alf with the bills and she didn't want to risk her job if Wayne was playing up for attention, a situation that had occurred so many times in the past. She took another look at him rubbing his stomach with his hand and looked back at her husband for a final decision. He shook his head and surrendered, advising her to ring the bakery to let them know what was happening.

In reality he was feeling a touch guilty. If Wayne's stomach upset was genuine then it may well have been down to the technique he'd employed on the barbeque the night before. He'd been set up to cook for twenty of their friends and was having trouble keeping up with the orders so he slipped a few undercooked examples to his son, sure that the lad's iron stomach could handle the influx. He was loathe to suggest his cooking may have harmed their only son and so made the strong point against the validity of his illness to cover his own misdemeanour. Had he not felt this way there was an excellent chance that Wayne would have been sent to school regardless with Mabel on standby for the call in the event of his sickness becoming physical.

As the door closed Mabel made the call to her employer, emphasising how dangerous it would be for her to work around food with her son in such a condition. As it happened her manager was sympathetic and understanding, offering her two days to get her son well again and giving them both a chance to fight any potential bugs. Mabel thanked him and replaced the receiver, calling up to the patient as she did so. The reply was stifled and weak, leaving her to believe that he was definitely not well. Within minutes he'd dropped back to sleep and was left there until deep into the afternoon when he woke naturally feeling a little refreshed yet still unwell.

Mabel sat at the edge of the bed when he'd regained consciousness and stared at her offspring with a smile as he prised his eyes open and yawned. She was pleased to see that he had some colour back in his face and was also relieved to think that Jill was away for the week on a school camping trip as, if Wayne had a bug, she was sure to get it twice as bad. She spoke softly to him, asking how he felt and making sure he didn't need anything before suggesting he made his way downstairs. This was to ensure he would use up what little energy he had and allow him to sleep that night and, although Wayne was still drowsy, he agreed with her sentiments and put on his dressing gown.

That night, once Alf had returned and Wayne had gone to bed, Mabel discussed his condition and confirmed that he had been genuinely ill. She told him that he would be home again the next day and he was alarmed to think that the situation may cost her job yet she relayed the details of the phone call and he relaxed a little. Knowing that Wayne was feeling better alleviated his guilt somewhat yet he was still reluctant to mention why their son may have been ill and put it to the back of his mind as his honesty was sure to betray him otherwise.

Mabel felt more tired from a day of seeing to her son than she ever had working at the bakery and was concerned that another day of the same would finish her off. Alf convinced her to stay up with him to watch a film they'd both been looking forward to but she found herself unable to keep her eyes open and finally went off to bed an hour later leaving him to watch the end on his own. He felt a little lost without her as he had so much to talk about concerning his day at work and, with no-one around to convey his feelings to, he was forced to save them for the following day. As it was his wife and son were in no fit state to wake at the same time as him and so he left them to rest, carrying the burden of his previous day with him for the first time in a while.

Mabel was a little heartbroken to see that Alf had gone to work without saying goodbye although she figured that he would have let her rest while she had the opportunity. His access to a phone at work was limited yet she wanted to be sure that he was alright and decided to phone him at lunchtime for a brief discussion. Wayne was still asleep as she dressed and readied herself for another busy day and she found it necessary to wake him for his breakfast, hoping he would be able to eat something to keep his strength high. As it happened he almost made up for the day he'd missed and she was pleased to see that his appetite was back.

Although Wayne was clearly in a better state she took the opportunity to cuddle close to her son and watched a few of his favourite films to cheer him up, giving her a chance to feel the contact that had started to creep out of their relationship due to his increased age and the need to look independent to his peers. The truth was that he enjoyed that moment too and Mabel could feel it from his reciprocation, however he wasn't likely to admit it. She didn't want to break the hug but knew that it would be up to her to make their next meal and she watched the clock tick round as she contemplated having to arise from the sofa.

When the time came Mabel had already squeezed an extra fifteen minutes out of her son and the thought had crossed her mind that she would need to ring Alf as she still felt that echo of guilt creeping up on her. She made their food a priority as it was so good to see Wayne eating again and then picked up the phone, initially speaking to the boss of the company before he put her on to Alf with a warning to him not to tie up the line for too long. Mabel apologised for causing the interruption but Alf was so happy to be hearing her voice that he put it straight out of his mind and finally unleashed the details of the day and a half she'd not yet heard about.

Her initial concern seemed to drain from her as she took on board everything Alf was relaying, mostly because she too had wanted to avoid confrontation with her husband. They laughed together as he recalled an incident regarding his workmate and a pallet load of wax crayons that had fallen from the forklift truck on to the managing director's car and they both stated their love for each other before hanging up and going back to the same situations they'd been in before the phone call; Mabel watching films with Wayne and Alf picking individual boxes of wax crayons off a brand new yet written off Ford. He had to force himself not to laugh as he remembered the hearty chuckles emanating from Mabel, although there was clearly a spring in his step now that he was sure it was a placid environment waiting for him on his arrival home.

Wayne once again demolished a healthy amount before the two of them returned to the TV for one last afternoon together. Mabel was already trying to decide what to cut from their food allowance that month due to the time she'd taken off work but she didn't hold it against her son as they'd derived more pleasure from the time spent together than they would have from a few extra desserts. Mabel pulled Wayne close and kissed him on his forehead to which he smiled and briefly closed his weary eyes.

That night, as Alf returned from his day at work and Mabel served a cottage pie to her ravenous family, the conversation turned to wax crayons and the sacking of a clumsy employee yet all three listened and conversed with light hearts and a realisation that they could never be without each other. Jill's absence was notable as she was not due to return until that weekend and so they all made a point of making the effort with her on her return as she was also a massive part of their collective spirits. Having not been a part of their realisation Jill found it very odd that her family was acting pleasantly towards her, more so her little brother, and had to ask what had happened while she had been away before concluding aloud that they must have been kidnapped and replaced by an intergalactic species. As she pulled a giant bag full of dirty washing into her bedroom she admitted to herself that she'd been pleasantly surprised by their welcome and made a mental note to appreciate them all a bit more.

THIRTY SIX

Alf sat on the hospital bed in a light gown that let a breeze up his back. He'd been a patient before and had worn such a garment during those times but at this point he was particularly uncomfortable, especially since he'd last slept on the floor of a cold building with no roof. He looked at the blanket he was sat on and tried to figure out how he could get the blanket over him yet it was to no avail as he was so disorientated. There was a nurse in the room with him who was moving objects around and preparing a wheeled table with implements that looked like they were for taking blood despite the fact they'd already taken some from him. He wanted to ask the nurse what he was doing or at least if he could have the blanket over him, stopping himself just in time as he didn't want to put him out.

He looked around at the room he'd been placed in, realising that there was too much medical equipment present to be a recovery room for patients and surmising that he'd probably be moved into another room soon. He had no desire to be on a ward as he didn't feel he could cope with the staff of the hospital, let alone the patients, and silently prayed for a single room even if it was just for a night. His mind wandered back to the last time he was with Mabel and he remembered every word of their final conversation before they were discovered and taken there. He briefly considered that he may have been dreaming and closed his eyes to transport himself back to the old fire station, realising that if he could go back a little then he could probably go back to the house when Mabel had been alive and spend the evening keeping her awake.

The sheer depth of Alf's exhaustion was clear when, within a few seconds, he dozed off while still seated and was in danger of falling from the side of the bed. This was only prevented by the nurse turning to see him swaying forwards and backwards and darting forward to help him into a lying position on the bed during which he barely stirred. The nurse needed Alf conscious to satisfy his paperwork and was torn briefly between allowing him to rest and moving on to other patients or waking him and getting his work completed. The decision was made on his behalf when he attempted to wake Alf and received no response so he lifted the barrier on the edge of the bed to stop Alf from rolling on to the floor and carried on with his various other tasks, alerting the desk staff that he was in there and promising to return within the hour.

Alf's mind was working hard to get him back to the place he'd wanted to see once more and he was lying in a deep, dreamy slumber for around thirty minutes before the room saw any interruption. As Wayne and Isobel burst through the door, with a receptionist explaining the very reason they couldn't visit Alf just yet and trying desperately to remove them from the room, he shot bolt upright and, with wide eyes and perspiration gushing from every pore, he tried to work out at which point in his dream he was actually present for. He'd managed to see right back to his time lying next to his healthy wife yet wasn't convinced that he was still there and was looking for the floor to determine whether he may have still been in the woods or at the old fire station. He thought the whole episode may have been a dream; perhaps he'd dozed off in the shed again and everything was fine, his son bursting in to complain that Jill had managed to borrow a few pounds off of him and seeing no reason why his father shouldn't be sharing the wealth both ways.

He managed to catch a glimpse of the glossy, white linoleum beneath him and reality came flooding back, confirmed by the syringes and sample pots lying on the shelves close to where he was now sitting. Wayne's temper was starting to flare but Alf was feeling terrible following his ordeal and lack of sleep and so he let out a violent cry for Wayne to leave the room immediately. His son stopped dead in his tracks and adopted the look of a toddler finding their favourite toy has been banned following misbehaviour. Without so much as a squeak he turned on the spot and led himself away from the room, taking Isobel with him as she twirled behind him and the receptionist who by now was feeling the guilt of waking an irate patient regardless of having no part in the actual act.

As the trio sought a suitable area for Wayne and Isobel to wait Alf lay back down on the bed and realised that returning to sleep was futile given his condition. He knew that, before long, doctors would be swarming around his bed as he came to realise exactly what he had done and tried to reason with himself as to why he'd done it. As this thought crossed his mind the door swung open more gently than it had previously and the nurse returned as promised to initialise the process.

Hearing a bellow from the bottom of the corridor next to the seating area she was occupying, Jill knew that she would soon be needed to calm her brother down. Isobel had a great knack of doing so but she knew that, when it came to family issues, nobody could calm him like his sister. Wayne was still trying to shake off the receptionist who'd blocked him from seeing his own father despite the fact that this was more her establishment than his. He felt useless and tried to make up for it by choosing his own waiting room and disturbing little pockets of unwell and seriously injured patients before his escort took charge and forced him to sit in the general waiting room that Jill had been sent to on her arrival. PC Drayson had been asked to help with the paperwork back at the police station given his involvement in the case of the missing parents and had promised to return, leaving Jill to ponder life without her mother on her own. In truth she was somewhat relieved to see Wayne regardless of his reckless behaviour and the childlike mannerisms of his flailing arms.

The siblings caught sight of each other and Jill moved forward to hug Wayne, leaving Isobel out of the huddle purposely to show that she would be there for him whether he was with someone or not. Isobel understood the gesture and watched the embrace, smiling politely as she realised how important they all were in his life. She would be doing most of the rebuilding once the information had settled in his mind yet Jill and Alf had a lot of groundwork to put in to enable him to return to his previous condition. At this point Isobel had no idea about the mental state of her future father-in-law and couldn't see just how much her input would be valued yet she prepared herself for what was to come.

The three of them sat silently in the waiting room, looking around at the small selection of empty chairs and reading some of the notices regarding hospital health and the intolerance of bad behaviour within the confines of the building. Wayne hadn't considered those around him during his unnecessary rant and felt awful for the way he'd burst through the corridors, making a mental note to apologise to the receptionist who was actually just finishing her shift and would never be seen by him again, a fortunate circumstance given his flaky nature in such matters. If nothing else the poster had managed to open his eyes for his upcoming conduct, a fact neither of his associates in the room really noticed.

Drayson managed to make it back to the hospital fairly quickly as he'd explained that he'd left Jill alone and had been reprimanded by his sergeant for doing so. He felt a little put out by this response due to the fact he'd had the same conversation before leaving her in the first place and he'd been told that he was a vital component in the completion of the investigation. He too made a mental note to correct his behaviour and vowed to stand by his customers before allowing himself to be conducted by other staff. As he walked into the waiting room he realised that Jill had been joined by others, although none of them had much to say to each other. He thought about attempting to lighten the mood before realising how sombre this was for them all and instead he simply announced his arrival and asked about the general feeling of the room. Receiving a handful of negative replies was enough for him to realise why they had all been silent, a situation he had rarely encountered during his time in the force.

It took a while for the acceptance to sink in with the two siblings, after which they started to exchange stories about their parents. Drayson was surprised to see such a rapid shift in the mood as they laughed about the past and recounted characters that had long been forgotten and he managed to chuckle along with them, pleased that the tension had finally been broken. He knew their moods would alter once more after seeing their mother though it was warming to see them animated about the people they'd been close to for so long.

THIRTY SEVEN

"Do you remember Mr Hodgkinson, Dad's old boss?"

As soon as Jill asked the question her mind went on a journey thirty years back to a time when Alf had been employed as a plumber's mate with a self employed plumber by the name of Geoff Hodgkinson. He'd been invited to the family home for an evening meal and Jill hadn't taken to him despite the fact he was friendly and talkative, perhaps because she didn't trust that he'd bought them both gifts. Jill wasn't used to such shows of generosity from her father's workmates and instantly put up a guard while trying to figure out exactly why she was doing so.

Mabel had met Geoff on a number of occasions and had managed to conclude that, although he had an odd look about him, he was harmless enough. His wiry grey hair stood out from his head and reminded most of grimy steel wool, although the condition of it was perfectly normal. He spoke as though he'd been shipped straight from the centre of London and, combined with his confidence, this gave the impression of arrogance yet anybody caught in conversation with him realised that it was simply his manner and nobody was ever wary of him for long.

Wayne could see that his sister wasn't her usual self and found an appropriate moment to corner her and find out why. She explained her position, stating that she didn't know exactly what the issue was but that she'd always been taught to go with her gut instinct and so had come to the conclusion that he was not to be trusted. Wayne immediately tensed at this suggestion and the two of them agreed that they needed to get him out of the house as soon as they could to alleviate the danger of him exposing his flaws and leaving them and their parents in a potentially risky situation.

Their biggest hurdle was Geoff's actual size. He was over six foot tall and, although he was slim, he was quite obviously toned and could more than likely handle himself in tough situations. The troubled pair made a plan to work together to scare him off subtly as they knew being caught would result in a punishment for them since Geoff had clearly cast a spell of charm over their parents. They agreed to take it in turns to make suggestions with Jill taking the first action following a game of rock, paper, scissors.

Walking into the living room, Jill studied the position of the three adults and was careful not to incriminate herself. Mabel was in the kitchen preparing the meal and Alf was talking to Geoff in the living room, a conversation she ceased by telling Alf that Mabel needed his assistance. Without question he left the room and Jill was then free to casually suggest that rats had been a big problem in the house recently; big, terrifying, hungry rats. Geoff took in the details of this statement and countered with a fact of his own, informing her that statistically every person is never more than a few feet from a rat at any given point. She listened intently to his information and nodded as he spoke, simply stating how interesting it was before turning from the room with a look of horror etched into her features. He hadn't meant to scare her as he'd simply joined in the conversation; however he managed to delay her sleep for the rest of that week and instilled a phobia of rats into her that would last a lifetime. As she walked from the room and her victim remained seated on the chair Wayne realised that his turn had arrived.

Entering the vicinity he started to shake and put his arms around himself, pretending to warm himself up as he looked from side to side and breathed in the manner of an arctic explorer. Geoff was still unaware that the two of them were working together and asked Wayne if he was alright, to which he replied that he felt as though a ghost had walked through him at that very moment. Geoff was sceptical when it came to such matters but asked what the young man knew about spirits and was advised that a man had taken his own life in the attic of the house and his soul wandered the halls of the building, desperate to scare away the inhabitants so that he could live in peace once more. The storyteller looked his solo audience in the eye with confidence and determination and this caused the latter to recount his own tale of poltergeists that had apparently plagued his own family when he was just ten years old.

Hearing the tales of plates crashing against the walls and vases chasing visitors through the corridors, Wayne suddenly started to wonder if there really was a ghost in the house and whether his own fantasy was actually a product of his memory. Considering this to be a possibility, though desperate not to lose face in front of a man he'd just met, he smiled a maniacal smile and vowed to return in an ethereal voice before he too turned to escape the room. As he left a trail of urine appeared vertically on his jeans and tears shot from his eyes as he suppressed the urge to wail frantically.

When Jill saw the state her brother returned in she was aware at how much trouble they would both be in if their plan was unveiled and so she took it upon herself to get Wayne into the shower and cleaned up. As soon as the water gushed from the shower head and her parents noticed that she was still dressed they quizzed her, asking how she had managed to get Wayne to get washed without having to fight with him beforehand. She replied that she'd educated him on the importance of hygiene to young ladies, a retort that wasn't very convincing given the fact that he'd been scolded very recently by a teacher for putting a dead frog into his classmate's bag with a note reading 'a gift fit for a girl' pinned to its back. Jill's insistence was the only reason for them to cease asking further questions and Alf made his way up the stairs to tell his son that dinner was nearly ready.

As the two children ate their meals in silence, both deep in thought about their new found fears and concerned that they wouldn't make it through the night, Geoff filled the gaps by talking about sewage pipes that had burst and devastated the lives of families by destroying their photos and belongings before chuckling like a broken drill. Mabel looked at her husband several times in a bid to encourage him to change the subject yet Alf remained fixed on Geoff's face, taking in every word and giving a half-hearted chuckle at regular intervals in an attempt to fit in. Before long Mabel gave up and looked towards her children, noticing their lost and worried expressions and wondering again how Jill had managed to get Wayne clean and fit for the table.

As Geoff left the house following a short coffee and Mabel's assertion that her yawning was genuine and she was feeling under the weather, Alf shook his hand and thanked him for spending the time with them all. As he was having a good time listening to the stories of people he clearly couldn't connect with emotionally Mabel had been growing tired of his boss's indifferent manner and was starting to grow concerned for her children who hadn't been that silent in so many years. They waved him off as he made his way out in the van and closed the door before Mabel gave Alf a look of contention.

Alf replied with a shrug of confusion and asked if anything was the matter which became the beginning of a long conversation about how he was constantly redesigning his personality to fit with that of the people he was trying to please. Jill and Wayne listened to what their parents were saying but were barely able to take any of the content in as they considered how lightly they'd be sleeping that night.

As the memory drew to a close Jill started to chuckle at just how long she'd spent being afraid of rats, all because she'd tried scaring away a guest of her parents. She could recall the exact look on Geoff's face as he gave her distinct details of the habits of the rats, a look of pride as he passed his knowledge to the next generation. The image was still clear in her mind as she asked her brother if he was still afraid of ghosts and looked towards him finally to be greeted with a look of confusion.

Isobel was sat listening with a smile on her face, pleased that she could be a small part of their reminiscing as it meant they were comfortable with her presence there. Drayson was similarly at peace yet he seemed to still be in a professional mood, not allowing himself to smile or laugh during such an occasion. Jill accepted both of their states yet was surprised to see Wayne looking at her as though she'd recounted an episode of a TV series instead of an event from their lives. She couldn't help but plainly ask if he had remembered the incident.

"No", Wayne replied. "I don't remember any of that."

THIRTY EIGHT

Following Wayne's departure from the room Alf and the nurse found some common ground to start a discussion. The nurse was a young man yet he had four children and showed plenty of empathy to Alf after the latter had offered an apology on behalf of his reckless son. The hospital staff had seen much worse before the incident and it calmed his mind to know that Wayne wasn't the worst relative they'd ever dealt with by quite a high margin.

The discussion continued as the nurse checked Alf's reflexes, blood pressure and pulse, all of which proved what a good condition he was in despite his age and the amount of hard work he'd done in his bid to support his family. The nurse was aware of the action he'd undertaken and so took it upon himself to stay in the room for longer than was necessary to reduce the gap between his departure and the arrival of a doctor. He was tempted to ask about where they'd been following Alf's initial idea to use the wheelbarrow but knew that it wasn't his place, instead opting for safe choices of conversation once they'd both recounted the most interesting moments of their children's lives.

As the doctor entered the room the nurse assured Alf that he was in good hands and made his way out of the door to find where Jill and Wayne were seated. After ten minutes he was able to locate them and assure them that they'd be able to see Alf once the doctor had finished with him, giving a timescale of about an hour. Wayne was starting to get visibly agitated and the news of the wait didn't help, though he knew it was out of his control and so he contained his feelings and simply gave a nod.

While the nurse was advising on the activities of the room, the doctor had already introduced himself as Dr Farley and was starting to quiz Alf about his movements in a bid to roughly analyse his mental wellbeing. He could sense that his patient was anxious and reserved, more than likely lacking trust in his care provider, and so he didn't push the issue. During his investigation Alf couldn't help but wish that the nurse had remained in the room to reduce the tension as he'd enjoyed discussing the past with someone who'd understood and been through similar situations. Dr Farley didn't strike him as someone who'd had to apologise to passing neighbours while removing suction darts from their back and this lack of connection left him withdrawn again as he had been on first arriving at the hospital.

It wasn't long before Dr Farley left him in the room on his own for a brief moment and a feeling of loneliness erupted throughout him. He called out quietly to Mabel to see if her voice was still present in the air, however her lack of response gave him the knowledge that he would never get to hear her voice again and, more importantly, he would never be in her company. This sent a wave of sorrow through his core and he felt a stream of tears escaping down his cheeks as he sobbed, at first trying to keep his volume to a minimum before fully taking on board the finality of the situation and allowing himself to grieve accordingly. The echoes of his cries rang out through the assessment centre of the hospital and at first were picked up by a young nurse dealing with another patient who alerted his doctor to the cries.

On realising how anguished Alf's call was Dr Farley immediately ran to the room to calm him down, knowing that an overload of grief could be harmful to his patient. He had always been fairly cold towards his clients as he'd had more than his fair share of attention seekers and those unwilling to help themselves, however he offered Alf an uncharacteristic embrace and felt the emotion draining from him as he wept. He was likely to say something unsuitable for the occasion given his nature and he realised this, opting to remain silent as he helped Alf to overcome this bout of mourning. He knew that this wouldn't be the last episode Alf would encounter, but depending on his strength, it may well have been the worst and Dr Farley was keen to create that scenario.

After a few minutes of anguish Alf managed to look up at his doctor and he felt foolish for his outburst, apologising and promising to keep himself contained. Dr Farley was astounded by this offering given the nature of the circumstances and assured Alf that he was well within his rights to react in such a way. The sheer quantity of feeling that had come over him left him completely exhausted and he advised his doctor of this who, in turn, suggested he sleep for as long as he felt necessary. This invitation was more than welcome and he nodded his head, lifting his feet back up onto the bed as the doctor helped him to cover himself with the blanket. He made sure his patient had reached unconsciousness before he left the room and he asked one of the nurses nearby to keep watch while he slept and to note any unusual activity.

Although Dr Farley had perused his notes before attending he felt he should return to them to get a better picture of Alf's general health and to ensure he hadn't missed anything that may need attention. He'd barely leafed through the first few pages when a pair of heavy footprints marched themselves to his desk and stopped just in front, the lead of the two belonging to a ruthless looking officer named DI Pittman and the second to a similarly brutal but slightly less arrogant PC

Mayes. As he looked up from the notes the two officers stared down at him with fixed stares and enquired as to his identity.

Dr Farley confirmed who he was and mirrored the tone of the officers in front of him, warning them both that they were on his territory and that they would need to carry out their activities on his terms. DI Pittman rarely came across such resistance and felt slightly intimidated by the nature of the obstacle; but his reason for being on the premises was a serious matter and this gave him the confidence to suggest that their enquiries would need to be started immediately. Suddenly it struck Dr Farley that it was his current patient, Alf, who was the subject of their investigation and Pittman confirmed the potential charge to be that of murder. The doctor knew Alf had been through too much already and needed to get his mind straight, his current period of rest being the first step towards this. However, the two officers were apparently in no position to allow this and threatened force if they weren't escorted to his location immediately. Dr Farley raised an eyebrow at the instruction, an image of the last patient he ejected crossing his mind, and turned away from them both as he stood up to hide the giant grin that had sprung across his face.

The three of them made their way to the room where Alf was still lying peacefully, dreaming of the time he'd met his wife once again and hoping the moment would finally last forever. Before they arrived, however, Dr Farley was asked to attend to a patient who was threatening to harm a member of his staff as she'd offered him some pain relief and the patient had deemed it not strong enough. As his presence formed in the bay of the ward the patient looked towards the doctor and started to cower, the demeanour of Dr Farley being enough to suggest he wasn't in a mood to deal with egos. The patient gave a formal greeting to which the doctor simply asked if there was a problem, only to be told that everything was peaky before the prescribed medicine was administered and all threats were immediately relinquished.

Given this situation at any other time Dr Farley would have been sure to suggest that similar outbursts be kept to a minimum or; in ideal circumstances subdued completely as it was, he knew he was in for a battle with the two officers in tow and so left the nurses to apply his suggestions for him. He turned back down towards the corridor and made no sign to the officers, figuring they would follow regardless. They both looked at each other and conformed, having to catch up a little until they arrived at the side of Alf's bed.

Dr Farley was still reluctant to wake him due to his condition but he knew that he could take his patient's side and hopefully be rid of the two of them before too long. As Alf opened his eyes he noticed the doctor and smiled, a reaction Dr Farley was less than used to. He explained who the officers were and advised his patient to sit up, filling a jug of water to ensure he could make himself as comfortable as possible. Without much of a pause the officers dove straight into the tough questions.

THIRTY NINE

A storm was brewing. Leaves were thrown around in unpredictable patterns as the trees they'd left struggled to remain upright and the power cables supplying the area threatened to distance themselves from their duties but not of their own accord. Windows rattled in their frames, doors banged from the side of buildings where built-in sheds were unsecured and the whole country was on high alert for what was about to hit.

Inside the hospital an unusual silence was creeping through the wards. Alf's visit was over six months away and, as such, when Dr Farley checked the notes from his GP he registered the name and forgot it within seconds. Alf had caused a minor cut on his finger and Mabel had encouraged him into the surgery to get it checked out, the result of which was a fairly short consultation, a bandage from an overworked nurse and a message to Dr Farley from the GP alerting him that he had one less patient to see. Had the cut resulted in a finger flying across the room then Dr Farley would have been required to stitch it back on. He produced an instinctive sigh of relief before deciding to take a break from the notes to refresh himself with a coffee.

His office was a fairly small room off the side of a corridor leading to two wards and it served as a good advertisement for how close he was to his patients while doubling as an excellent retreat, the one small window having blinds to alert the staff to his busy periods. He would be the first to admit that he closed the blinds more often than he was busy yet he never offered this information as he knew the trouble it would cause. Instead he kept his little secret close to his chest and revelled in the opportunities to detach himself from the stressful environment surrounding him.

As soon as he left his oasis he knew there would be a swarm of people looking to disrupt his mission. The whole infirmary seemed designed to stampede through his agenda despite the fact coffee kept him in a state to work effectively so he always exited his office quickly and with his head down in the vain hope anybody looking would think he was a visiting doctor. This rarely occurred but seemed like his best chance of getting away and he was ready to duck as soon as he opened his door, only to be greeted with the incoherent yelling of an obtuse, intoxicated male.

There were other doctors around and he didn't doubt their abilities to calm patients and get them back on the right track yet the bellows slipping through the quiet on his ward suggested the man would be difficult to sedate and an unusually high amount of paperwork had created just the right mood in the doctor for him to head straight towards the fracas. Instead of bowing his head he raised it towards the ceiling and the rest of his tall, well built frame followed.

He was known within the building as a gentle giant. At six foot five and with broad shoulders he tended to dominate any room he entered and his dark, curly hair caused a necessary distraction at times. Children loved to play with his locks, pulling individual hairs and watching them spring back into place, yet adults seemed to think it would be the chink in his armour, a reason for his self esteem to be sent plummeting to the ground whenever it was acknowledged in company. Unfortunately for a lot of them, it wasn't.

Dr Farley had been scared of dogs as a child which was brought on by the constant barking of a neighbour's mongrel when he was a child. The deep, throaty barks resonated throughout their estate and he'd built up an image of a hardy Rottweiler with a penchant for chewing children and an eternal lust for blood. A year or more had passed with the noise echoing inside his ears during the night yet he'd never actually encountered the beast. Finally, with a fear deeply set into his frame, his mother dragged him around the corner and towards the street where the dog lived. He was clearly pulling away from the sound but he had an appointment with the dentist and his mother had put his tense nature down to a phobia of the drill as was common in children his age.

Before long the two of them came within a few steps of the dog-filled garden and the ferocity of the barking increased leading the future doctor to believe that the dog could smell his fear and was drooling at the prospect of feasting on his insides. They turned the final corner and he could barely look as the garden came into view and the sound continued. He tried to stop, pulling his mother's arm and finding it locked in place. In a moment of terror he looked straight at the dog only to find it was a Jack Russell with an unusually deep voice. In reality the tone wasn't particularly strong, however his young ears had believed what they had heard and exaggerated this to form a demon in his mind, one that he could now replace with the image of a hyperactive mutt who refused to be silenced until he received the ball that had been stuck beneath his owner's shed for over twelve months.

Dr Farley had completely forgotten the days of the evil dog right up until the point when he entered the ward and found a stocky man shouting obscenities at his nurses, his deep voice creating a false impression of his build. The doctor felt himself unwind in an instant, realising that he'd tensed up despite his confidence of resolving the situation. As he entered and once again seemingly filled the room the drunk, loud gentleman caught a glimpse of his foe and stopped immediately, looking skyward at the obstacle before him. Dr Farley said nothing, communicating his contempt for the man's behaviour by simply crossing his arms and staring into his eyes. Two final words exited the man's mouth before he closed it for good and he realised that the care provider stood in front of him wasn't likely to allow him to stay on the ward for much longer. As it turned out the drunk man was absolutely correct.

    Dr Farley was aware of the boundaries when it came to ejecting unruly patients from his premises and so he was careful not to hurt him as he guided him towards the nearest available exit. There wasn't so much as a crease in his shirt as he found himself beneath a cloudy sky and he braced himself for the flurry of clothes that was about to follow. The nurses cursed the paramedics who had taken him to hospital in that state however they were happy to swear that he was co-operative when he had left, a fact that couldn't be denied by anyone witnessing his departure.

    He'd only started to become unruly when a care assistant from the community entered the ward on her way to procuring some necessary items and had turned down his advances. Her brash and intolerant manner seemed to rub off on him and he'd started shouting in a desperate bid to win her affections. She'd left before the doctor had made it on to the ward yet he was still eager to win the affections of *somebody* on the ward and had continued his rant. Suddenly, with the rain refusing to avoid his head and the wind blowing his jumper across the small car park at the back of the hospital, he realised that his actions had been senseless. As he began the long walk home that would sober him up he cursed his stupidity, a feeling that doubled as he watched his last potential bus pulling away from the stop beside the hospital.

Back inside the building the doctor had maintained his reputation by not allowing the incident to sway him in any way. He knew he was committed to a big pile of notes and he'd remembered his reasons for leaving the office in the first place. He'd all but ignored the round of applause from the staff and patients who had seen him eject the unruly former patient and had made his way to the only machine on the floor that offered frothy milk and two sugars into an already sweet beverage. Once he'd procured this he made his way back to his office, resumed his former position and started reading from the next set of notes that was glaring at him from the desk. The only difference between his demeanour then and that of his pre-ejecting self was that he'd allowed himself to smile slightly, satisfied with the way the event had unfolded and safe in the knowledge that the staff still saw him as the last person anybody would pick a fight with in the entire hospital.

FORTY

"Murder?"

DI Pittman had never been afraid to look a suspect right in the eye and suggest the worst case scenario to shake the guilt from within them while his colleagues, in this case PC Mayes, looked on with a straight expression. Pittman loved the surprise that came from the faces of suspects whether they had committed any offence or not and felt it was best to draw a confession from them and to have this retracted later rather than allowing innocence to be applied and then withdrawn as necessary. Dr Farley could see the man for what he was and, regardless of his status within the hospital, wouldn't tolerate bullying whether it was to a youngster with their lives ahead of them or a frail elderly man who was clearly in need of positive attention.

Alf was still in a state of confusion and couldn't remember what the word meant, causing him to say it out loud. His perplexity altered the tone of his response and the officers picked up on this immediately, causing them to think that he was likely to be guilty of causing Mabel's death even if he hadn't originally intended to kill her. Pittman continued his questioning while Alf descended further into bewilderment, answering as best he could while trying to recall the definition of the words being thrown his way. He kept Mabel's post-death conversation to himself but this in itself was causing a great deal of distress and Dr Farley could see the situation for what it was - two letter-of-the-law officers trying to get their work done on a budget.

He knew he should have terminated the interview earlier yet Dr Farley finally snapped and gave his verdict on the circumstances to the officers before requesting their departure. Both refused, claiming they were dealing with a dangerous subject who should not be allowed to interact with his peers again and, at that point, Dr Farley began his trademark ejection. Pittman looked at Mayes as his collar left his neck, the DI being the initial target due to his position as chief interrogator and therefore the biggest issue within the room. The doctor knew that Mayes would follow as he witnessed his formerly confident colleague being dragged through the ward of the hospital and Alf simply saw a blur where the three men seemed to vanish in front of his eyes. The relief of seeing the two officers disappear caused Alf to have another uncomfortable episode of emotion which made him weep quietly to himself as he overlooked his legal position and once again wished for his wife to return to him in the state he'd left her during their last night together.

As Pittman's body landed upon the grass at the front of the hospital he could see a look of horrific intent on the doctor's face and it made him feel twelve years old again. He briefly considered threatening the doctor with legal action, however his method of questioning was his little secret and he knew that by dragging this scenario through the courts there would be uproar about his techniques, particularly if the old man proved to be innocent. He studied the expressions in front of him as he tried to make out what Dr Farley was saying, surrendering to the pain in his head and back once he was left alone. Mayes tried to fill him in on the details he'd missed yet Pittman was in no state to listen and abruptly ended their conversation in a way that suited the potential families close by.

Fifteen minutes after his short-lived confrontation Pittman felt well enough to attempt to stand and successfully righted himself with the aid of his colleague. He knew that Alf would need to be questioned eventually yet his inability to do so at the first instance was taken into consideration by his chief and the conclusive story was eventually assembled by PC Drayson. As the officers walked towards their car Mayes tried once again to console his partner, only to be told to button it. A short meal at a local drive through was all that stood between them and the completion of the report in which the officers exaggerated the doctor's actions, yet another point that was dismissed immediately.

Back inside the hospital Alf had almost calmed down by the time Dr Farley made it back to his room. The doctor asked if he could get anything for his patient to which the latter simply asked for a cold drink. Before he left to fulfil the request Alf's trust in his doctor led him to make the confession about the discussions he'd had with his wife and the reasons they had decided to leave the house when he realised their position. Dr Farley knew it was his duty to listen, particularly when it came to referring his patient to the psychiatric team. He assured Alf that it wasn't uncommon for patients to see and hear echoes of their departed loved ones despite being unsure as to whether it was true or not, however he knew it would help Alf to recover faster if he didn't have concerns of abnormality on his mind. The two of them discussed Alf's actions and the doctor was sure to entice the whole story out, offering sympathy and warmth whenever Alf struggled to remember details.

Tiredness gripped his entire body after his declaration and Dr Farley knew that Alf needed time to relax. Dr Farley was also aware that the family were waiting to see him and so offered Alf an hour to rest up while he reassured the restless loved ones. Alf once again took a horizontal position on the bed and quickly dozed off as the doctor closed the door behind him. He asked a few of the nurses if they knew the location of Jill and Wayne, finally getting to the bottom of their position when he was well clear of Alf's temporary accommodation and he made his way to the waiting room where four individuals were sat. His first job was to get to the bottom of how PC Drayson fitted in with his colleagues who had just been removed from the hospital and, once he was satisfied that they were all on the same page, he introduced himself to Isobel who had caught his eye the moment he made it into the room. His disappointment in the fact that she was attached to Wayne was buried deeply in his mind as he explained what had happened, causing Jill to cover her mouth and Wayne to feel a mini flare up of temper. The doctor finished the story of his forceful ejection without realising that he was playing up to Isobel, however her reaction of relief and immediate consolation of Wayne made him realise just how little attention she was returning.

Dr Farley left the family in the waiting room after proposing refreshments, an act that was forbidden in the hospital due to budget restrictions. He was never one to offer much consideration to his superiors and was quite happy to give out sandwiches to relatives, often doing so to spite those who held the purse strings. During his time away the siblings managed to discuss what may be wrong with their father, starting with a complete mental breakdown and ending on the possibility of him having obtained psychedelic drugs and partying with his now deceased partner well into the night.

As promised the doctor woke Alf from his slumber, ensured he was comfortable and confirmed he was suitably attired before he invited Jill, Wayne and Isobel into the room. He was still a little wary of the police officer and held tightly to the rule of family only to avoid any further scenes. As Alf saw his son for the second time in that room he apologised for the way he'd reacted and they embraced, Jill coming in to join them as soon as she knew they were happy for her to do so. Isobel's eyes watered as she witnessed the three of them looking so elated to be in each other's company despite the air of uncertainty concerning Mabel's situation.

After a few minutes of discussing Alf's health Jill asked the question of where he'd been, forcing her father to become cautious about what he told them. He looked coyly at Dr Farley who agreed to leave the room for the conversation, making a mental note to quiz Jill regarding his answers in the interest of making an accurate diagnosis of his mental health. Alf tried to make light of the situation, referring to himself as daft, old fool while his daughter took in the severity of his actions and became anxious at the thought of him on a murder charge. Given his explanation she was sure that he would barely have to get through the questions of compassionate officers before they were satisfied with the case, however he clearly needed some help and was not dealing with the death of her mother at all well. Jill was struggling with the fact, although she knew she had to be strong for her father.

Wayne on the other hand was crying for both his loss and the state of their father. He'd always been a firm and confident man, providing the boundaries and sticking to them without swaying for either him or his sister. Now he didn't seem to know what day it was and his recovery was going to be a long process. Alf saw the mess his son had become and tried to alleviate some concern, realising that he wasn't really in a position to do so. Isobel managed to fill the gap temporarily before Dr Farley re-entered the room to give the family a warning that they would need to leave Alf soon. He explained the methods the hospital used for grief recovery and assured them that he was in good hands, a proclamation that was unnecessary as they were all certain their father was in the right place. The doctor gave them some time to say their goodbyes and saw them out before returning to Alf and finalising the arrangements for his stay.

As the younger generation were leaving the grounds of the hospital, deep in conversation about the next steps for both Alf and themselves, Mabel was taken to a table in the mortuary. Two technicians worked together in a bid to find evidence for the murder charge, neither of them really believing they would given their experiences with subjects who *had* come to a grim finale. They found plenty of small marks across her body and had been briefed on her journey around the town with her husband, finding on examination that the story matched the imperfections they were finding. Without discussion, Mabel was telling the tale of her final hours with her husband and clearing him of a charge that never would have befitted him.

FORTY ONE

Wayne had never seen a dead body before. Jill had, although it was that of the family cat after a run in with a bad driver. Despite this neither of them objected to the viewing and went straight up to the body, kissing the elderly woman in front of them upon the forehead before saying goodbye. Alf looked over them, ready to provide the comfort they may have needed while holding back his own tears. The funeral director could see that she was in this position and offered to comfort him, his courteous rejection leading her to stand at the back of the room once more.

Mabel looked completely at peace, her hands together and hiding the front of her favourite dress. She had a smile on her face as she remembered the enjoyable times she'd had with her mother, this being the only way she could cope with what she was witnessing. She'd struggled at the thought of her two young children having to say goodbye to their grandmother as they'd all been so close yet she knew she couldn't separate them from death for their entire lives. As it happened both were comfortable with the circumstances, asking plenty of questions about where she would be now and accepting that she was no longer in pain following the leukaemia that had eventually taken her from them.

Mabel allowed a tear to fall while her children were looking away from her and Alf caught sight of this, moving towards her and blocking the funeral director's view of the casket. This took her focus from her subject to the grieving couple in front of her and she smiled inside at the pleasantness that emanated from the two of them. It was important to detach herself from the people who were brought in to her but she always had great empathy for those who were affected by her work and this scene was a classic example of why she'd worked for so long in a career most people stated they couldn't even consider. She moved forward as the children came away from their grandmother since she knew that, following the sighting of the body and the final goodbyes, most people felt unsure of exactly what they were expected to do next.

As it happened Mabel wanted to know how her two children were feeling about what they had just seen. She left Alf's embrace and knelt down to their level, searching for the answers to guide her verdict on how they were coping. Once she was satisfied that both were fairly content with what was happening she couldn't help but feel a little concerned that Jill was smiling while her little brother was crying to the point that mucus was leaving his nose in streams. The funeral director also caught sight of this while Alf tried to settle his son and she listened intently as Mabel took Jill to one side and tried to establish why she was so accepting of a family member's demise.

Her answer warmed the hearts of the two women as she stated that she was staying strong for her little brother. Crying, she had gathered, was better done away from the company of others as it was easier to move on from grief if everybody remembered the positive times had with the deceased rather than mourning their own loss. This philosophy seemed straight from the mouth of Alf as opposed to the young girl in front of them, however Mabel was proud to see her daughter acting so selflessly when it came to her brother's feelings.

Once she was sure the family were ready the funeral director moved them out to a small room for refreshments and they discussed the arrangements for the funeral. To Mabel's relief her mother had paid into a scheme that would cover the expenses and so her only considerations were the choice of music and who she agreed should attend. Mabel had come from a large family and she felt it only right to invite as many of them as possible to give her mother the ceremony she deserved and was pleased with the number of people who confirmed their attendance, giving her confidence that the day would run smoothly.

Eight days later Mabel found herself at the church where her local vicar gave personal memories of her mother and she was able to laugh at some of the occasions they'd shared, such as the incident involving the family's Jack Russell and the vicar's biscuits, that had left the latter covered in tea while the energetic pup had run for fear of reprimand. Following the vicar Mabel's sister provided a full eulogy that had been comprised from the recollections of her four other siblings and provided a full picture of how caring their mother had been despite such a shortage of provisions while they were growing up. Having all been born around the time of the Second World War meant they were subjected heavily to rationing and yet still had everything they'd ever needed with the protection of a happy and healthy home thanks to the hard work and diligence of their parents.

Mabel had declined an invitation to speak and was satisfied with her decision during the service as Alf had needed to comfort her on more than one occasion. Wayne felt his mother's grief and tried to keep it in, allowing himself short bursts of emotion when he felt the congregation were least likely to hear it. Jill was in a state of some concern regardless of the occasion, however as her cousin Henry was sat to the right of her and was looking terrifically green.

He was only three years old and was well known for his vitality and mischief particularly when compared to the relatively quiet behaviour of Mabel's children. On this day he was inaudible and swaying suggesting he was unwell but had been brought along anyway. Jill was trying hard to concentrate on all that was being said and had a genuine interest in the upbringing of her mother yet she had to keep looking to her side to ensure Henry was still upright and awake. As it happened tiredness wasn't the issue and this became apparent on the seventh occasion of Jill turning her head somewhere towards the middle of the ceremony. As her face aligned with that of the wall behind him, he let out a belch that could be heard echoing throughout the church. Jill's eyes flew open at the sound and she was about to shout a warning when a flood of vomit emerged from his mouth and covered him from the neck down.

The smell was ghastly and Jill finally managed an incomprehensible scream when Henry turned to look at her, still feeling more than a little under the weather. The second stream that exited his person was directed towards her and managed to coat her shoulder despite her attempts to back away from the human fountain. Henry's mother was now looking horrified as she contemplated the clean up of both boy and pew, receiving a grand view of his sharing habits. The altar fell silent as everyone in the church turned to witness the horror and Jill's audience managed to catch the second wave to cover her, filling her favourite handbag with the remains of his last meal and rendering her outfit suitable only for the waste.

Henry, now covered with vomit and struck with remorse for his victim, was duly reprimanded for his actions and marched out of the church; his mother endearing herself to the family further by telling them to move out of her way. The odour of the vomit was too much for Jill who allowed her cousin and aunt to pass before adding to the mess on the floor with her own contribution. Fearing the wrath of the congregation Mabel immediately stood up and removed her daughter, considering the best way to clean the poor girl after her ordeal. The two of them caught the final sentences of Henry's heated dismissal before he was bundled into their transport and taken away for good, neither of them returning for the wake later that day.

Fortunately Mabel was able to clean Jill in the sinks adjacent to the toilets by the church and they managed to return to hear the end of the service. A few too many family members turned around for Jill's comfort but Mabel buried her head in her arms and returned a frown, leading them to swiftly turn back and face the service. The vicar was unmoving during this action and managed to finish as expected with plenty of time to see out the grieving relatives.

As the church emptied and Alf gave his review on the whole occasion Mabel spoke to her children about their feelings, Jill giving nothing away due to the attention she was receiving and the extremely negative spirit she was experiencing about her dress. Wayne managed to ask a barrage of questions, some of which involved the possibility of getting toy soldiers into Heaven and others that were so far out that Mabel didn't know what to say for the best. The question that touched her most involved whether his grandmother was feeling any pain now that she was no longer alive.

"No, sweetheart", she replied, "All of her pain is now gone forever."

FORTY TWO

It had been a few days since Dr Farley had ejected the officers from the hospital and Wayne was remembering his mother's words about his grandmother as he looked at his own mother now lying in a similar position. Her face had been made up which covered the bruising Alf had caused by moving her around the town in what he now realised was an unsuitable mode of transport and she seemed to be smiling, a look of peace radiating from her. A blanket had covered her body but was removed so that the family could see how beautiful she looked in the formal red dress she'd worn to a ball accompanied by her husband, a dress that had been selected by Jill and that took the others by surprise. Alf was speechless as he contemplated life without the woman in front of him; someone who'd picked him up at his lowest points and had reminded him of how hard he'd worked to keep the family together and healthy. He knew he would miss the simple things too, such as having someone beside him at night who would happily discuss the state of their local football team despite the fact she had never enjoyed the sport.

Jill and Wayne also considered life without the woman who had taught them so much; however their main concern was for their father. In the short term they would be more than happy to look after him as much as possible but they knew that consistency was the key and they were apprehensive about whether they were able to keep the level of care up after a few months had passed. Isobel could see the concern on their faces, and to bring them back to the present she commented on how beautiful Mabel looked. Jill and Wayne immediately snapped out of their trances and looked to Isobel as she smiled before she nodded towards Alf, highlighting the need for them to comfort him.

Alf felt Jill's arm around his shoulder and turned to face her as Wayne came in from the same side. The two siblings felt their father break down beside them as they held him closer, the occasion becoming too much for Isobel as she sat in a chair to steady herself. Her tears were hidden by her hands and she forced herself not to make a sound as she considered this to be their moment yet she still experienced empathy for the grief her husband-to-be and his family were feeling.

The family had been taken to the room by a nurse who was experienced in such occurrences and she knew that this was an appropriate time to give them time. She excused herself and exited the room, promising to return in another thirty minutes. As the door closed Wayne noticed that Isobel was struggling to control her emotions on her own and he invited her into their huddle, telling her that she was a massive part of the family and should feel entitled to be a part of the moment. She smiled briefly, noticing how red his eyes were and how wet he'd made his father's shirt. All four had shed tears but Wayne's stream of emotion had covered his father's apparel and made it look like he'd been in a gym for an hour.

Isobel made her way over to the three of them and they embraced for a brief moment before she announced her intention to help Alf in any way possible with Jill and Wayne confirming they would do the same. Alf's sense of loneliness was briefly replaced as he realised he still had so many people around him who also needed his support and he managed to pick himself up momentarily, vowing to keep his strength for them. In truth he knew that his moments alone would be the hardest as Mabel had so often been there to fill them and he now had to motivate himself to push on for the sake of those around him.

Before the subject of time was mentioned the nurse returned and advised them to say their goodbyes as the funeral directors were due to return for the body. Alf had remained in hospital for observations and had already undergone initial examinations from a psychiatrist but he knew to expect more intense questioning and was sure that they wouldn't want to keep him in for too long. As he said a final farewell to his wife he listened for her sweet voice, his disappointment at the silence showing as simple grief for his lost love. He then watched his children wishing peace in the afterlife and couldn't help but allow a further tear to fall as the experience was still so fresh for them. Alf had lost both of his parents over the years yet he knew this would be the hardest parting he would ever have to endure under normal circumstances and both Jill and Wayne were potential recipients of this dubious honour in the future.

Alf led the four of them out of the room as the nurse readied Mabel for her penultimate trip and he stopped at a small café in the hospital to treat his family, realising at the wrong moment that he didn't have any belongings to hand. Jill took care of the bill and told Alf not to worry since the amount was so small, after which they found a table allowing them to face each other and continued the discussion about how Mabel had enriched their lives. As they did so a nearby gentleman with bandages around his head and one of his eyes listened in before enquiring as to whom they were discussing. Alf was reluctant to disclose any information yet Wayne, who had failed to grasp the suggestion of stranger danger as a child and often saw himself in dangerous situations because of his naivety, told him about their recent bereavement.

The coincidence was astounding as the family of four listened to the bandaged man's tale of how he'd lost his wife the year before. The circumstances had been more expected as she had been diagnosed with a terminal illness that he neither named nor was asked about, however his words seemed to penetrate Alf's mind and put his position into perspective. He was now a widower and that could never change, however he had a beautiful family that were all sat around him and he was assured that it was important to remain grounded for them as they were likely to be grieving in a similar way. The bandaged man advised Alf that he would feel the most pain due to the fact that he spent every day with his wife but he also had more experience of loss than his two offspring and needed to apply that understanding to their current situation.

Once he had finished talking the bandaged gentleman removed himself from the café and walked slowly down the corridor away from where Alf was due to exit shortly. Jill looked slightly uptight at the casualness the man had taken to provide the information of his loss but she was quick to hide it as she could see a ponderous look on her father's face. The four of them quickly reiterated the main points of the discussion they'd just been involved with before returning to their original topic of events Mabel had been involved in. As they talked Alf's consideration remained and he finally managed to break into a smile. He knew the heartbreak wasn't over and that he was likely to have episodes of recurring grief yet the gentleman had given him hope that he could be happy again, maybe passing his knowledge on to another grieving relative in the future.

He was still considering this as Jill finished the last of her coffee, a beverage that had turned cold in the time they had spent sat down. As she did so Wayne caught sight of a vending machine and excused himself for a moment, leaving Jill to ask if the bandaged gentleman had upset Alf. Pleasingly he replied that he was alright and he smiled widely as if to prove it to his daughter, taking great pleasure from seeing her return his gesture. As they embraced they shared a chuckle before they started to walk away from the café at which point Wayne returned and, with an outstretched arm, waved Alf's favourite chocolate bar slightly too close for him to be able to see it. He figured it must have been a gift and so took hold of the outside, grinning when he saw the bold writing on the shiny wrapper and stuffing into his pocket as he assured his son he would keep it out of sight of the nurses and other patients. Wayne had wanted to see his father consume the treat but had settled for his promise as Alf had never turned one down in the past. With the chocolate safely hidden in his hospital gown, the four of them made their way back to Alf's bed to discuss a schedule for visitation over the rest of his stay.

FORTY THREE

Frank entered the room with his mother's permission and tried to stare into the cot from the time he passed the doorway until he made it to the bars. He was so small that he couldn't see Mabel until he was almost stood right next to her but as soon as his eyes locked with hers he started to coo and smile. He'd only ever seen babies from a distance, however the partial distance and knowledge that they would be keeping this baby around made him especially excited. His first instinct was to continually say hello to her until she responded, a feat she was never likely to achieve but not to his knowledge. After his twenty third attempt at getting Mabel to reply his mother delicately requested his removal so that she and the baby could get some rest and his mother's brother was happy to oblige.

Frank and Mabel's father had long since left the household as he'd been unable to cope with the attention required from a young son and a pregnant wife and so their mother vowed to give them everything they needed and she worked hard to maintain that promise. Upon the birth of her daughter she decided that a dog would be a great way of ensuring the children bonded with each other and that watching the young girl growing up with a canine friend could only be a good thing so she rescued a puppy from a nearby litter, which had the threat of extermination upon him. Frank named the dog Thadeus, which quickly became Thad; however he was always Mabel's dog and proved this point by protecting her whenever she seemed to need it.

As the years passed Frank became less and less involved with Thad and Mabel took on the responsibilities of his care from feeding and playing with him to walking him when she became old enough. He'd been a useful ally at times, particularly when a group of lads from her school had started to pick on Mabel during the day and she'd returned home in tears as she replayed the incident in her head. To calm her down her mother suggested a longer walk with Thad and Mabel obliged, feeling the tension lift with every step. As they crossed the park close to Mabel's home the group of lads appeared and continued their taunting in a manner that reduced gradually upon sight of the dog's behaviour. He had started by baring his teeth and a few of the lads noticed this quickly, yet some were slower to respond. By the time the comments silenced Thad's growl was echoing between the trees that surrounded them all and his eyes were wide, giving no doubt as to how he was feeling about the incident.

    The leader of the group uttered a solitary word before he too widened his eyes, his reasons for doing so being much the opposite. He fled after a majestic turn on the spot and his followers replied in the same fashion as Thad let out a ridiculously loud bark that rang in the ears of the lads and disrupted much of their sleep for nights to come. Mabel knew that letting him off his lead would have meant hospital for whoever was unlucky enough to get caught and so she let him show off, keeping him tight to her and smiling as she watched her potential assailants flee. The biggest of the lads was the last to leave and, given his instilled fear of dogs from a previous incident, he was required to do so with the contents of his breakfast staining the seat of his trousers. Mabel saw this as rough justice as he had been particularly involved in the chanting and had threatened violence at one point, an action he would never take again as Mabel now had a solid method of embarrassing him.

    Although frightening to young lads Thad was a fairly small dog and, as such, he lasted well until Mabel was around eleven years old. The family were by no means well off which meant that when he started to look ill and his motor skills were affected Mabel's mother put off a visit to the vet until the last moment possible. She went alone, leaving Mabel and Frank at the park with a group of their friends to ensure she could make the best choice for him without the emotion of the children swaying her decision. It was confirmed that Thad was succumbing to age and that an operation was necessary to reverse the effects of time, albeit temporarily, and she knew that they could not afford to treat him and feed themselves adequately for the sake of a few extra days or weeks. The vet tried to encourage her as it was clear how much they had all grown to love Thad but her decision was made with the children as priorities and the vet couldn't help but agree with her ultimately.

Returning home, Mabel's mother prepared a fairly lacklustre meal as though to emphasise their living conditions and broke the news to the children, claiming there was no choice to operate but that they would have to make the most of the time they had left with their companion. He struggled on under almost constant supervision past both his and Mabel's twelfth birthdays and finally gave in to the pain two months later during a mild November. Mabel and Frank were at school when he passed in his sleep and their mother noticed early in the afternoon with just enough time to move his body into a fairly large cardboard box she had prepared for the occasion. Mabel had decorated the outside with pictures of flowers and her mother wept as she placed his lifeless body into the bottom of the box and sealed the lid.

Later that afternoon Mabel begged her mother to open the lid once more, so that they could both see Thad for the final time and it looked to both of them as though he may still have had some life in him as he remained in the position he regularly chose for resting. Frank stroked him first, taking in the coolness of the skin beneath his fur and submitting to the fact that he would never be available to play again. Mabel was harder to convince and stroked him for over ten minutes as her mother dug an over-sized hole beneath the only tree in their garden as agreed by all concerned. It was a further five minutes before her mother insisted on closing their time together and moved the sealed box into the garden beside the prepared memorial area. Mabel watched her with agony coursing through her body and finally she lay down where the box had been and sobbed.

An hour passed before she felt anywhere near ready to say goodbye to her dear friend yet Frank and his mother waited patiently in the garden recalling stories of times they'd shared together. As she emerged into the garden they fell silent and Mabel's tear-soaked face bore the expression they were all feeling; that of utter grief and unfathomable loss. The children had prepared poems and read them to a meagre crowd, thinking only of the pup who had come to their aid on so many occasions. Their mother said a few words before placing him into the freshly dug grave and filling over the top of it, finishing the decoration with a home-made stone that simply displayed his name and the years of his life.

The clichéd rain started to fall halfway through the simple ceremony and, by the time they were finished, their mother was concerned about the threat of lightning and so insisted that the children made their way indoors. Mabel was too distraught to respond to the suggestion and watched the two other mourners making their way slowly toward the shelter while she sank to her knees and, before long, lay down on top of where her friend since birth was now resting. The mud soaked her clothes and coated her skin but she was relentless, taking in the last precious moments of their time together and adding to the moisture that was blending into the soil.

    Mabel finally gave in when the sky turned dark and she realised that her mother was worried about her wellbeing. The rain had come in with a chilly wind and she was shaking as she made her way into the house. Her mother greeted her with a blanket and suggested she take a bath before making her way to bed, something she was keen to do by that point. Her every thought was occupied with the image of her beloved pet and she had to fight to stay awake in the tub before she finally made it to her bed. Fortunately the weekend was upon the three of them and her mother let her sleep in fairly late on the Saturday. When she rose they all made their way out to the site one more time before their mother took them out to maintain the bond between them all. She asked if Mabel wanted another dog to which she could only decline swiftly. The thought of losing another friend was too much for her to bear.

FORTY FOUR

Alf had lost more than a friend. Growing up he'd only ever wanted to be a husband and father, the opportunities for which Mabel had provided him. She was his soulmate and, by the time they were married, he lived purely to please her. His friends had suggested body parts they would have surrendered for the chance to copulate with various ladies over the years yet Alf knew he simply had to work hard and to be present as often as possible to satisfy her needs and he was more than obliging. Now he felt his reason for being was fulfilled, right up until Jill, Wayne and Isobel joined him at the church.

The occasion was in doubt for a while as Alf was still under the care of the hospital and had required a chaperone in order for his attendance. Perhaps more important was the case DI Pittman and PC Mayes had considered, although they'd finally cleared Alf of any wrongdoing and had allowed the family to proceed as normal. The event felt anything but normal, however, and as Alf took his seat he stretched an elbow out for Mabel to hang on to before looking towards a confused gentleman and dropping his arm once more. What made the act more poignant was the familiarity of the features on the gentleman's face and, as he looked back up, he realised that he was looking at Mabel's brother, Frank.

Alf apologised for the gesture and offered a formal handshake to which his brother-in-law grabbed his limb and pulled him closer for a hug. The two men had been brought up to believe that hugging between men was unnatural and both felt a pang of belief springing up yet refused to abide by it. They had both lost someone very dear to them and each acted as a link to their dear Mabel, meaning they completed their embrace and separated on their own terms.

Any strangers catching a glimpse of them both would have thought they regularly kept contact; however it had been over five years since the two of them had seen or spoken to each other and both simply put it down to life getting in the way. Neither had harboured ill feelings for the other and had become good friends when Alf and Mabel had started dating which was obvious during their latest encounter. Little was said between them but each other's presence was comforting to both and they were certain to make this known before the service began. Jill and Wayne greeted Frank with small gestures as they were concerned about conversing when Mabel was brought in and so they agreed to catch up during the wake.

The congregation filled the pews of the church, the back row of standing room and the neighbouring streets. Mabel had been an active part of the community and had touched so many lives that they all felt it necessary to attend her final farewell. Many hadn't seen her within the past year yet they still harboured a strong connection with the woman who was all accepting and spent a lot of her time fulfilling the needs of others. Alf showed no surprise at the size of the crowd surrounding him and managed to postpone his nerves at having to speak at such an occasion. Frank had asked to present an obituary of her early years with the vicar and confirmed his wishes with Alf who was more than happy for him to do so. In truth he wanted to hear some of the stories again despite having heard them so often as he knew it would bring some positivity and laughter within such a sombre time.

As the first tune began Alf's stomach tightened and he almost couldn't stand unaided to watch his wife being escorted in. His chaperone was seated at the other end of the pew with Wayne, Isobel and Jill between them and so she couldn't act quickly enough. She breathed a sigh of relief as he made it off the chair and Frank confirmed his condition before they all fell silent. The coffin was covered in flowers from well wishers and, sat in the middle of her gifts, was a small bear Alf had won for her at a local fayre when they were in their twenties. He'd never been much of a shot with an air rifle, a crutch that had aided his victory due to the questionable sights on the weapon. He thought about that day as he watched the hired pallbearers lift his wife towards the front of the church and smiled, an act that was noticed by a large number of the congregation. Some wept to think that Alf could achieve such a feat at that point and his nurse noted his reactions, realising that he was almost ready to depart the hospital for good. Jill took his hand and smiled with him to which he allowed a tear to roll down his cheek and gave her a very specific smile in return.

A few of the congregation were struggling with their emotions and the family listened as some members audibly cried. Alf, Mabel and Frank had all received a fairly strict upbringing that had made it difficult for them to cry in public and the two remaining members knew they would take a private moment to allow their emotions to escape. Wayne knew he had to be strong for Isobel and silently joined his father in his thoughts, taking his fiancée's hand as the coffin came into sight and she buried her head into a hanky she knew she'd require. Jill allowed herself a couple of tears as Mabel had encouraged her to release her emotions, however she knew that her father's grief was likely to be much higher than hers and took this into account.

The service was much like any other the congregation had seen with Mabel's two children reading short passages about their mother and intertwining them with poetry that was appropriate for the occasion. Frank delivered a beautiful piece on the early years of his sister and the congregation appreciated the humour of the stories he included in his delivery. Two local ladies gave their very high opinions on Mabel's work with others before the vicar turned to Alf and asked him to make his feelings public. He nodded to confirm he was up to the task and made his way to the front as Frank and his nurse looked on with a view to aiding him if necessary.

As he looked out over the congregation he caught a vast number of familiar faces and thanks them all for taking the time out to attend his wife's funeral. He then went on to give some details about their early life together and how he had felt the first time he and Mabel were officially an item. He held back tears through confidence and told all in attendance how proud they'd both been of their children as they reached maturity and how they'd both become a little lost when Jill and Wayne were able to fend for themselves. He acknowledged to himself how this period of their lives had given them so many opportunities to travel and enjoy each other's company yet he kept this thought private as he didn't want his children to think they'd altered his life for the worse when they'd brought so much joy into the household from the moment of their birth.

Alf gave personal thanks to a few members of the congregation who had been particularly helpful to the couple as time slowly took their independence from them. Many had helped in small ways but there were a select few who couldn't do enough for the couple and seeing them sat before him made him realise how powerful their friendship was. Some of them had personal struggles but they always put them aside for the couple, dealing with their own issues separately. He knew how tough that was and gave a nod to those he knew in such a position.

Special mentions went out to Jill, Wayne, and Isobel while Frank was thanked for being there on such a big occasion. Alf gave highlights of the days since his beloved wife had been taken from him and he assured the crowd that he wouldn't be in such a good condition on that day had it not been for the support of his children and the staff at the hospital. He asked for donations to the ward as they had gone out of their way to ensure his health returned and he had to pause to allow his feelings to subside before he finally started to talk at length about the time he'd spent with Mabel, the only time in his life he truly acknowledged. He'd managed to cope with the difficulties of his upbringing, however meeting Mabel had altered the way he looked at everything and, in his words, had opened his eyes to the very fabric of being. He tried to avoid clichés as he spoke about wandering through a fog yet seemed to make the words his own, particularly to those who had known them both.

He completed his speech by thanking Mabel for their time together and almost made it back to the pew before he broke down, causing a large number of the gathered crowd to do the same. He'd been able to keep his strength for longer than seemed possible and no-one could deny him the opportunity to release his emotions following such an event. The vicar completed the service with a few formal words and the congregation emerged from the church to a hymn Alf knew well. He'd picked it for the service as he and Mabel had sat up late on a hill when they'd first become a couple and he'd sung it to her, inviting her to dance with him. He could have chosen a song that was popular at the time yet the melody of the hymn was so striking and uplifting that he couldn't help but offer a rendition. Mabel had blushed upon hearing it and they both completed their version together looking over the town that had always been their home.

As the coffin was taken from the church all looked on and their thoughts turned to the future for Alf. Jill and Wayne had vowed to be there for their father and that was a great comfort to all who were still involved with the family, a few of whom made similar, silent vows. Alf made a whispered apology to Mabel for any time they'd ever fought before ending with the words that had counted for most during their time together.

"I love you."

FORTY FIVE

"I'm going to live with Mum, you can stay with Dad."

It was said through tears as Wayne hadn't wanted to choose yet the situation had forced him to pick which parent was the kindest towards him. It had been a close run decision and one that Jill seemed to agree with as they both started to open negotiations to resolve who would be staying where following their parent's pending divorce. Wayne was in his bed, however he'd previously removed his pyjama top due to the heat and had needed to put it back on to listen to the noise that was rising from the living room. Jill had meandered past the noise and ended up in Wayne's bedroom knowing that he would be upset to hear raised voices.

As they both listened in they realised that they could only hear high volume muffled rage and Jill collated all of her knowledge about adults to establish a discussion on what would happen next. She concluded that they would both go their separate ways with Mabel choosing to reside in another location as her friend Pippa's mother had done. They would then be used as bargaining tools to enable each party to achieve their aims and, to keep the peace, one child would have to live with each parent. Wayne questioned whether Mabel would be granted custody of them both yet Jill knew about these things and assured him that he would have to make a decision.

Once they had both agreed on where they would be placed Jill hugged her brother loosely, conscious of the amount of sweat that was pouring off him. She suggested he remove his pyjama top once more but he communicated that he wanted to be ready in case Mabel was to leave that night. Jill had managed to convince him that he would also be leaving with their mother at the same time and he would have to say goodbye to those he left behind which he refused to do half dressed in front of the neighbours. Jill agreed that he was making a wise choice and he continued to slowly bake beneath a duvet that could easily have been removed to ease his comfort, a point neither of the siblings picked up on.

The reason for their concern came from the fact that their parents rarely argued and, if they ever did, it was over pretty quickly. Alf was always quick to back down during heated confrontations, preferring to allow situations to run their course before using hindsight to conduct his analysis later. This evening was playing host to a particularly high intensity debate that seemed to go on past the usual point of closure and neither of their parents seemed content with failure. Points of debate were repeated more than necessary and an hour passed before any signs of fatigue came forth. By this time Wayne could feel his eyelids drooping and Jill hugged him closer in the hope that he would fall victim to sleep, disregarding his smell temporarily as she realised that his anxiety was still high.

Downstairs the argument was anything but muffled. Most of the words were being lost through the ceiling due to the slurring nature of the two parties who were certainly inebriated, unbeknown to their children, yet they seemed to be able to communicate adequately despite this. It had started when the couple attended the party of their neighbour, Nancy, who was trying to impress after moving in to the area. Mabel had struggled to find something she considered appropriate for a low end, high brow soiree yet Alf knew exactly what he would be wearing as soon as the invitation brushed their welcome mat. He had one suit for all occasions and almost mocked his wife for the fact that her efforts were so much higher than his.

Mabel was able to ignore this as her mind was on the type of occasion she had been asked to attend. The couple had been used to barbeques and general get-togethers yet Nancy seemed to be the type who was always trying to impress which made her believe that a number of these types of occasion were on the horizon. How they would cope with the attitude adjustment was her biggest concern and it had come to fruition almost immediately once they had entered the house.

Alf had always been adept at putting up an appropriate front for any occasion. He had once gone to a scrapyard with his cousin and had given the impression he knew what different parts of an engine were called when the reality was that he took his car to a garage at the first sign of trouble and barely even topped his own oil up. Likewise, when they had crossed the threshold at Nancy's party he had transformed into a sophisticated entrepreneur who was playing the markets and enjoying freedom in his career. Mabel could put up with his instability in employment as he always provided for his family; however she couldn't abide his dressing up of their struggle to put food on the table over the years. She tried to play his situation down by injecting some realism into their conversation and this had prickled him, seemingly for no reason.

As the story swapping continued Mabel noticed that Alf was looking more at one of the guests than at any of the others. He had gone to school with the woman, Henrietta, and she had noticed her gratingly false laughter at all of his terrible jokes. This in itself was no issue but his continued attention towards her was starting to cause resentment and she left the conversation to find Nancy and thank her for inviting them despite their lack of connection before the evening. As she did so she noticed Henrietta stroking Alf's arm and was trying to decide whether he was pulling away or whether he was indulging her interest. The next morning she considered that alcohol had played a big part in how she was feeling yet at that particular moment she only had eyes for her husband and the woman who was beyond flirting by that stage.

Without so much as an utterance of caution Mabel marched over to her husband and pulled him by the arm his old school friend had been pawing, giving him no indication as to why he was being relocated at such speed and causing a great deal of embarrassment to all who had joined their circle to his mind. Mabel was beyond reason and managed to find a quiet spot outside the house that gave her an opportunity to confront him about his lack of action. He had denied any knowledge of her advances, claiming that any contact was simply friendly assurance. The heated conversation continued back into the party where they were both sniping at each other, onto their street once the party had finished and finally back to the house, disturbing their children and causing unnecessary concern.

Deep down Mabel knew that Alf harboured no feelings for the woman and that he was simply being his inclusive and charming self, however he could see by her mannerisms that she was willing to approach Henrietta with some choice words and possibly attack her with a beverage to spotlight the woman's ridiculous behaviour. He had watched many a guest attempt to woo her away from him in the past by kissing her hand and putting their arm around her waist yet Mabel was witty and cutting with her put downs, embarrassing the attention away before it continued any further. Alf's connection with the woman and the length of time they'd known each other meant that it was possible he'd meet her again and he was loathe to put himself in an awkward situation if at all possible so he'd simply tried to brush her away.

This information managed to make its way into their discussion but neither party was ready to back down as both believed they had acted correctly under the circumstances. Exhaustion called time within a couple of hours and Mabel made her way up to the bedroom leaving Alf downstairs with the insinuation that he would be making use of the sofa for comfort that night. Jill and Wayne heard their mother climbing the stairs dramatically and held each other for the rest of the night, finally catching their slumber around thirty minutes later. Alf was sure to explain the situation in the morning once the intoxicants had worn off as he was certain they'd been able to hear everything but was afraid he may have given the wrong impression had he gone in straight away.

At around four that morning the refreshments from the evening had all but left Mabel's system and she had woken up feeling very cold as she lay in bed. She turned to face Alf's side of the bed and found plenty of available space which made her frown before she remembered why she was alone. A tear formed in her eye as she considered how sharp her tongue had been previously and she made her way downstairs, wrapping herself in the duvet beforehand to warm her back up. Her foot touched the bottom of the stairs as Alf came into view, his body lying diagonally across the sofa with his head almost touching the floor. He looked in the most discomfort of anyone she'd ever laid eyes on and he hadn't woken on her return so she gently woke him and tried to place him back on to the sofa.

His eyes gently opened and he was pleased to see his wife coming into view. Her smile warmed him and he returned the gesture, neither of them saying anything as she climbed onto the sofa beside him. He was keen to secure a part of the duvet as he too had become cold and Mabel was more than happy to surrender half as she placed her arms around her husband and drifted back to sleep. The sight of them both together in the morning was a relief to the children and Jill hugged Wayne as they came into view, telling him it was going to be alright. Their family was back together again.

FORTY SIX

Alf was starting to feel like a social experiment. He'd undergone a vast range of psychological testing after his admission of hearing Mabel's voice and was down to just regular counselling sessions by the time he was allowed to leave the hospital. Dr Farley was still showing signs of concern but those around him knew that Alf was much stronger than he'd been during his initial week in the hospital, an observation first made by his nurse, Shirley.

Although Shirley hadn't admitted Alf initially she was on duty and took great interest in his wellbeing as she could see that he'd suffered a great trauma and needed more assistance than most on the ward at that time. Whenever her availability allowed she attended to Alf, bringing him water and fruit as an example to the other nurses yet sneaking him desserts out of their sight to bring his weight back to an acceptable level. He could barely eat half a trifle after his admission however his appetite slowly returned and she wanted to be sure that he would have enough food to hand should it rise to a more normal standard.

He grew to appreciate how much extra effort Shirley was putting in for him and, as his strength returned, he started to notice her long, black curls and smile that lit up the room. If she suffered stress it was impossible to tell as she was fully committed to her patients while on the ward and she never spoke of her home life, leading Alf to think that her career was her priority. Shirley was a full figured woman but it suited her and she was clearly never worried about how she looked as there was never any intention to hide her curves. A number of the men on the ward were particularly forward towards her yet Alf was always a gentleman, asking after her own health and smiling politely as she answered him. He felt she must have enjoyed the attention she received but the amount of time she spent with him suggested that he served as a welcome change in her conversational needs. This lifted his spirit more than any snack could have and seemed to make the time pass more quickly while he was on the ward.

The time had come for him to leave and he knew that saying goodbye to her would be difficult. He wasn't completely certain how long he'd been in for but knew it had been a number of weeks and the two of them had shared so much. As he packed his small amount of belongings, Jill having taken his old clothes to wash already in a bid to get used to helping him with chores, Shirley made her way across to bid him farewell. His time had started in a single room but he was now in a ward with three other men, all of whom had offered very little conversation or exchanging of ideas due to the nature of their illnesses and so he didn't feel uncomfortable allowing her to embrace him as she spoke. As much as Shirley had encouraged Alf towards better health, she had enjoyed his company and always looked forward to seeing a patient who had gone through so much in returning to his former self. There was a clear void within him that would probably never be filled yet he was starting to cope with the idea in a way that didn't seem possible upon his arrival.

As Alf made his way towards the exit of the ward Shirley remained by his bedside and waved him off, a tear threatening to appear as she did so. The other occupants watched him leave but said nothing, continuing with their usual states. As he walked out of sight a short pause marked the end of his stay before Shirley returned to her tasks, thinking about the impact he'd made on her during his stay. She was used to seeing patients leaving but had rarely felt so connected to them, a feeling she would need to shake as soon as possible to allow a sense of normality to return.

As she did so Alf made his way down the corridor to Dr Farley's office and knocked on the door, half expecting the doctor to be away on an errand. As it happened he was in and Alf made his way to the other side of the door for a final conversation with the doctor before receiving a reminder that he was to attend the hospital regularly for updates. Dr Farley insisted that Alf see him as opposed to another doctor as he was still concerned for his long term health and wanted to ensure that progress was being achieved. Alf was humbled that someone could exert so much attention on him and so obliged, taking the first appointment card and promising to attend.

The doctor shook his hand and made one last check on his health before allowing him to leave, ensuring he knew to attend the hospital pharmacy first to pick up his medication. Alf acknowledged this and promised to head straight there before saying goodbye and thanking him for all he'd done. Dr Farley sighed when the door was closed, remaining thoughtful and still as he listened to his patient's footsteps making their way up the corridor. He was trained to look for the worst yet could only imagine the best for Alf now that he had recovered from the worst of his ordeal and he was pleased that he could feel that way about him. Alf had been a very agreeable patient, taking his medication as prescribed and listening intently to any advice he was given. He could only think that if every patient was that way inclined there would be very little stress in his career, chuckling to himself at the notion before picking up a bundle of notes for his next patient.

The corridors felt very brightly lit compared to the ward and Alf was struggling to see where his next stop was, particularly as the signs had a reflective coating that only served to enhance the beams from above. He rounded a corner he thought looked like it led to another department but stopped suddenly when he noticed a sign that read 'Fire Exit - Alarm Will Sound If Door Is Operated'. He immediately pulled his hands back from the metal bar and breathed sharply in fear, realising he'd nearly caused unnecessary panic and looking around to find that, worse still, he was walking around a burns unit. He took a moment to steady himself and returned to the head of the corridor, making the decision to walk back the way he'd been and look for the canteen as he'd seen several people making their way outside for a cigarette using the back door. He figured he could always take the long way around the hospital to the front doors as he knew where the pharmacy was once he was out of the maze of corridors.

It took him almost an hour to make his way to the pharmacy and he was overwhelmed with relief when he saw the illuminated green cross suspended over a cloud of pharmacists and technicians working their way around the vast array of medical paraphernalia. He took one final look at his prescription before calling the attention of the closest attendant and receiving a promise that he would be served as soon as possible. He took a seat in a waiting area and noticed the four other patients already seated there looked anything but pleased about their presence. A long wait was clearly inevitable and so he took his mind elsewhere, studying the posters on the walls and imagining himself in some of the locations despite none of them being particularly exotic.

The one that kept his attention the longest was a picture of a cocktail party with young ladies in long, elegant dresses and a young man dressed as a waiter with a tray of drinks who had his finger up to his mouth in a 'shhhhh' pose while he winked with his left eye. Although this was an advert warning of the effects of Chlamydia he put himself in the waiter's place and imagined that he was carrying the tray for himself and Mabel, giving them something to enjoy before they stood to dance together. Once they were exhausted from their movement around the room he could see them attending a plentiful banquet with rich, succulent food the likes of which he had never really been able to afford. Having closed out the scenario of the party he moved on to the next poster and did the same, allowing his imagination to take him out of his actual location and placing himself with Mabel until he was suddenly woken by a technician who, after hours of failing to acknowledge his daydreaming, was finally ready to serve him with his prescription. Alf wasn't sure if he'd dozed off in that time but assumed he probably had when he looked up at the clock on the wall in front of him.

By the time Alf left the hospital at four o' clock that afternoon both Dr Farley and Shirley had finished their shifts and left yet, had his two primary care givers still been on shift, they may have asked him about his transport home. As it was Alf picked up his belongings, walked slowly out of the hospital and made his way to the front of the Accident and Emergency department where he knocked on the door of an ambulance that housed two medics and politely requested his transport home.

FORTY SEVEN

The family had been visiting the same GP for so many years that they usually spent five minutes of each appointment catching up on news before they even started to discuss symptoms, however this time it was different. Mabel was obviously fraught with concern and Alf went straight into the problem leaving no detail unspoken. They had left Jill with their next door neighbour as she was still quite sensitive and struggled to understand that medical issues weren't necessarily severe which was highlighted by her questions towards her parents as they left her briefly.

Wayne's hearing had always been a little wayward but he always seemed to cope well despite this. After his fifth birthday his sense clearly declined until he could barely hear his own name. Mabel had called to him repeatedly from the kitchen to the point that he usually heard, after which she made her way into the living room and shouted his name across the room without an obstacle in sight. She was horrified to see that he didn't turn his head and tried three more times before raising the alarm to Alf who picked up the phone and made an emergency appointment with the GP.

As they sat in front of him they repeated the experiment, first with Mabel calling his name and then with the GP trying different tones. There was clearly something getting through as Wayne turned his head on two occasions but seemed undisturbed during the other calls. The GP checked his ears and found an unhealthy amount of wax had built near the eardrums, causing the sound to distort by the time it reached Wayne's interpretive organs and giving him an option to ignore the signals by labelling them as background noise. Drops were prescribed to reduce the build up and the GP advised that he would need regular checks to ensure he was progressing healthily but assured Mabel that the condition was fairly common and that she needn't worry. As the mother of two young children, one a five year old, near-deaf boy, she couldn't help holding on to her concern yet she shook the hand of their GP to ensure she wasn't noted as an over-protective mother and they left having finally shared their news.

Mabel's look on the journey home was one of sorrowful anxiety and Alf tried to reassure her that Wayne was on the right track. He left them both in the car as he picked up a prescription and Mabel spoke to her son from the front, realising that he was smiling to mirror her demeanour and could probably only pick out key words from what she was saying. She persevered, taking some comfort from the fact that he wasn't in any visible pain and seemed to be enjoying life.

As Alf made his way back to the car from the pharmacy he looked over towards his family and saw them both smiling, causing him to break into a grin. As he did so Mabel caught his eye and looked up, breaking her communication from her son. In doing so she missed the moment her son turned his head to the sound of a siren and watched intently, soaking in the piercing noise and looking wide eyed at the blue lights of the vehicle as it passed. However, Alf noticed this and knew exactly what had happened and therefore what he needed to do. Excitedly he moved towards the car and proclaimed that a detour was necessary and they would be home a little later because of it. He kept his idea to himself as he considered it fairly radical yet he had a strong feeling it would work and so followed his instinct immediately.

The car pulled into the road behind the gardening centre and Alf once again left his wife and son in the car, this time with both wondering where he was going and what he was up to. Mabel turned to her son again and asked him for his views in a cheerful voice, receiving the same smile of approval but no spoken communication to confirm that he'd understood the sentence. Before long Alf had returned with a wheelbarrow, stoking the interest of his wife as Wayne's eyes widened and his smile spread right across his face. This was also noticed by Alf and missed by Mabel who would have been more confused than ever had she caught sight of his new expression.

Stepping out of the car upon their return home Mabel couldn't help but ask why he had bought a wheelbarrow when he was so terrible at gardening and seemed to have no inclination to become a builder. A glint appeared in Alf's eyes as he wheeled it into the garden and then left to collect Jill, leaving Wayne with Mabel one more time. She picked up her son and he started to convulse with excitement, making it clear that he wanted to play with the barrow but being informed that it was Alf's tool and not a toy. He still didn't respond appropriately to Mabel's voice and she sighed, resigned to the fact that she would have to wait for the effect of the drops.

On his return Alf sent Jill and Wayne into the garden before placing his son into the bucket of the device. He then proceeded to wheel him around the garden while imitating the noise of the ambulance that had passed earlier that day. In doing so Wayne nearly exploded with excitement and Mabel was struggling to believe that she could hear her son making the same noise. Jill took over the driving of the barrow and Wayne continued to make the shrill, continuous siren noises that would have driven most parents near insanity, though Mabel could only feel elated that her son had finally heard and registered a sound after months of obvious decline. His smile had been a comfort that he could tolerate the discomfort but to see such joy etched into his face was enough to make Mabel laugh along, hugging Alf as she did so.

Over the next few days visitors to the house were greeted with the same sound of a wailing siren and the occasional interruption as Jill donned her nurse's apron and saw to the array of patients Wayne brought in to her surgery. Every bear and stuffed toy in the house had their medical conditions seen to and there was nothing the duo couldn't cure, including total loss of hearing. As they administered care to the inanimate members of the household Mabel played her part and kept Wayne's ears topped up with the prescribed drops which had the desired effect after six weeks. A return trip to the doctor confirmed that the unreachable build up had all but disappeared and gave the young patient a hearing test that was passed with ease. The parents had seemed a lot brighter at the start of the visit and the doctor was sure that the diagnosis had been accurate by their manner, although they told the story of the wheelbarrow and laughed at the way Wayne's face had lit up at the sight of something so unusual. As they left the surgery they thanked the doctor and Mabel hugged her son tightly, elated at the news that he was well again.

That night Mabel spoke to Alf about his idea and thanked him for bringing such a vast smile to their children's faces to which he simply shrugged and concluded that it was all part of being a dad. Mabel lay with her head in her husband's lap so they could both watch a documentary together and, as she did so, Alf smiled with the satisfaction of his actions. He thought about how the children had enhanced the household and how their lives had changed since the birth of Jill and Wayne, an experience that most had said would either bond them as a couple or tear them apart. The devotion they provided to each other was enough to afford them the former and he was always quietly grateful that he was offered this opportunity and promised himself that he would never take a moment for granted.

As this thought crossed his mind he slowly drifted off to sleep with Mabel following shortly afterwards. They were awoken the next day by the wailing of a mock ambulance followed shortly by a plastic thermometer in Alf's ear and a damp cloth on Mabel's forehead. Jill suggested they were both very unwell as they'd spent the night sleeping on the sofa and prescribed them a course of antibiotics followed by a shot from a very large plastic needle. The thought of the needle was enough to get Alf up from the sofa just in time to see his son wheeling the peat from the flowerbeds throughout the downstairs carpet and across the skirting boards. Children were a blessing for sure, he thought, but he could see why they might be the end for some couples. This thought continued as he searched for the cleaning products and started to remove the remnants of his bright idea from a carpet that was only a few months old.

FORTY EIGHT

It was gone six by the time Alf made it home. The young female paramedic he had spoken to beside the ambulance had been kind enough to call him a taxi when she realised that he didn't have any change for the phone but he'd had to wait until one had become available, meaning another short stay in a bland room of the hospital. He pondered how people normally arrived home given that they'd been transported to the hospital, especially as he rarely carried more than a few pounds on him. Once he was through his front door all of these concerns were banished and he placed his bag and coat on the floor beside the stairs.

A small glint of light caught his attention in the kitchen and, as he made his way through, he noticed that pictures had been knocked off the walls and a few of Mabel's figurines had either been moved or had developed limbs and walked off. He summoned up the last of his energy and wandered around the downstairs of his house, putting his hand to his mouth when he realised that someone had broken in through the kitchen window and had helped themselves to his valuables while the house had been empty. He looked again for Mabel's figurines, a collection of which she'd brought together over a period of a number of years, but found no evidence of them. He wasn't sure if this was a cruel dream or an even crueller act of fate until he picked up a large piece of the broken glass and felt the smoothness for himself.

Having just recovered from a mental state that had worried so many Alf was in no place to keep himself together as he took in the amount of damage and theft that had occurred in his own property. He wept to think that the last remaining artefacts of his soulmate had been taken from him as well, although he couldn't think what to do to adjust the situation. He made his way to the sofa to sit down and he felt ready to succumb to his exhaustion but a wave of panic hit as he considered that his house was unsecure and he worried for his own life, fearing further opportunistic thieves would find their opening and dispose of him quickly before making off with what little was left.

The answer was obvious; he had to ring Jill and ask her what his next step was meant to be. In doing so he was assured that she was on her way and that PC Drayson would be along soon to take some details and to secure the house. It took a further fifteen minutes before they both arrived almost simultaneously and Drayson went to work immediately. Alf was close to breaking at the thought of someone rummaging through their belongings and Drayson knew that he needed to rest elsewhere, suggesting he went with Jill to her home to get the sleep he desperately required. He had no choice but to agree given that his decision making was suspended and he followed her to her car, looking around with fear as he crossed the threshold into the street.

Drayson had seen cold hearted acts of this nature all too often and his experience helped him to react quickly. He called Wayne and advised him to take Isobel to the house after relaying the details of the incident. Isobel was otherwise engaged at the time but he promised they would make it to the house within the hour and Drayson assured him that they would look far and wide for the burglars, knowing there was little chance of catching anyone or finding the perpetrators.

True to his word Wayne made it within the hour and escorted Isobel into the maze of broken glass and belongings. The thieves had left photos of the family in shattered frames but she knew that it would be easy to replace those. The hardest part of her task was replacing the figurines and tableware that had disappeared or perished in the attack and she took Wayne straight out to find suitable objects to make the house look like her future father-in-law's home once more. Drayson was left to speak to the insurance company who were happy to take his word given his position and closeness with the family and Wayne was relieved to hear that there would be financial compensation to replace what Isobel had managed to spend that evening. Given that it was for his father he couldn't complain, however he was in no position to give away such an amount without seeing some effects. He managed to keep these thoughts to himself and, on the journey back to the house, breathed a silent sigh of relief at the thought of receiving some of the funds back.

Isobel set to work as soon as they arrived and Drayson was keen to watch her methods. She'd only recently been at the house yet the time she'd spent admiring the décor of the building meant that replacements were in keeping with previous themes. Exact replacements were impossible to come by but the alternatives sat as though they'd always been and, with the damage to the kitchen window repaired before night fell, Drayson, Wayne and Isobel felt hopeful that Alf would be able to settle back into his home.

It took a further week before Alf was rested enough to make it back to the house and Jill knew that he was better off under her supervision as he started to adapt to life on his own. Recognising the sincerity in his face she was relieved when he asked to return home and she offered to stay with him for the first night, an invitation he couldn't refuse. Alf packed his belongings once more and made his way to his daughter's car, smiling as he did so to think that she could be so empathetic. As Jill locked her front door she looked over to the car and caught sight of Alf's joy, an expression she had missed on her father given the length of time since she'd last encountered it.

As they arrived back at the house Alf visibly tensed and Jill was concerned that he wouldn't make it after all. They'd received a guarantee that the security had been upgraded and, as long as Alf remembered to lock the doors and windows, nobody would be able to get into the house unaided again. He had yet to confirm this and was relying on his daughter to get him through the door, her presence being the only reason he had the courage to do so. As she parked the car he waited beside the front door and, reaching in to his bag for his key, only placed it in the lock when he was sure that Jill was on her way.

Alf was lost for words when the two of them entered the house as the redecoration was so radical that he barely recognised his own home. The photos were the same but each was housed in a different enclosure, the carpets had been replaced where the burglars had destroyed the old ones with their clumsy mannerisms and the paintwork had been updated by Wayne to freshen the interior as much as possible. Alf caught sight of the new figurines and recognised some of them as potential targets for Mabel had she been given the opportunity to collect them and tears formed once again as he wept with joy. The overwhelming familiarity of the house had been replaced by a tribute to their former life and he was comforted to think that he was moving into a new chapter, a part of his life where Mabel was no longer around but where he had the memories and essence of her being and his fear of being alone finally evaporated. The final transformation of his emotions came when he caught sight of the new double glazed windows and doors, helping him to finally feel safe after a week of doubt and grief. He knew that this house would remain his home for as long as he needed it.

That evening he and Jill were joined by PC Drayson, Wayne and Isobel who brought over a cheeseboard and a bottle of port to help him get his strength back. He declined the port knowing that his medication would not agree with the alcohol yet he made light work of the cheeseboard having been a guest in both the hospital and Jill's house and abiding by both sets of mealtime routines. Jill would happily have indulged Alf but he felt obliged by the fact it wasn't his residence, a feeling that waned now that he was back in his castle. Drayson had originally attended to complete some paperwork but had been drafted into a game of Monopoly and ended up staying with the family well into the night. Jill and Isobel saw to the bottle of port and both were in no position to look after the eldest of the gathering who needed assistance getting ready for bed. He knew his strength would return but, in the meantime, Wayne was on hand to help him in a number of ways before he retired for the night.

That evening was the first time he'd returned to his bed since he'd woken up beside Mabel and he was concerned on the journey up the stairs that he wouldn't be able to face a room so full of bad memories. He put it to the back of his mind until he was at the door of the room and he said goodnight to his son, assuring him he could complete the journey alone. Isobel had been into the room and had replaced some of the silverware that had adorned the Welsh dresser but he noticed that, beneath the fresh linen, the bed and mattress were still the same. He gingerly climbed under the duvet and waited to see how he would react to being back in this position before, five minutes later, he considered that he was ready to rest. As he rolled to face his wife's side of the bed he realised that he did miss her presence and turned her pillow through ninety degrees so that it lay next to him. Within a further ten minutes he was lying with one leg over the pillow, one arm under the pillow and dreams of his sweet wife playing within his unconscious head, the front of which housed another smile.

FORTY NINE

Alf dreamed about the first time he and Mabel had shared a bed. At that point they had been together for over twelve months yet their status as a young, unmarried couple meant that the closest they could get to each other when they were out in the open was holding hands in the park. They were both sure that they'd discovered their life partners as they'd never felt such a strong attraction to anyone else before, however they respected their parents and would never have acted in a way that would have angered or embarrassed them.

Mabel's stepfather was loath to leave them both alone in the house for the evening as he knew the worst possible outcome for such a scenario. It was her mother who had finally managed to entice him out of the house with the promise of a few drinks at their local ale house, leaving Alf and Mabel watching a film with a few snacks that had been bought for them both. They had sworn to each other that they would ignore their teenage urges and concentrate on the feature as both had been keen to see it since it was released at the cinema. As the action took place on the screen in front of them the two viewers took turns in staring at the other, Alf unable to resist Mabel's youthful charm and radiant looks while she imagined his sculpted body from his evenings helping his father move blocks for local builders. Eventually their stolen glances coincided and both looked away quickly, blushing as they did so to think that they had been caught.

Less than ten minutes passed before he could stand the tension between them no longer and he went to suggest they hold hands on the sofa, his words being stifled by her suggestion that they make their way up to her bedroom. She surmised that her parents would be out for at least the duration of the film and, since she was well aware of what may have happened if they went too far, she made him promise that they would stop before any carnal knowledge was realised. On agreement they made their way up the stairs with Mabel chasing Alf for the distance and pushing him onto her bed.

His biggest concern was the lack of time they may be granted for their activities as he knew that there was no way to explain why they'd left a film that had created so much excitement for the two of them to retire to Mabel's bedroom other than to confess what was actually happening. Her only thought was the dependency she could place on her parents to be out for a safe period of time and, with that, she placed him under the duvet and gently pulled his shirt over his head. Pulling back slightly she could see the indentations surrounding his muscles and her eyes widened at the thought of placing her hands on his body. He picked up on her awe and smiled with confidence that he could be the owner of a body that someone considered attractive, particularly a young lady of Mabel's standing.

He quietly reminded her that it was her turn to match his state of dress and she grinned at the suggestion, licking her lips before undoing the buttons on her light top and humming seductively as she did so. As the top fell to the floor she laughed and Alf pulled her close to him, ensuring his pleasure at her state was well hidden as they embraced. She caressed his physique lightly, tickling at first before applying a firmness that they both appreciated. He tensed his biceps in an attempt to highlight his features and she kissed them gently, keeping to a peck to ensure she didn't lead him on. The longer they lay beside each other the more adventurous they were willing to become and she asked him to close his eyes while she removed her bra, struggling in an effort to make the gesture seem smooth and elegant. Finally she wrestled it off and assured him it was safe to look to which he threw his eyes open and stared.

Mabel let him look for a few seconds before she took his hand and placed it at the top of her shoulder. From there he lightly brought his fingers around the outside of her breast and they both beamed as he made his way inwardly towards her nipple. Her intention was to call time on their actions once he had experienced the feel of her but their time was interrupted by an enormous bang and the pounding of footsteps on the stairs. They both jumped in shock and Alf's face became a portrayal of fear as he imagined the figure bursting in on them and seeing them both under her duvet with their clothes half removed. She hurried to get her top back on in the hope she could do so before such an incident occurred, giving her a more plausible alibi for their presence in the room that would only be hampered by his inability to do the same.

The noises drifting in from the rest of the house were of no help to his position. They heard shouting which included the phrase, "That damn boy!" which was closely followed by the cocking of a shotgun, an implement that was kept loaded for the event of a burglary. Mabel's stepfather hadn't been out of the house long enough to be drunk and his often serious demeanour made their position even more dangerous as there was very little chance of him believing the two of them were planning to stop once they'd felt the contours of each other's upper body. Alf managed to fumble his shirt back on after whispered advice from Mabel and was just about to take a step towards the landing when she grabbed his arm, her eyes silently screaming at him to stop. He felt he could have justified their actions now that they were fully clothed once more yet, just as he thought this, the footsteps bounded down the stairs and were followed by an apology to the living room for the disruption. The front door slammed and the shouting continued as Mabel's stepfather made his way back to the ale house, leaving the two occupants of the house agitated and confused.

Knowing they were once again alone they made their way quickly downstairs and into the living room where Mabel placed a kiss on Alf's forehead in an attempt to seal their actions and calm him down simultaneously. He smiled and breathed a sigh of relief, confessing his certainty they would be caught and that his head may have been brushed with shot as he tried to escape the house. He bravely offered a hug to Mabel and she accepted before they returned to opposite ends of the sofa to watch the end of a film they couldn't follow due to their absence during the main plot points.

Following the film Alf offered his goodbyes and the two of them kissed once more before he made it to the front door since a kiss in view of the neighbours would have made him eligible to be the next target of the shotgun. They confirmed their next meeting and he tentatively made his way back to his parent's house, looking everywhere for the presence of an angry man sporting a weapon. Although he'd escaped a potentially terrible situation there was always the chance that he'd end up in the line of fire and be accidentally killed, a possibility that kept him entertained for the duration of his return home.

When the two of them were together once more Mabel was much less concerned about the fact that her stepfather had exited his property with a tool of execution and a growl that matched any wild animal. He had been halfway through his second pint when a group of men on a stag do had entered the ale house and had promised to stop for a single drink before turning up the juke box and dancing drunkenly on the tables within a few minutes of entering the establishment. The locals had tolerated their bawdy behaviour as they knew young lads had to perform once in a while to get it out of their system, particularly when they were celebrating the nuptials of a close friend. After an hour it became apparent that the lads were enjoying themselves and continued ordering drinks, spilling most of what they were paying for in their drunken state and making no apology for doing so.

One member of the party was a lad Mabel's stepfather had known as he was growing up and he chose this subject as the target for his displeasure. The lad in question hadn't recognised the bearer of the suggestion to leave and had retorted sarcastically before attempting to seduce Mabel's mother with a demonstration on the length of his tongue. As she winced and pulled away the front door of the ale house slammed shut and Mabel's stepfather had disappeared, causing the bar staff to yell obscenities of alarm and to push the members of the stag do out of the door as quickly as possible.

The lad in question was outside when Mabel's stepfather returned with his pride and joy, giving him no protection from the further suggestions of a man he suddenly brought to memory. His father had known Mabel's stepfather for a number of years and he had been warned never to breach the line when it came to acts against the man in front of him. He made a case for his defence, apologised hard to the victim of his advances and sped away with the rest of his group following swiftly. The gun was made safe and the local patrons returned to the bar, never uttering a word of the incident again. The last word on events came from the best man at the wedding who summed up the regret they all held for disturbing a night in their local ale house, to which Mabel's stepfather grinned in satisfaction at having ruined what was meant to be a hilarious anecdotal account of the night in question.

FIFTY

Alf woke with the memories of that event still fresh in his mind, the bang of the front door as crisp as it was when it had occurred. He had to readjust for a moment to confirm that he had seen a lifetime of events since that night and his heart sank when he remembered that the girl he'd shared such an intimate moment with was now no longer by his side. He reached out for her in a final attempt to correct the truth, finding the empty space and filling it with his own limbs. He sighed loudly, knowing that no-one was there to hear it and therefore free from the concern of nurses misjudging his complaint and surrounding him.

Jill and Wayne had agreed on their turns to visit their father as they knew how colossal a change he would be undertaking and they attempted to keep the conversation light, restricting themselves to exchanges about their mother only when Alf felt the need to discuss her. They spent long periods of time at the house although occasionally they would wander to the local pond or venture to the gardening centre to buy low maintenance flowers. Alf routinely watched the shows that he and Mabel had enjoyed together and found himself laughing or enquiring towards her chair from time to time. He also knew how colossal a change he needed to undertake after cementing so many habits yet he was pleased that the hospital were taking less interest in his condition as this could only mean that he was getting better.

He considered what this actually meant for his situation. After his wife's initial passing he had still been able to have a conversation with her yet weeks had passed since her voice had disappeared and he was certain that he actually felt better when he could hear her voice despite her lack of physical interaction. He was still close to her and they were able to take on the world but now he could only feel distant and alone. This would pass in time, of course it would, though Alf needed to know if he could ever get the voice back to save him having to wait so long to appear normal again. Eventually the contemplation became an experiment as he had to be certain that having her spirit back was no longer an option.

After a friendly visit from Wayne and Isobel, who prepared his meals and kept him company until gone 8 o' clock that evening, Alf stood up and made his way to the coat rack, wrapping himself in a long, blue, faux suede coat that he kept for formal occasions. He felt the need for some spiritual guidance and so he ascended the stairs to get a locket from his wife's dresser as a symbol of optimism. He didn't consider that the photo inside was of himself and the two of them would have chuckled at what may have looked to some like an act of vanity but it was the first thing she donned before they went out for an evening together and so was the closest item to her. He placed it in his pocket and made his way to the front door to carry out his final research into voices of the deceased.

The night air was still and the streetlights surrounding the town were perfectly placed for his journey. He planned to retrace the steps he had taken with Mabel in the wheelbarrow but, to do so, he first had to avoid the gaze of the neighbours and escape to the woods. He took a torch with him to light the murkier areas, only really requiring it when he started to walk beneath the trees. With each step he listened for a faint whisper that couldn't be attributed to the wildlife and he started to notice how much faster he was able to move without the impediment of the wheelbarrow. He soon made it to the hollow that he and Mabel had occupied and looked around for any trace that they were there. The tracks had worn away quickly, largely due to the rain that followed their journey, yet there were still offcuts of wrappers from some of the snacks he had consumed before their position was compromised. He wondered quietly to himself how he had ever survived overnight in a place that offered minimal shelter such as this before considering that his adrenaline must have been high and his mind was working overtime to keep them both as out of sight as possible. He picked up the litter out of consideration for the environment and moved on.

It was a long walk from the woods to the old fire station and Alf recounted the struggle of the hill without difficulty. In his current condition it would have been impossible, such was his lack of strength and the overwhelming fatigue that flowed through his body. The chance of hearing Mabel's voice once more was the only motivation to keep going yet it was too big a prize to surrender and so he went on with the knowledge that he could sleep as long as he needed to during the next day. No visitors were due until later in the evening and this thought hung for a brief period until he heard a whispered echo in a breeze that seemed lost in the calm air. He stopped immediately and looked around, his body frozen in one spot in an attempt to determine whether the voice was that of his wife. Seconds passed before he heard another noise, this one clear enough to give him confidence that he'd heard his own name. The voice was certainly female and had a delicate nature of the sort he'd heard previously. He knew about the power of three and stood motionless once more for the final, concrete sign.

"Alf..?"

It was unmistakably aimed at him and came from a far off place. The word was surrounded by a glow that seemed ethereal and gave him the inclination to respond. He shouted the name of his departed wife into the darkness of the night and smiled at the possibility of a final conversation with her. A chill ran down his spine and, as quickly as it had arrived, the voice disappeared. He gave it time to return before calling out once more, putting his remaining energy into the reply as he felt the smile drop from his face. He looked around at the flickering stars, giving them no consideration as he did so and only hoping for one outcome. He felt it necessary to move towards the source of the voice as though it may have briefly forgotten where he was and he made the decision to climb the hill, sure that his hard work would grant him the return he so desperately wanted.

Another call into the night sky was required and he knew that he would have to rest before he was able to provide it. He took a seat on the wall of a small community garden and breathed deeply in an attempt to fill his lungs and diminish his need for such a heavy intake. Time was against him but he was careful not to rush his rate of breathing as he knew how catastrophic that could be. As he made it halfway to a steady rate he heard his name once more and his eyes widened while the sound enveloped him. A fresh surge of adrenaline was released and this gave him the strength to stand and move up the hill once more, hoping to determine exactly where the voice had come from. His optimism was high and he prepared his opening speech for when he and his wife were together once more.

Rounding the corner towards the top of the hill, Alf was in the midst of confirming his dialogue when he came to a sudden halt and was forced backwards causing him to fall and land on the floor. He almost rolled back down the hill a little until the source of the voice leaned forwards and pulled him to his feet once more. His hands were grazed from his landing yet he was grateful that he'd been able to save himself from a hard impact and had even more gratitude for the hand that had launched forward and stopped his inevitable course. He looked into familiar eyes and his heart sank as a dawning realisation set in; the voice hadn't belonged to Mabel, it was Jill's. The distortion from the night air had made him believe he would be able to communicate with his beloved once more but now he knew that he had simply caused another alarm by wandering out so late at night.

Jill offered her concerns about Alf's state of mind, particularly relating to him being alone during the day. He admitted that he had gone in search of Mabel's voice but his daughter was relieved to hear that it wasn't a search for a voice he could already hear. She assured him that the lack of contact from a deceased party was a good sign and he transferred his opinion to her consideration. It was time for him to move on, to take charge of his life and to live it in honour of Mabel. Jill smiled and kissed Alf on the forehead upon receipt of his words before guiding him back to the house. While there she promised to make arrangements for a carer to attend once a day, relieving her of the cleaning chores and allowing some conversation to take place. This seemed an excellent idea and he nodded along with her plans, knowing the transition wouldn't be easy but conceding that it was the only way forward.

FIFTY ONE

It was a surreal experience and one that he knew would require adaptation of his state of mind but he made the most of the quiet within the house and poured the biggest bowl of cereal he had managed for a long time. He kept the radio and television off, absorbing the absolute silence that crept around the house and capturing every crunch of his jaw against the fresh boulders of food. Mabel's voice was nowhere to be heard and he felt good about that as he could finally appreciate his own company. He knew Jill and Wayne would not be disturbing him and it was this knowledge that had sparked his low key but enjoyable celebration. He placed the last spoonful of cereal into his mouth and went to wash the bowl, hitting the side with the ceramic dish and cursing himself as he did so.

"Alf?"

He closed his eyes. The voice was unquestionably Mabel's and he willed it to disappear. He didn't want to appear harsh and would never have admitted to a soul that the peace was the only noise he was open to hearing but he kept his eyes closed and waited for a few seconds more. Sure enough he wasn't free from her and he heard his name a second time. He sighed quietly so as not to cause offence and went to the foot of the stairs to see where this exchange might take him.

His plan was to move into the living room quietly, close the door and watch the highlights of the football from the night before. Mabel had never been keen on sport and only allowed him to watch games of any apparent meaning such as cup finals or international matches, however occasionally at weekends he was able to leave her sleeping while he caught up on the regular week-to-week matches that made up the conversation at work. This week was a write off and he had to accept that as he looked up to the top of the stairs and saw his wife in her dressing gown looking dishevelled and exhausted. As he looked up he could see how miserable she appeared and he made his way up the stairs to console her as she had clearly missed out on an essential night of sleep.

They were both adapting to a massive change in their lives. Jill had been slow to move out as she had no steady partner to rush out for and had discarded the idea of getting a roommate before anyone had even put it forward. Her parents were happy for her to stay as long as she was contributing to the household and she had done so incredibly well, providing a small weekly sum to subsidise her expenditure while increasing her cleaning of the house tenfold. It seemed she appreciated the house more after paying to live there and took the chores less for granted, turning her hand from the washing of the clothes to repainting the inside after a spring clean that had involved the whole family. Eventually she managed to save enough for a mortgage deposit and had moved into her own home, leaving just Alf and Mabel to clean as Wayne had remained as reluctant as ever.

Despite this Mabel enjoyed having someone there who depended on her. She relished creating his lunches as he made the transition from school to college and finally into work and was happy to pick up his clothes as long as he didn't leave them lying around his bedroom and moved them into the bathroom. She loved to be busy during the day and Alf often enquired about it, to which she would retort that it kept time ticking away before his return. He loved to hear this more than anything else and, after the first time of asking, simply put it to her in the hope of receiving this reply.

Wayne's relocation from his parent's house to a shared house with two of his friends hadn't been wholly unexpected as he'd talked about his considerations in the past yet his usually inconsistent nature meant he dropped most ideas well before they were even formed. To take a step as big as this was most out of character and Alf was quietly convinced that he would be back soon, however Mabel was certain he was gone for good and was struggling to imagine how she would fill her time now that her particularly unclean son was messing up the house of someone else.

Wayne had known his two associates since they were all eleven and had started at secondary school together. His best friend was Hayden, a short lad who was never really gifted much extra height during his school years and had been picked on for wearing glasses from his first to his last day at the school. Their regular guest in the friendship was Gaby who could be seen drifting towards different sets of girls within their school year before inevitably ending back with Wayne and Hayden. She had never wanted to leave their company, more she felt that she could get the three of them into a different group if she spent enough time talking to fringe members. As it happened she was wrong and ended her time in school having spoken to everyone but still only having much time for her two companions.

Hayden's father had owned the house in the middle of the town and had rented it to enough antisocial tenants for him to consider letting it to his son and two friends. Wayne knew that the house was well maintained and the location was so close to his parents that he didn't have far to move his belongings, a big plus when considering his part in the institution. He signed on the Friday, made the necessary changes to parties who sent him any post during the following week and moved in the next Saturday. Alf knew the Sunday morning was going to be hard and had accounted for it, promising his wife they would go out to take both of their minds off the relative emptiness of their house. He turned the football highlights off with a sigh and made his way to the car.

They were on their way out of the town when Mabel asked Alf to drive past Wayne's new house, slowing down as they did because a van was parked dangerously across the road and a small crowd of people were surrounding a selection of white goods. Alf parked as close as he could get and they both walked up to the front of the house to see what the disturbance was, finding Wayne standing next to a washing machine wrapped in plastic with labels attached. Hayden and Gaby were standing nearby and Hayden's father was talking at an increased volume to three delivery drivers who had all coincidentally turned up at the same time. Hayden's father was discussing how, although the coincidence could not be accounted for, their decisions to pull up together and deliver their loads regardless had caused mayhem that was likely to attract the attention of the local constabulary. Alf looked beyond the argument and could see a queue of traffic building on the other side of the vans as evidence of the most vocal individual's complaint.

In an unusual act of forethought Alf assessed the amount that needed to be moved into the house and suggested those in attendance got to work clearing the side of the road and concerning themselves with the installation of the appliances when they were in place. This gave the delivery drivers the opportunity to clear the road while Alf used the knowledge he'd gained from his various occupations to plumb, wire and fit the machines as necessary. Hayden's father looked over the operation and was dumbstruck as he saw the processes in action. Within less than an hour the traffic was moving once more and the house was completely in place. Mabel used the occurrence to make a case for how much Wayne needed his parents, in doing so confirming to him that he had made a good decision in relocating and learning to provide for himself. He thanked Alf for the hard work and hugged his parents as appreciation for their visit, leaving no insinuation that they were welcome to stay. He was genuinely pleased that his father had come through for him but was keen to start his new life and knew this couldn't occur if he was constantly being checked on. Knowing this, Alf ushered Mabel to the car and took her out as planned for the afternoon while Wayne and his roommates recovered with uninterrupted drinking games.

On their return the couple felt the familiar feeling of isolation from within the house they had left that morning and Mabel was sure she would struggle to sleep that night. Alf promised to help her in any way he could and spent the night preparing drinks and snacks to aid his wife's relaxation. This would be the first night of many as she found the adaption difficult, however time was on their side and Alf was looking forward to spending more time with the woman he'd devoted his life to.

FIFTY TWO

The isolation Alf had felt following the departure of the children was coupled with thoughts of freedom and adventure, however the isolation he was feeling without Mabel simply held promises of dread and finality. He had never been one to sit in silence for long periods and decided he would fill the motionless air with waves of music, setting up a stereo system with a speaker in each room so that he could surround himself with the beauty of the melodies. His first source of entertainment was a collection of Mozart, a great artist he had revered and recommended over the years, that had come free with a copy of his regular newspaper. His carer had helped him to set up the system and was quite content with sitting for a while and listening to the breathtaking sounds that were emanating from every corner off the house.

Alf had warmed to his carer, Lizzie, very quickly. She was a young lady of medium height with very dark hair that covered her back, although it was her gentle touch and considerate nature that had made him appreciate her so much. He had tried to prove his independence on a few separate occasions, failing drastically and merely emphasising his need to have her around. By the time Wayne and Isobel had planned their wedding and the date had arrived Alf and Lizzie had spent a great deal of time laughing about the past and communicating in a way that meant she knew when he needed something even when he tried to deny the fact. She had been invited to the wedding as a guest but had received her own request as Wayne wanted the seat next to Alf's to be free at all times out of respect for his mother. He agreed that this was a fitting tribute and wondered if he would keep himself together during the service as Lizzie tightened the top button on his shirt before applying his tie.

Wayne was more nervous than he'd ever been and was pacing at the front of the church in a bid to put his concerns out of his mind. He knew what people had said about the couple when they thought he couldn't hear them and was concerned that Isobel would see the difference for herself before committing to him, leaving him devastated and alone for the rest of his life. Similarly, Isobel was shaking as her hair was given a few final touches at the thought that he would never turn up and would leave a note with the vicar stating his relocation to another part of the country and bidding her goodbye forever. Their nerves were a part of their make up and helped in their relationship as neither took the other for granted and both made a special effort when they were in each other's company.

Wayne spoke to Alf briefly before Lizzie walked him in to the church and he confessed his apprehensions, tripping over his words as he did so and waiting for his father to interpret the mess of questioning before he was able to answer. Alf simply confirmed that, over the times he'd seen them both together, he could see how devoted she was to him and that he should have absolutely no qualms about giving the rest of his life to the woman he clearly loved so much. Wayne smiled at the reply and hugged his father tightly, relieving him of his duties and watching him walking delicately to the second pew with Lizzie offering her arm for the distance. She sat him in his position and made her way back two rows as requested; giving her assurance that she was close by if he needed anything.

Once the church had filled and the vicar introduced the bride and groom the whole congregation watched Wayne's nerves in action as he sweated and shook the words out of his mouth. Isobel smiled at him for reassurance but he didn't take the hint and continued staggering towards the end of the ceremony. By the time he was asked to kiss the bride his back was dripping and he was only spared from informing those watching him by the black jacket that refused to separate the wet and dry sections covering him. Most observers thought it was sweet that Wayne could be so nervous but Alf empathised, remembering his own doubts about his and Mabel's future simply due to the inability of his own mind to accept that positive outcomes could occur to him. He stood and applauded the couple as they walked to the back of the church and gave his son a look of confidence that he would be alright, the congregation following his cue for a standing ovation and cheering loudly enough to make the groom blush.

Isobel had melted several hearts with her everyday wardrobe but she stole the show in her wedding dress and her new father-in-law could see the jealousy raging in some of the male guests to think that they'd never had a chance with her. Some of the female guests were showing signs of envy too, although these were mainly due to how well the bride looked. Regardless of their feelings nobody could deny them the best day of their lives as they were both so kind and helpful, ready to assist in the most unusual of situations. All emotions were put to one side and the group took turns to congratulate them both for making it down the aisle and into a commitment that secured their futures for the rest of their lives.

Lizzie was quick to help Alf out of the pew while the crowds gathered outside and she walked him straight up to the couple, waiting only for a few friends who were confirming details of the reception and giving their plans to the couple. Once they were free to talk Alf reached out to shake his son's hand and congratulated them both, discreetly wiping his hand before moving on to an embrace with his new daughter-in-law. He asked her to look after his son as they both knew traditional methods of care would never apply in their situation and Wayne gave a half-hearted protest suggesting he would be the provider of care for the family. As he said that his hand went straight to his mouth and Isobel's face widened, both acts that confirmed they were harbouring secrets. Alf's inquisitive mind jumped in at that point and Isobel looked at Wayne with a ponderous glance, the two of them clearly trying to decide whether they could keep their secret for a little while longer. Wayne knew they didn't stand a chance and promised to explain all during his speech, leaving his father to consider his ideas a little longer.

The guests all made their way to the hotel for the reception and, as they filed into the foyer, Jill noticed one of Isobel's friends walking in without a chaperone. She was extremely attractive, slightly shorter than Jill and had flowing blonde hair that went over her shoulders and covered the front of her white jacket as well as the back. Her facial features were almost perfect, reminding her observer of the dolls she'd played with as a child, but the feature that most struck her was a round, pink badge with a rainbow emblem in the centre attached to her white, leather bag. She knew this may simply have been a badge that the guest liked the look of but she was keen to know for sure and had just enough courage to walk over and introduce herself.

The guest's name was Charlotte and she had indeed received an invite from Isobel as they'd attended the same college and had kept in touch ever since, meeting at least once a year to reignite the excitement of their younger years. Charlotte was fairly bashful and only admitted her rowdy lifestyle later in the evening as she met up with Jill following the reception and the two of them spent most of the night talking to each other. Romantic intentions were never discussed during the evening but it was clear to those around them that both only had eyes for each other and they exchanged phone numbers at the end of the evening with both of them realising what the other's thoughts had been. They both felt they were at a point in their lives where they were happy to discuss children and both agreed that it was an option they wanted to look into once they were certain they were in a partnership that could handle such a big change. At that point their futures were undecided but fate seemed to have brought them together and their discussions made the evening pass so quickly that they missed most of the evening's activities. Fortunately they had been at different tables during the reception meal as it meant they both got to hear the news Wayne and Isobel had nearly spilled to Alf at the church.

The speeches all went as planned with one exception; Wayne's speech was left until the end and he'd managed to scribble a small note at the bottom of the last card. It was at this point that he asked his wife to attend his side and he held her hand as he announced that they were going to have a baby and that Isobel was around fourteen weeks pregnant. They'd wanted to keep the baby as a surprise for after the wedding as Wayne never wanted anybody to believe that he'd simply married her because she was pregnant, however it had always been clear to those who saw them together that their love was strong. The room erupted as the news emerged and Alf gave a wry smile at the confirmation of his presumption. Congratulations were handed out following the announcement and the reception went on as planned, the guests melting into the evening disco and finally making their way out once Wayne and Isobel had formally left the function. Good wishes were spread but at that point nobody knew that the couple would be having a boy, that he would be healthy and happy or that they would both be excellent, patient parents. The only thing that was certain to the family was that Alf would be a fantastic grandfather and he felt warm inside to think that he now had a new mission.

FIFTY THREE

It was a day like any other. The couple rose at 7 o' clock, the postman visited around midday and the tortoiseshell tabby stopped by that afternoon to dig up one of the flowers in their garden for the sole purpose of defecating beneath it. There was nothing incredible for the newspapers to discuss and the newscasters on television stumbled through some minor, uneventful stories to justify their existence. Behind the houses opposite a young lad from another estate fell off his bike and almost scraped a car that was parked nearby in doing so but it went completely unnoticed as he managed to right his vehicle and cycle off before anybody could see him there.

    The phone rang early in the afternoon, an occurrence that was becoming more frequent due to the amount of sales calls their landline was experiencing yet Mabel had perfected her technique for dealing with the companies and looked forward to the ringing of the handset when it seemed due. The theme of the call on this day was home insurance, a product they had taken out years before with their own bank and were more than happy with, a statement that didn't seem to sway other insurers anymore. With that she confirmed the details that were provided to her and listened to the script that was delivered, fading out after a few words and returning when he sounded like he was about to ask a question. Four long minutes had passed since the phone had been answered yet Mabel was unfazed, waiting for the speech to cease before she implemented her devious plan.

    Events usually went one of two ways; either Mabel would tell them that she was partially deaf and they would have to recap everything they'd just said, repeating this over and over again if they fell for her fictional words, or they would hang up immediately and allow her to get on with the rest of her day. In this case the caller was keen for her business and repeated his jargon word for word before receiving the same instruction and finally realising that he had been caught out. Mabel's laugh was always hearty and had slightly evil undertones when she came off the phone which regularly caused Alf to smirk at her prank.

He made his way from the kitchen to the living room having prepared cheese and pickle sandwiches for their lunch and sat beside her on the sofa, picking up a magazine about tuned cars. He's never owned an example of such in his life and certainly never made any attempt to obtain the magazine in the past and so when he returned home with it the day before Mabel had laughed at him and advised him that he was far too late for a mid-life crisis. He rolled his eyes at the sound yet kept his reason for buying the magazine quiet as he placed it beside his usual spot on the sofa to return to later. He'd heard through a friend of his that somebody had bought and restored his old Granada, a car that had caused Alf an incredible amount of trouble in the six months he'd owned it. Car maintenance was a bugbear of his and had caused him to sell the car cheaply to a local man who, he now realised, had kept it in storage for his son. The two of them had returned the car to a factory state and were getting the most out of it which included a spread in the magazine, something Alf shouldn't have researched but couldn't stop himself from doing. Worse still, the journalist had suggested a price that had made the former owner's eyes water.

Alf would have spent the entire day pining over the magazine had Mabel not interrupted and suggested they go for a walk to get a little fresh air. They both tried to get out as much as possible during the good weather as they had often been sat indoors for days on end as showers overlapped and the warm weather was far too enticing to ignore. Neither felt they needed a coat and stepped straight out into the glow of the sun, deciding on where their route would be as they went. They reached the outskirts of the town and Alf noticed a damp patch where someone had been washing their car that extended into the grass beside the residential road. Mabel was chatting to him about the area as they'd often looked at property there when she lost her footing and fell into the muddy centre of the patch. Far from rushing to her aid, Alf burst into laughter that mirrored hers from the previous day and Mabel couldn't help but feel that the score between them was now even as she picked herself off the ground, rubbing the dirt from her hands and realising that she was covered from her face to her knees.

Mabel decided to call time on their jaunt as she hated to look foolish and would never have paraded her poor fortune for others to see. They made their way straight back to the house in time for Mabel to get showered and ready for the evening. Donning a nightdress, she emerged to Alf questioning her attire in relation to the time of day to be told that, in her house, she could do as she pleased. She offered a self-assured smile and Alf chuckled before curtseying in her honour. They sat down together to plan the evening's entertainment and saw that it would mostly consist of the usual soaps, a crime drama they both enjoyed and a documentary about black holes that would leave Alf feeling insignificant while it played until he forgot his feelings immediately afterwards.

The sun set late as it had done recently and Mabel commented on the lack of contact they'd had from their offspring for the day. Alf retorted with confirmation that it wasn't out of the ordinary and Mabel made him promise to sort the arrangements with Wayne as she was sure they were due to be attending dinner that week as a chance to meet his partner. He promised to get in touch, trying to recall the exact date to alleviate Mabel's concerns before giving in to his dreadful memory. She reiterated the importance of the call and he repeated his vow, knowing Wayne was likely to be in touch beforehand anyway as he was so keen to show off his new lady friend.

The credits finally fired on the final program they watched together and Mabel commented that she had a void to fill, a suggestion that prompted her husband to occupy the kitchen and prepare a healthy supper for them both. As he returned he could see how tired she looked and he suggested they take their meal to bed to which she declined for reasons of mixing crumbs and bed sheets. He watched as she yawned through her late snack and then took the plates out to ensure the living room was ready for the next day, kicking his magazine beneath the table as he did so but in no state to pick it back out again as his own weariness was closing in.

They both climbed the stairs leaving the bottom of the house in darkness and prepared themselves for the evening, the two of them brushing their teeth after which Alf got out of his clothes. He went to ask Mabel about their plans for the next day before realising that it was likely to be very much like the period they'd just had with a few extras thrown in to keep them on their toes. Instead he revisited Mabel's muddy fall and laughed again, causing his wife to flash him a hurt look that he knew wasn't genuine. He sat on the bed and swung his body in so that he was lying beside her, offering consolation and feeling her move in towards him. She purred like a content cat and rubbed her head against his chest as she had done when they were younger, closing her eyes and smiling as she did so.

He held her close to him and kissed the top of her head as she reached for the duvet and pulled it up over them both.

They lay beside each other for a short while before Mabel noticed how quiet Alf had gone and she enquired as to whether he had gone to sleep, receiving confirmation that he hadn't. When she asked why he was so quiet he simply replied that he could feel her love radiating through him and he thanked her for their time together to which she assured him that it was mutually agreeable. She also stressed once more that he had no reason to thank her as he had put in his fair share within their relationship and he was pleased to hear her words affirming their time together. He was looking forward to spending the next day in her company without realising that it would be her last night alive and that he would be so busy during the next day. As she looked up from his chest he placed a kiss on her lips and allowed her to get comfortable before he did the same.

With both of them ready to settle for the night Alf turned the light off and bid sweet dreams to his wife. She reciprocated and they both closed their eyes, the darkness offering a promise of a restful night. Silence filled the empty space and remained until Alf completed their nightly ritual by telling Mabel that he loved her, an act he'd completed every night they'd ever been together. At that Mabel spoke her final earthly words and settled with a smile on her face.

"Goodnight, Alf. I love you."

THANKS

Many thanks to all those who helped and supported this project, it exists purely because of your efforts.

Christine Whyte Hahn
Allan Osborne
Paul Sheridan
Mark Hendy
Rebecca Plunkett
Sean Campbell
Dan Campbell
J-F Cuvillier
Claire Atkins
Kate Budd
Barry Lander
Becky Kemp
Helen Ruse
Mary Lander
Karen Monhemius
Mathieu French

Michael Williams
Jake Riding
The Collick Family
Chris Stringer
Helen Nutt
Gemma Strong
Michael Lander
Julia Hughes
Tiernan Douieb
Helen Rule
Debbie Fry
Simon Strong
Alya Bessex
Aaron Lander
David Hunt

COMING SOON...

From the authors of 'Dead on Demand' and 'Cleaver Square' comes the third instalment in the DCI Morton series. Entitled 'Ten Guilty Men', the book will be available late in 2015.

Ten Guilty Men

Reporters, photographers and a television crew camped out opposite the home of Ellis DeLange. Rafe Soros had been outside since daybreak, his camera remaining focused on the DeLange Residence for nearly six straight hours. It was fast approaching midday and Ellis DeLange had yet to show her face.

Rafe didn't blame her. In her place, he'd be hiding behind an eight foot high wall too. If he had one anyway. Such things were the preserve of the successful. While Rafe rarely grumbled about his lot in life, he had managed to sleepwalk into his forties with sod all to show for it. Twenty five year old Ellis however had never had to struggle. She was the daughter of steel magnate Gregory DeLange and had been born with platinum spoon planted firmly where it still remained.

A bout of schadenfreude had struck Rafe when he got the call that morning. His wife didn't understand why he was grinning as he leapt out of bed at four am. Little Miss Perfect, the darling of the fashion world, had been caught smuggling coke into the country hidden inside Daddy's private jet.

Ever since, she had holed herself up in her Richmond home. The only sign of life was the occasional curtain twitch but Ellis was too smart to give the mob a chance to catch her looking out.

It was at precisely half past twelve, after half of the reporters had adjourned to a nearby pub for a working lunch, that the front door swung open with a creak. A young man stepped out and strutted towards the gate. The front gate slid open as he approached it, as if by magic, and then closed the second he was beyond the boundaries of the DeLange residence.

A dozen cameras leapt into action, though quite what his colleagues thought they were photographing, Rafe had no idea. Likewise, microphones were thrust towards the man and questions shouted at him.

The man waved an arm for silence as if to make a statement.

'She's not here,' he announced flatly.

'Hokum!' One journalist, a noxious old scab by the name of Gifford Byrnes, spat. 'We've been camped out all morning. We know she hasn't had a chance to leave.'

'Look, she's not here. Why don't you lot clear off?'

'And who might you be?'

'Never you mind. I'm only here to tell you to clear off. This is harassment.'

'Can't be harassment if she isn't here to be harassed,' Gifford said with a look of smug satisfaction. 'And hang on, I know who you are! You're Kallum Fielder, the Fulham striker!' The same dozen cameras immediately began snapping away in his direction. Rafe reluctantly joined in and snapped a quick shot of the young footballer. He glanced down at his camera screen and smiled. The picture was perfect. Kallum stood shoulders apart with his arms folded tightly across his chest. At six foot six, Kallum nearly stood as tall as the gate but the house loomed larger still, three storeys of stonework which framed the photograph. It would be an easy sale to one of the weekly gossip magazines.

'So I am.'

'Are you dating Ellis?'

'None of your business.'

'If you're not, why were you in her house?'

'That's totally irrelevant. I told you she isn't home. Now you can either believe me which will save you from blocking up the pavement all day, or you can sit here and waste your time.'

'And why would we believe you?'

'Because in the,' Kal glanced at his watch, 'four and a half minutes we've been chatting, she's gone out the back door and down the private alleyway at the back of the property. Thanks for the chit chat.'

With that, Kal strode back towards the security gate, which opened again just for a moment, and then he was gone. The press would still get a story, but it wouldn't make the front page. Job done.